Matthew ... **working with the camera crew...**

He scowled as he noticed an appreciative grin from one of the gofers. "I'd like to see you in my office," he said sharply to Teresa.

Surprised, she nodded. "I'll be with you in a few moments."

"It's urgent." Without pausing to think, he took hold of her arm and propelled her toward the door. "Come on."

They were outside in the corridor before Teresa could jerk herself free. "Just what do you think you're doing?" she demanded. "I was only getting a few problems straightened out. That happens to be my job..."

"So is doing what the anchorman tells you," he shot back....

"The news team is just that—*a team*," Teresa continued. "I, for one, intend to keep it that way, provided you don't make a habit of dragging me off by the hair."

"It was your arm, not your hair," Matthew insisted. "And I wasn't dragging."

"Details. The point is I expect you to treat me as a professional. Whatever happened between us personally has nothing to do with what goes on here."

"Happened? You make it sound as though it's all in the past."

"Isn't it?" she whispered....

Books by Maura Seger

EYE OF THE STORM
ECHO OF THUNDER
EDGE OF DAWN

HARLEQUIN TEMPTATION
69–UNDERCOVER

HARLEQUIN SUPERROMANCE
181–SPRING FROST, SUMMER FIRE

These books may be available at your local bookseller.

Don't miss any of our special offers. Write to us at the
following address for information on our newest releases.

Worldwide Library Reader Service
901 Fuhrmann Blvd., P.O. Box 1397, Buffalo, NY 14240
Canadian address: P.O. Box 2800, Postal Station A,
5170 Yonge St., Willowdale, Ont. M2N 6J3

EDGE OF DAWN

MAURA SEGER

W RLDWIDE

TORONTO • NEW YORK • LONDON • PARIS
AMSTERDAM • STOCKHOLM • HAMBURG
ATHENS • MILAN • TOKYO • SYDNEY

First published February 1986

ISBN 0-373-97017-X

Printed in Canada

In dreams begins responsibility.
                              —William Butler Yeats

Chapter One

A DOZEN LONG TABLES were set out on the stone terrace of the house overlooking Long Island Sound. The white linen cloths covering them fluttered gently in the August breeze. Since early in the day, the caterer and his staff had been on hand, setting the tables with gleaming china, crystal and silver and beginning preparations for the dinner.

The florist had delivered arrangements for each of the tables and various rooms throughout the house. From the liquor store had come cases of champagne and other wines. Every detail down to the color-coordinated toothpicks and cocktail napkins had been seen to.

White-jacketed waiters circulated among the hundred or so guests gathered in the garden, offering drinks and hors d'oeuvres to tide them over until dinner. Frequent bursts of laughter punctuated the steady hum of conversation. It would be dark in another hour or so. Chinese lanterns hung from the trees, waiting to be lit. The underwater lights were on in the pool. Hawaiian-style bamboo torches had been set up around it.

In the nearby cabanas, towels and suits had been laid out for those who decided to take a dip. The grass had been cut that morning, and the air smelled sweetly of it above the tangy bite of chlorine. A string quartet played, one of two that would alternate throughout the evening.

Teresa Gargano paused at the top of the steps leading down into the garden to observe the scene for a moment before joining it. She needed to catch her breath after the interminable train ride from New York in the airless Long Island Railroad car and the cab drive from the station. Someone would have gladly picked her up, but she had wanted to come on her own. At nineteen, having recently completed her freshman year at Barnard College, such gestures were important.

She was a tall, slender girl with a heart-shaped face, waist-length black hair, a warm Italianate complexion and finely molded features. Her long, bare legs were tanned from afternoons sunning on the roof of the building in Morningside Heights where she shared an apartment with two other girls. They showed to advantage in the suede miniskirt fresh from London, which she suspected would raise eyebrows among at least a few at the party, including her father. The defiantly short length made her self-conscious, but she had decided to wear it for the same reason that she had taken the train.

It seemed that she was among the last to arrive. Both sets of her grandparents were already there. Joseph and Maria Gargano were seated at a small table by the pool along with Will and Elizabeth

Lawrence. Grandfather Lawrence had changed little since his retirement from the army a few years before. He was still straight backed and square jawed, looking a bit uncomfortable at being out of uniform.

By contrast, Grandfather Gargano looked more relaxed but no less impressive. He had also tried retirement, found he didn't like it and had recently gone into partnership with his son-in-law, Salvatore, who owned a string of restaurants in New York and New Jersey. His wife, Maria, silver-haired and a little frail in her navy-blue silk dress, was deep in conversation with Elizabeth. Grandmother Lawrence kept busy with a host of volunteer activities that would have exhausted a woman half her age. She retained the slender beauty of the Southern belle she had once been, tempered by the accumulated wisdom of decades as an army wife.

Teresa's smile was fond as she surveyed her grandparents, but it sharpened with amusement when she caught sight of her younger brothers, Joe and Anthony, Jr. Two years apart in age but close enough in appearance to be taken for twins, Joe and Tony both had the black hair and broad shoulders inherited from their father. The light of unholy mischief burned in their dark eyes. Eyes of cherubim, a frustrated parish priest had said once just before he had thrown up his hands at their latest escapade. They had been the bane of Teresa's existence when she was living at home, yet she loved them both dearly.

Just as she loved her other "brother," Matthew
Callahan, the son of her father's business partner
who had been so much a part of her life from its very
beginning that she could not imagine being without
him. Was he there yet?

Hazel eyes sought the telltale glint of golden-brown
hair, without success. Her shoulders drooped slightly
as she wondered if he might not be able to attend. His
job on the *New York Times* often kept him working
late. A shadow moved over her features, only to
vanish as, with one of the swift changes of mood that
had become so typical lately, she shrugged it off. She
was certainly capable of enjoying herself without
him.

Her father was standing at the center of a circle of
friends near the pool. He was dressed in a dark-blue
pin-striped suit of conservative cut and looked remarkably fit for a man who spent most of his time
behind a desk. His thick black hair, so like her own,
was streaked with silver at the temples. There were
lines in his face that were always a surprise to her
since frozen in her mind was an image of him as he
had been when she was a child. When he saw her, he
held out a hand. There was the briefest frown at the
miniskirt before he smiled. "Have any trouble with
the train, honey?"

"No, Dad, everything was fine." She kissed him
lightly on the cheek, grateful that he hadn't made any
comment about her clothes in front of the guests.
Several were neighbors whose children she had grown

up with in the upper-class Long Island community, the others were men she recognized as executives at IBS, the television network founded and run by her father and James Callahan. "Happy anniversary," she added softly.

"Thanks, though I have to admit it kind of snuck up on me."

"Twenty years, Anthony," one of the men said jovially. "How's Maggie managed to put up with you so long?"

"I keep wondering the same thing myself. Guess there's just no accounting for taste."

Teresa laughed along with the others. She took it for granted that her parents had a good marriage. She presumed that had always been the case and always would be. It was when she tried to think about ever having something similar for herself that she ran into difficulty.

The older she got, the less sure she was of anything. "It was easier for our parents," one of her friends at college had said recently. "They came out of World War II knowing exactly what they wanted and the rules of how to get it. For us, nothing is as simple."

Listening to the familiar sound of her father's voice as he told a story from the early days of his marriage, she felt a pang of envy. What must it have been like not to be filled with doubts? To have instead a clearly defined path through life, values one could believe in and presumptions about the innate nature of the country and the world that were not questioned?

In this summer of 1965, slightly more than twenty months after the assassination of John F. Kennedy, there seemed to be nothing but questions. "Who really did it?" fueled the late-night bull sessions in the dorms. "Can we trust Johnson?" was another in the aftermath of the president's landslide victory the year before.

But beyond all other consideration was the half-sad, half-angry plaint of "how could they do that to us?" *They* being simply the adults, the people who were supposed to be in charge. *It* being the shattering of innocence, the sudden realization that the world was not the benign place where Beaver Cleaver and Ozzie and Harriet lived, but was instead a bewildering, frightening arena from which no one escaped alive.

"We were living in a trailer back then," Anthony was saying, "and Tessa had just been born." He looked down at her fondly. His eldest child and only daughter, she had always held a special place in his heart. That hadn't changed even though she had insisted on moving into New York rather than commute to college, living in a lousy neighborhood when he would have gladly paid far more in rent to have her somewhere better, and wearing skirts that looked as if half of them had gotten lost in the wash.

Tessa had heard the story before. She let it drift over her as she continued to scan the crowd. James and Alexis Callahan were deep in conversation with a man everyone expected to shortly run for the senate. Alexis looked beautiful as always in a dark-red silk dress perfectly fitted to her slender figure. Few women could have gotten away with such a dramatic color, but with Alexis's silver hair and ivory skin, it was perfect. How old was Matthew's stepmother now? Mid-forties certainly, and James was older than that. They didn't fit the prevailing wisdom that reserved physical attractiveness and vigor for the young. But then neither did her own parents.

"I'm going to give Mom a hand," she said when her father had finished the story. She smiled politely at the guests and slipped away, heading across the garden toward the house. As expected, her mother was in the kitchen, checking the final details of dinner.

Maggie had her back to the door when Teresa came in. She was talking with the caterer who nodded several times as she spoke. Her daughter couldn't hear what she was saying but she was sure that whatever it was, Maggie was being very nice but also very firm. As chief surgical nurse at the local hospital, she was accustomed to having her instructions followed.

When she had finished, she turned around. Her face, heart-shaped as Teresa's own, was a little flushed and she looked preoccupied, but that was only to be expected considering the event. She also looked quite lovely. Not in the glamorous way of Alexis Callahan but in a quieter and more understated style that suited her. Chestnut hair going gracefully silver was cut short and brushed away from her face to reveal the smooth line of her neck. The soft blue gown she wore bared her slender arms and shoulders, kept firmly muscled by frequent games of tennis and the physical demands of her job. With it she wore the sapphire and diamond necklace Anthony had given her on her last birthday.

"Now where did I put the...?" she murmured to herself, breaking off when she caught sight of her daughter. Her smile was warm and relieved. "Teresa, I'm so glad you got here. Your father has been looking at his watch every two minutes, worrying that something had happened to you."

"It's okay, Mom," Teresa murmured, bending to kiss her. "I'm capable of getting myself on and off a train."

"I know that, darling, but does your father? You'll have to forgive him if he worries about you. What a marvelous skirt. Where did you get it?"

"A little shop near school. You don't think it's a bit . . . short?"

"Well, of course it is. That's the point, after all. Besides, you've got the legs for it." Linking arms with her daughter, Maggie drew her out of the kitchen. "I absolutely must stop worrying that everything won't go all right. The caterer has it all under control."

"You've always said he's the best," Teresa said soothingly. "Besides, you've had parties like this before."

"And been a nervous wreck every time! Worse yet, this one I brought on myself."

"Let me guess. You said 'why don't we have a few friends over to help us celebrate our anniversary.' Then Dad started reeling off names and the next thing you knew . . ."

"Exactly. Oh, well, everyone seems to be having a good time."

That was certainly true. The party was in full swing with several couples on the dance floor and the rest gathered in boisterous knots around the garden. Maggie surveyed the elegantly dressed, sociable crowd with a faintly bemused smile.

"Something wrong?" Teresa asked.

"No . . . it's just that this is so different from when we were married."

Teresa knew her parents' wedding had taken place in the Philippines toward the end of World War II when her father had been a marine officer and her mother an army nurse. They had expected to be separated shortly thereafter by the invasion of Japan, but instead had been spared that by the sudden end of the war following the atomic explosions over Hiroshima and Nagasaki.

So much she had grown up accepting in the blithe way of children glossing over anything that had happened in which they were not central participants.

But now, looking at her mother in the beautiful blue dress with the jewels gleaming at her throat, she had a sudden flash of insight into what it must actually have been like to be young, in love and engulfed in war.

It was only a fragmentary sensation that passed in an instant, but it was enough to disturb her, as though she had trespassed onto a private landscape where she had no right to be. A place where her parents did not exist, but two strangers did: a man and a woman who had never heard of Teresa Gargano but who would shortly bring her into being.

The look in her father's eyes as he came to claim Maggie for a dance stayed with Teresa for a long time. She wandered among the clusters of people, a glass of wine in her hand, smiling and chatting automatically while her mind remained firmly elsewhere.

Distantly she noticed Amanda Callahan and her brother, James, Jr. Fifteen-year-old Mandy, tall and blond with the precocious maturity bestowed by beauty and privilege, was busy dazzling the guests. Meanwhile Jim was . . . Jim. Taller than his twin sister and well-built like all the Callahan men, he looked somehow less than consequential beside her. His features were slightly blurred as he stood in her shadow, and he slumped a little in his evening jacket as though hoping not to be noticed.

Teresa shook her head impatiently. She didn't understand Jim. Why couldn't he be more like his half brother, Matthew? Which brought her back full circle to wondering if Matthew was coming.

She glanced at her watch. It was 8:00 P.M.; the Chinese lanterns and bamboo torches had been lit. They would be sitting down at any moment. It occurred to her to simply ask if he was still expected, but she hated doing that. Instead she waited, still hoping, until her Uncle Dom came to offer her his arm and take her to dinner.

"I thought I'd claim the prettiest girl," he said with a smile. "How have you been, honey?"

"Fine," she assured the tall dark-haired man, her father's youngest brother. "How are Auntie Katie and the kids?"

"Fine, I guess. They're off visiting her folks."

"I'll bet you're having a great time on your own," she teased, knowing how much Dom missed his family.

"Yeah, it's terrific. TV dinners and long nights at the office. At least I'm getting plenty of work done." Dom was a former major league baseball player who had joined IBS when his batting days were over. He had single-handedly created the highly successful sports division which he now headed. In his own way, he was as tough as her father, but he masked it under a more jovial, relaxed manner.

Which did not affect his keen-eyed perception. As he held out her chair, he asked quietly, "Seen Matt lately?"

"No . . . not in a couple of months." Which was why she had been hoping he would be there tonight.

Dom took his seat beside her. "They keep him pretty busy at the *Times*. I read his stuff; it's good."

Teresa thought it was more than that, but she refrained from saying so. She didn't want to sound gushy. The other guests were taking their places as the waiters began to serve the first course. Anthony rose from his place at the head of the table and gently chimed a spoon against his glass.

When he had everyone's attention, he proposed a toast. "To Maggie," he said softly, "the gentlest woman I've ever known, and the strongest. All my love." At the opposite end of the table, his wife blushed like a young girl. Her eyes were warm as they met his. When the approving comments had died away, it was Dom's turn. Rising, he said gracefully, "To Maggie and Anthony: they showed us that love endures and with it everything is possible. May the next twenty years be at least as good."

That brought a round of cheers before everyone fell to, Teresa along with all the rest. The food was delicious—especially after long months of cafeteria fare—and the conversation entertaining, but her gaze kept drifting to the empty chair on the other side of the table. That it hadn't yet been removed was a good sign.

Thin slices of rare roast beef were being served when her hopes were at last rewarded. Matthew slipped into the party quietly. He spoke for a moment with Maggie, apparently apologizing for his late arrival, and was rewarded with an understanding smile. Then he took his place at the table and said hello to several other people.

Meanwhile, Teresa watched him, hardly able to do otherwise. Whenever they had met in the past year, she had felt faintly disconcerted, as though an extra layer of perception was intruding between them, changing the way she saw him.

For all his specialness to her, he had been someone she could always count on and therefore inevitably came to take for granted. She had known he was handsome, with all-American good looks given added depth by the clarity of his light-blue eyes and the frequent quirk at the corners of his well-shaped mouth. But lately his appearance had begun to affect her oddly.

Matthew was six years her senior. At twenty-five, he seemed to her to be very much a grown man, part of the adult world she was only just entering. When she tried to think of him as anything but a friend, she was struck by a sense of her own inadequacy. If he knew how she felt, she did not doubt that he would be embarrassed. Certainly he would be nice about it, but she would end up seeing even less of him. A fate to be avoided at all costs.

He turned to speak to someone across the table and caught sight of her. For a moment he frowned, as though something about her puzzled him. Then he smiled and she quickly did, too. After that she enjoyed the dinner more.

At the end there was another round of toasts to accompany the cake that her parents cut together. As the guests drifted away from the tables, the string quartet struck up a dance tune. Waiters circulated with snifters of brandy and goblets of champagne on silver trays. The noise was louder now. Ties had been loosened, and here and there a few stray wisps of hair slipped from elegant coiffures.

It was the time Teresa normally liked best at a party, when the success of the occasion was assured and whatever stiffness had existed at the beginning was long since gone. Yet she found herself unable to completely relax, though she danced with several young men and chatted with others.

Tiredness was creeping up on her when she excused herself and went back into the house to comb her hair and freshen what little makeup she wore. Back on the stone terrace, she began to think about leaving. It was getting on for midnight; she didn't want to miss the last train. Her parents would be happy for her to stay over, but she didn't feel comfortable doing that. Perhaps when she had been on her own a little longer.

"Leaving?" a quiet voice asked behind her. She turned to find Matthew standing in the shadows near the house, his hands in the pockets of his evening trousers, his tie loosened and the collar button of his shirt undone.

"I was thinking about it." In the darkness, she couldn't see his face, but the lights from the lanterns turned his hair a shade of beaten gold. The elegant attire he wore so casually made him look even bigger and solider than usual. He moved then, coming toward her as she stood with her arms at her sides, not taking her eyes from him.

"Nice party," he said. "Your folks look great."

"So do yours." Though Alexis was technically his stepmother, he did not think of her as such. James Callahan's first wife had died some twenty years ago after a bitter divorce and on the eve of what promised to be an equally bitter custody battle. Before his marriage to Alexis, and for a few years afterward, Matthew had lived with Maggie and Anthony, hence his close relationship with Teresa and his tendency to think of her as his little sister.

Except that he was having some trouble remembering that lately. Since she had started college the year before she had become different. Less the little girl he had always thought her and more a stranger. Someone new he didn't know but wanted to.

"Did you come by train?" he asked, his hands plowing deeper into his pockets.

"Yes." He looked tired, as though he weren't getting enough sleep or eating properly. The job on the *Times* was tough, but he had wanted it so much. She hoped it was turning out to be everything he had hoped.

"I'd be glad to drive you back."

"Oh . . . you've got the MG with you?"

He smiled faintly. "I know it looks disreputable but it still handles pretty well. I'd hate to part with it." His father had given him the little red sports car when he had been accepted at Princeton seven years before. Teresa was willing to bet that he held on to it for a lot more reasons than the way it handled.

"That would be great," she said, "that is, if it's no trouble?"

He assured her it wasn't, and they made their farewells to her parents. Anthony in particular looked relieved when he heard Matthew was driving her home. "Great," he said, "and while you're at it, try talking her into moving to a better neighborhood."

"They still treat me like a kid," she murmured as they walked down the footpath to the road where the cars were parked.

"You can't blame them. They love you."

"That's no excuse for refusing to recognize that I've grown up."

"Is that what's happened?" he asked lightly. Teresa shrugged and didn't answer. After a moment he said, "Sorry. I guess I'm as guilty as the others. It's just hard to realize that someone you've known all your life is turning into an adult."

"You did," she reminded him. "I remember when you had arms and legs that stuck out all over the place, and you looked like you'd never grow into your ears."

"What's wrong with my ears?" he demanded teasingly.

"Nothing, now. But for a while there you looked like Dumbo the flying elephant." She laughed and added, "I also remember when you got sweaty palms worrying about what to do on a date and spent your allowance on Clearasil."

"Never my *whole* allowance," he insisted. "I always saved part of it to buy those disgusting little candy things you liked so much."

"The colored ones that came stuck to long sheets of paper?"

"Yep. It's a wonder you've got any teeth left." As though struck by a sudden doubt, he said, "Or do you? Maybe I'd better check."

"Oh, no!" She dodged away from him laughing and ran down the path. Matthew followed, not fast enough to catch her, which he could have done easily, but staying close enough to enjoy the sight of her long legs in the moonlight.

They were both a little breathless by the time they reached the car. As he opened the door for her, he said, "I hope you didn't pay much for that skirt."

"Twelve dollars."

"Jeez, you got taken."

"It happens to be the very latest from London."

Actually, the skirt looked great, at least with her in it. If current fashion trends continued, leg men were in for a very good year.

"How did you like it over there?" she asked as he got in behind the wheel and turned the ignition key. The paper had sent him over to London the month before to do a series of stories on Britain's most recent hit export, a shaggy haired group of Liverpudlians called the Beatles.

"It's interesting in England just now," he said as he switched the radio on. Not surprisingly, a Beatles' tune was on. They seemed to run night and day. Teresa's foot kept time with "You've Got to Hide Your Love Away" as he explained, "There's still everything we associate with Great Britain—bowler hats, rolled umbrellas, stiff upper lips and all that. But it's rubbing up against something explosive, original, filled with energy. I'm not explaining it very well...."

"You're doing fine." A little shyly, she added, "I read all your articles; they were wonderful."

"You really liked them?"

"More than that. You made me feel as though I was actually there."

He exhaled sharply. "I wish my editor felt the same way."

"Surely he appreciates you?" How could he possibly not?

"I don't think he quite knows what to make of me. That's why I got sent to England. They wanted to do something on the Beatles, but none of the older guys would touch it. Thought it was beneath them somehow. So they sent me." He grinned ruefully. "I'm their token representative of wild youth, which they have decidedly mixed feelings about. The other day I was told to get my hair cut.''

''But it isn't even that long.'' The thick golden-brown strands barely brushed the collar of his dinner jacket. Granted several fell over his broad forehead, giving him a vaguely disreputable look, but to her eyes at least that only made him more appealing. *Times* editors must see things very differently.

''I thought you'd be happy there,'' she said softly. ''You wanted it so much.''

''I still do. Print's the only place to be.''

''They do news on television, too.''

''No, they don't. They read the headlines, throw in the weather and fill up on commercials. That isn't journalism.''

''What about Winston Harcourt? Isn't he a good journalist?'' The anchorman of the IBS evening news and several regularly scheduled in-depth news programs had helped Matthew get his job on the *Times*, where Harcourt had once worked. Teresa knew it was unfair in a way to mention him since Matthew would never say anything bad about him, but she was trying to make a point.

''Winston's the exception,'' he insisted grudgingly, then relented enough to add, ''Cronkite's all right, too. So are Huntley and Brinkley. But they just don't have enough time. Important issues can't be presented in a couple of minutes.''

''Your father says that you have to take the news to the people, and the people are watching television.''

"If he really believes that, he should be doing more. There's so much to deal with today: civil rights, the white backlash, the whole business in Vietnam. You know our guys are actually fighting over there now, have been since June."

Teresa nodded, her eyes somber. She didn't know what to make of the war being fought thousands of miles away. "I saw it on television."

He made a small sound of disgust. "I hope you've read about it, too."

"Of course I have. But television adds something. Reading about a situation isn't the same as actually seeing it. There's a power to pictures that words can't replace."

"If that's what you think, why don't you go to work for IBS? It's as much your family's business as mine."

"I might just do that. At least I'm not prejudiced against an entire form of communication. You know what I think? That you're just trying to prove your independence from your father. You don't want anyone to think you had to go to work for him because he said to."

"Thanks for the two-bit analysis. Maybe you should switch your major to psychology."

"I'll stick with history, thanks. Someday I'm going to be a writer."

"Writers major in English."

"Maybe that's what's wrong with them then. All they know is what other people have written. I'm learning what they've done."

Matthew had no comeback for that. He and Tessa—Teresa as she now wanted to be called—had always argued; that was the nature of their relationship. But it had been in a lighthearted way, not about anything serious. He wasn't used to her standing up for her opinions so determinedly.

"I guess you're entitled to your own point of view."

"Thanks loads." Unaccountably, she was angry with him. Not because they had disagreed, but because he was being so blindingly stubborn about a situation she believed could only hurt him. The *Times* men knew his background, knew who his father was, and who had helped get him the job. He would always have to prove himself to them, to demonstrate again and again that he could be a real journalist despite the taint of television.

Meanwhile, the pressure would continue from the other side. James Callahan wasn't the sort to meekly give up. He wanted Matthew at IBS; Teresa thought it likely he would eventually get his way. She just hoped they wouldn't both be hurt in the process.

They drove awhile in silence before at last he said, "Let's change the subject, okay? How's your social life these days?"

"All right, I guess."

He cast her a quick look out of the corner of his
eye. "Are you seeing anyone special?"

"No. I spend most of my time studying." She
hesitated a moment, then asked, "How about you?"

"What about me?"

"Anyone special?"

"No . . . not at the moment. I don't seem to have
the same interest in it I used to." He was surprised he
had said that. It was more personal than he had intended, but he and Tessa—Teresa—had always
shared confidences. Still, he wasn't about to let her
think there was anything wrong with him. "I'll get
back to it, once things settle down some."

"Do you think they will?"

"I don't know. It depends on what happens in a lot
of areas."

"Such as?"

"What Johnson does, for one. He's got so much
to take care of here at home I can't figure out what he
wants to get involved abroad for."

"We were attacked in Vietnam, remember? That's
why the Tonkin Resolution was passed last year."

"I know . . . but it doesn't feel right to me, somehow. I keep thinking we're being . . . distracted."

"I'm not following you."

"It just seems that whenever there are internal
problems that might threaten the established order,
someone manages to come up with a war to keep
people preoccupied and make them feel they
shouldn't be questioning their government."

"Do you really think Johnson is so cynical?" Teresa was not a big fan of the new president's; the mere thought of what had happened at Dallas was still enough to make her want to cry. But she was willing to give the man the benefit of the doubt.

"I don't know," Matthew said tiredly. "He may not even be aware of what he's doing. Look at what he's got to deal with. Martin Luther King can preach all the nonviolence he wants, but it's radicals like Malcolm X who are grabbing the headlines these days. Some very serious people are starting to say that we're in for another revolution in this country. That kind of talk rocks the establishment right down to its boots. And on top of everything else, we've now got the biggest generation of young people to ever exist in this country at one time. Somebody has to find jobs for us, give us a sense of opportunity, or at the very least keep us too busy to think about what we're missing."

"And a war would do that?"

"It might. It worked with our father's generation."

"You're not saying that Roosevelt and Churchill . . . ?"

"No, of course not. Then it was Hitler and that bunch trying to keep the lid on. But the effect is the same. War unites the people, fuels the economy and maintains leaders in power."

He slowed down for a tollbooth and they were silent again until the car picked up speed once more.

Then Teresa said, "Why don't you write about this?"

"The *Times* has plenty of political reporters."

"You could still try."

"Maybe I have. That doesn't mean it will be published." In fact he knew it wouldn't. The article analyzing the underlying causes of the war in Vietnam had been returned by his editor before his trip to London with the comment that it was a nice try for Poli. Sci. 101 but didn't belong in a reputable paper. Johnson wasn't particularly popular at the *Times* but that didn't mean they were going to let some green kid run all over him.

"Have you talked with your father about this or with Alexis?" His stepmother had the distinction of being the only woman head of a television network, having taken over UBC from her brother several years before in a move the industry was still talking about.

Instead of answering directly, Matthew said, "Alexis wanted to do an in-depth program on Vietnam years ago when Eisenhower sent in the first advisors. It never got on the air."

"Maybe it would now."

"I doubt it. If anything, there's even less of a tendency to rock the boat these days."

"We've been through so much lately. . . ."

"And we may be headed for a hell of a lot worse unless someone pulls us up short."

They were entering the outer fringes of the city, passing neat rows of houses with patchwork lawns. Teresa stared out of the window wondering if any of the people whose homes they passed were thinking about the same things. She rather doubted it. Matthew seemed to be running these days on a fine, bright flame of anger whose source she could only guess at. Was it simply frustration with his job and perhaps conflict with his father, or was there more involved? Something akin to the sense of restlessness that gripped her from time to time no matter how much she tried to ignore it.

At nineteen, it was tough enough to be no longer a child yet not quite an adult. How much harder that must be for a man of twenty-five who chafed under the restraining hand of an older generation not yet ready to share power.

"Thanks for listening to me," he said when he left her at the door of her Morningside Heights apartment. He had insisted on walking her to it even though that meant leaving the MG double-parked.

"I liked it. We used to talk so much."

"It was easier then."

"It won't always be like this. Things will get better." She had no idea where her certainty about that came from but it was real nonetheless.

He smiled gently. "Little Tessa, you always were an optimist."

"Teresa, and I'm not so little anymore."

"I noticed." God help him, he really had. The urge to touch her was almost more than he could resist. If only she were older, closer to his age, or if he had only just met her. But she wasn't and he hadn't. He could remember her as a baby lying in a pink and white crib, a tiny child toddling over the lawn into his arms, a little girl riding high on a swing he pushed. All his life he had protected her; he couldn't stop now.

"I've got to go," he said, turning away. Down the three flights of stairs, back into the car, a quick trip across town to his own East Side apartment, and he'd do some writing before trying to sleep. That always helped.

"Thanks for the ride."

"It was nothing."

"I appreciated it." Her hand was on the doorknob. She'd go in now, wouldn't she?

"Matthew... I was glad you were there this evening."

"Well, sure, I wouldn't have missed it. Twenty years, that deserves celebrating."

"They've been very happy."

"It works out like that sometimes. You'd better go in, it's late."

"Yes, all right. I just wanted to say... I've missed you."

The words were muffled; he could hardly make them out. By the time he did, she had opened the door and closed it again. He stood on the landing for several minutes, staring at the cracked, peeling wood. Then he dug his hands deeper into his pockets and walked away.

Chapter Two

"WE WILL NOT BE USED as cannon fodder! We oppose this war and we intend for everyone to know it!"

Teresa listened to the shaggy-haired intense young man from the back of the crowd. She was at Columbia University, where women attending Barnard were allowed to take some classes. The rally against the war had been going on for about half an hour. Several dozen students had drifted up to join it. Most were dressed in drooping dungarees and loose-fitted khaki jackets. The few other women wore miniskirts, T-shirts and sandals like Teresa's. Most had long, straight hair—if only because they had ironed it—and several wore wire-rimmed glasses. Like her, they kept to the back of the crowd.

"The military-industrial complex has no respect for the integrity of human life," the young man went on. The high-pitched hum of the bullhorn he was using drowned out his next words and he had to repeat them. "They have only one way to justify their existence—through killing. We will not be a party to that. The illegal war in Vietnam must end now!"

There was a smattering of applause before he stepped down and yielded the podium to an older black man dressed in a dashiki of vibrant African print with beads strung around his neck. "Brothers," he began, then paused and smiled benignly, "and a few sisters are here, too, I see. We need volunteers to help with the mailings and other office work, so I hope you'll all be signin' up. Now then . . ." As he buckled down to his main point, his voice became more sonorous and took on the swinging cadence of street rhythms as though to emphasize that he felt no need to talk "white" to them.

"What ah came here to say is that ba-ad as this war is, we all know who it's really hurtin'. You white boys got your student de-fer-ments, you don't have to worry long as you don' flunk out." He paused a beat for nervous laughter. "But the black man, he's got nothin'. He's jus' prime meat on the hoof to the Pen-taa-gon. They send him over to Vi-et-nam, he get shot up, you think they care? Noo-way, noo-how! Jus' one less black man t'make trouble here. You think that's right?"

"No," the crowd responded obediently.

"Lemme here it louder."

"No!"

"That's better. We gotta stand t'gether against this war. We gotta tell those fat, rich honkies runnin' this country that their time is over. It's our time now! Our time! We in charge now and they gonna know it! Am ah right?"

"Right!"

"That's good. You got it now. But wha' you gonna do with it? Talk is cheap, brothers! I wan' you to dig

your hands down deep into your pockets and·find me
some money. Money for the movement, brothers!
Money for the black man who's given his sweat an'
his blood for this country for too damn long now an'
never got a thing in return. Money, brothers. Show
me you ain't just mouthin' off. Show me you really
mean wha' you say!''

They showed him, in the dollar bills folded up and
pushed into the can that was rapidly passed around.
The few who dared to drop in coins were glared at.
Teresa walked away before the can could reach her.
She didn't necessarily disagree with anything the
man had said, she just didn't like having her ideals
taken advantage of.

The few trees scattered around the campus showed
the soft green leaves of spring. Her sophomore year
would be winding up soon, but instead of feeling any
satisfaction, she was burdened by a disquieting sense
that nothing was as it should be. Something was
happening beyond her understanding, perhaps beyond the understanding of any one person. Something huge, amorphous, multifaceted was seeping
over the country of the young, sharpening the line
between them and the generation of their parents
until it began to resemble a battlefield.

Battlefields were very much on her mind these
days. American casualties in Vietnam had been
mounting since the new year. Spokesmen for the
Johnson administration—Robert McNamara, the
Bundy brothers, Walt Rostow and so on—kept in-

sisting that the war was being won. In his rare press conferences, the president did the same. But the evidence said otherwise.

Men were dying, that much was sure. Young men her own age who had really had no chance to live. And those that were still alive didn't seem much better off. She saw them on television every night, looked into their empty eyes and felt fear at the bottom of her soul.

The day was warm, the sun shining, birds singing, yet she shivered and wrapped her arms around herself as she walked. When had it all started to go wrong? Most picked the day in Dallas as the turning point, and she supposed that was as good as any. The litany of events since then was a tale of madness told by a lunatic to an audience of the damned. Protest marches, riots, murders, police assaults, it went on and on.

Barely had the buildup begun in Vietnam the previous year than the black ghetto of Watts in Los Angeles had erupted in an orgy of fire and death. In October, thousands had marched down Fifth Avenue to demand peace, ''doves'' daring the jeers of ''hawks'' along the parade route. A young man had burned his draft card. Two others had found an even more personal way to protest; taking a lead from the Buddhist monks opposing the government in Vietnam, they had burned themselves to death. Both had made the evening news.

AS THOUGH ALL THAT weren't enough, there were other elements at play that might have been almost comical had the situation not been so grim. A former Harvard professor espoused the creed of better living through LSD and advised followers to "turn on, tune in, drop out." Marijuana was becoming almost commonplace at college parties. Teresa had tried it but didn't particularly like the feeling of being somehow disconnected from the rest of the world. Apparently that didn't bother many of her friends; on the contrary, they seemed to crave it.

What they also craved was sex. Most girls she knew were on the Pill, whether they really needed to be or not. She had thought about getting a prescription herself, just in case. Not that she had much motivation. The young men she met were for the most part humorless, self-important and insecure. Hardly what it would take to inspire her into bed. She resented the idea of sex being an obligation, one more rite of passage to be gotten through. Maybe it really wasn't anything more than that, but she could wait a while longer before finding out for sure.

She hadn't seen Matthew since Christmas, and then only briefly. He had been off to Europe again, this time on his own, though she suspected he would be looking for stories. If he was any more content at the *Times*, he didn't show it, yet neither did he seem prepared to join IBS.

Thinking about that, she took the subway downtown to where she was meeting her father for lunch.

In deference to his susceptibilities, she had chosen not to wear the pantsuit she had recently purchased, since women in such attire were not permitted in many of the better restaurants. Though she thought the prohibition outrageous she didn't intend to fight it at his expense. Besides, he was doing his best to adjust to the length of her skirts and should get something in return.

He was already there when she arrived. As the maître d' escorted her over, Anthony rose. She thought he looked elegant as always, but unless she was very much mistaken, his hair was a bit longer than she had ever before seen it.

"Your barber on vacation, Dad?" she asked teasingly as she slid into the chair the maître d' held out.

He grinned a little self-consciously. "No, your mother just thought I should let it grow. She says short hair is out of step."

"It looks good," she assured him, "just please don't decide to give bell bottoms and paisley shirts a try."

He looked genuinely horrified at the prospect, which made her laugh, and they settled down to lunch in a companionable mood. "So how's school?" he asked after the waiter had taken their orders.

"Fine. I should make the dean's list again this term."

"That's great! We'll have to celebrate." When she didn't respond, he asked, "What's the matter, honey? You should be proud to be doing so well."

"I am, I guess. It's just that . . . it doesn't seem to mean as much to me as I thought it would."

"You've always done well in school. Maybe you're too used to it to see how special it is."

"Perhaps." She didn't want to talk about school; it was too disturbing. "How's everyone?"

"Your mother's fine, busy as always. Joey wrecked his car the other day, so he's grounded for a while."

"He wasn't hurt, was he?"

"Only his pride. Maybe it will be a good lesson for him. Tony's dating a new girl; she seems nice."

"He'd better be careful. He'll have gone through the whole neighborhood pretty soon."

"Just as long as no fathers show up with shotguns."

The waiter returned with the first course, and they ate for a few moments in silence before Teresa asked, "Anything particular going on at work?"

"We're acquiring a couple more affiliates, one in California and the other in Texas."

"You're going to end up owning them all."

He laughed gently. "I doubt it. The government might have something to say about that. However, we are doing very well. Enough to be able to hire a certain college girl if she decides she wants a job this summer." They had talked about the possibility of Teresa going to work for IBS; she liked the idea but didn't want to be accused of taking favors.

"I wouldn't want any special treatment for being the boss's daughter," she reminded him.

"Only one of the bosses."

"Would Uncle James mind?"

"Of course not. He's all for it." He hesitated briefly before going on. "As you may know, James has been trying to interest Matthew in coming aboard."

"He still hasn't had any luck?"

"No, the kid's as stubborn as his old man."

"Maybe Alexis could persuade him."

"Possibly, but the last thing she needs is to get caught between the two of them."

Teresa could understand that. In Alexis's place, she would feel the same way. "Matthew may yet come around," she suggested. "He's not happy at the *Times*."

"Has he told you that?"

"He didn't have to in so many words. It's obvious."

Anthony looked at her for a moment before he nodded. "The two of you have always had a special relationship, so I'll take your word for it. Do you have any idea what kind of work you'd like to do for us?"

She grinned irrepressibly. "Running the place would be fine."

He laughed. "That will have to wait awhile. We can put you in entertainment, news, sports, production, accounting . . ."

"Not accounting, please. And not sports, since I don't know anything about them. Production might be interesting; I'd learn how things work. On the other hand, I wouldn't mind seeing the news division from the inside.''

"Good enough. I'll put you on Winston's staff."

"It might be best for him to talk with me first," she suggested diplomatically, "so that he can decide whether or not I'm suited to the job."

Anthony hid a smile. It pleased him to see her being so adult, thinking of others, insisting that things be done properly. On the other hand, it also made him even more conscious of the fact that she was no longer a little girl. It was a lovely young woman who looked back at him from across the table. In her, he saw both himself and Maggie, yet also someone else. Teresa herself. Children, he decided, were a classic case of the whole being more than the sum of the parts.

And before he got any more maudlin than that, he'd better get back to the office.

TERESA STARTED WORK at IBS the first week of June. Winston and the other members of the news team made her feel welcome, though it was clear she was expected to carry her weight. Officially, she was his assistant but in fact she did anything that was needed. She quickly became adept at keeping track of which crews were covering which stories, what film was in, what was coming, where celebrities of all stripes were expected to be at any given time in case they had to be reached in a hurry, who was coming into town, who was leaving, and so on.

She also learned how everyone in the newsroom liked his coffee, who took what kind of sandwiches for lunch, and which bars, hotels, steam baths and the like to check when certain members of the staff turned up missing close to airtime. Winston was tolerant of such peccadilloes as long as they did not interfere with the quality of his programs. When anything did threaten them, his patience ran very short very fast.

Teresa did her best to stay on his good side, not out of any fear of him but because she valued his respect and wanted to keep it. About a month after she started work, it was evident that she was succeeding.

"You're doing a good job," he told her one evening after the broadcast. He was sitting in a barber chair getting the small amount of makeup he grudgingly wore on the air removed. His silver-gray hair was neatly combed and his gray-green eyes were pensive as he watched her in the mirror.

"Thanks," she said with a smile. "I've been enjoying it."

"More than college?"

"Yes," she admitted. "I like that, too, but here I have a sense of...excitement, purpose, I'm not sure exactly what." She shrugged apologetically for not being able to put it better.

"I understand what you're saying," he assured her. "You've got what, two years left at Barnard?"

"Yes, and frankly they seem very long."

"This is a tough time to be in college. For that matter, to be young."

He spoke matter-of-factly, but not without an underlying note of sympathy that touched her, if only for being unexpected.

Winston had no children, in fact had never been married. There were rumors that he had never met a woman he wanted as much as Alexis Callahan, whom he could not have. Teresa didn't know if they were true or not, but she did know that there was a glimmer of sadness about Winston that made her feel closer to him.

In her second month with the news division, she and Winston fell into the habit of talking together briefly each evening. Sometimes they went out for a quick meal. There was nothing even remotely romantic about their association; they were simply friends and to a certain extent, student and mentor. She could talk to him about things she would never mention to her parents or anyone else of their generation. And from him she could learn.

"I'm worried about my brothers," she said one evening as they were having dinner at a little bistro on the West Side. "Joey will be eighteen next year, eligible for the draft, and Tony's only a couple of years behind him. The way this war is going, they could both be swept up in it."

"They'll go to college surely," Winston said, stirring his martini idly. Martinis weren't as fashionable these days as they had been in the fifties, but he stuck to what he liked.

"Yes," she agreed, "but I'm not sure how much protection that will give them. Johnson is getting so much heat about the draft being unfair that he may have to change it."

"Don't you think he should? The way it's set up now, young men are vulnerable from eighteen to twenty-five. That's a big chunk of your life to live with uncertainty."

Teresa was well aware of that. She had breathed a sigh of relief when Matthew turned twenty-six. Even though the vast majority of inductions were among kids just getting out of high school, she had hated even the thought that he might be affected.

"Forgive me for putting this so bluntly," Winston said, "but your father isn't without connections. He can protect them."

"He'd hate having to do that."

"I know, but he'll do it nonetheless rather than see his sons be caught up in this insanity."

She knew Winston was right. While most members of the older generation still seemed unsure about whether or not they approved of the war, her father made no bones about how he felt. "Either we go in there with everything we've got," he had said, "short of nuclear weapons, and finish it once and for all or we get out. Anything in between is just slow suicide."

Accustomed as she was to the moral arguments she had heard on campus for why the war was wrong, Teresa was a bit taken aback at his unapologetically pragmatic stance. But she thought she understood what it stemmed from. Unlike so many of the men making the decisions about Vietnam, he had actually fought in a war, taking part in innumerable island invasions and seeing for himself what combat really involved. He didn't believe in putting the lives of soldiers at risk if they had less than total support.

He wasn't the only one at the network who felt that way. IBS had recently broadcast a special on the fighting that focused very heavily on the daily lives of American soldiers in combat. It showed them tired, discouraged, frightened, and more often than not, bewildered. There had also been strong indication that to escape the misery of their situation, more and more of the troops were turning to drugs. A similar program had been broadcast on IBS's sister network, UBC.

"Would you mind explaining something to me?" she asked Winston over the spaghetti. "How is it that IBS and UBC, technically separate networks, are run by the same people?"

He coughed in his Chianti, excused himself and said, "Dear child, don't let anyone at the office hear you say that. It is a doctrine of pure faith that distance is maintained between the two operations."

"But James Callahan is president of IBS, Alexis Callahan is president of UBC and my father is vice president of operations for them both. So how can they really be separate?''

"They are, for one very simple reason: Alexis was determined to have her own network. You know UBC was founded by her father?''

"I've heard something about that.''

"He was a remarkable man, not someone you would have liked but admirable nonetheless in a ruthless sort of way. He built UBC from nothing to the most successful string of radio stations in the country. Then TV came in right after the war, and he refused to see where it was leading, even though Alexis did her best to try to convince him. The upshot of it all was that she married James in a huff and went to work for IBS. When her father died, he left UBC to her brother, Graham, who did a fine job of running it into the ground. Alexis bided her time, bought up stock and, *voilà*, got what she wanted.''

"You make it sound easy," Teresa mused, "but it couldn't have been. She must have wanted it very much.''

"More than anything . . . almost. The only thing she ever wanted as much was James and she got him, too." The hint of bitterness in his voice was faint but Teresa caught it all the same. Her conviction that the rumors about him and Alexis were true grew stronger, and with it her sympathy.

How terrible it must be to go through life caring for someone who did not feel the same way. While she did not doubt that Matthew's stepmother liked and respected Winston, she knew her well enough to realize that all her most private feelings were reserved strictly for her husband.

Why then did Winston stay within her sphere? Granted he didn't work directly for UBC, but he must certainly see her often nonetheless since, despite what he had said, relations between the two companies were extremely close. He could have gone to work for any of the other networks and not encountered her more often than at an occasional industry dinner. Why put himself through such torment year after year?

For the same reason, she supposed, that she longed to see Matthew even though she knew it would hurt her to do so. Determined not to think about him, she asked, "What happened to Graham?"

"He owns a couple of little literary and art magazines. I think he fancies himself a cultural arbiter or some such thing. Goes to a lot of parties."

The mocking drawl of his voice and the cutting gleam in his eyes told her more than his words themselves. Winston had only contempt for Alexis's brother. Even as she wondered at the cause of it, they moved on to talk of other things.

That summer was not all work for Teresa. She wandered around Greenwich Village with friends, listening to the folk singers and enjoying a sense of kinship with the young people there. She went to parties on the upper East Side where society matrons with hair by Sassoon and clothes by Rudy

Gernreich lamented the bourgeois attitudes of the middle class who didn't understand the needs of the underprivileged. There was a war on hunger and a war on poverty to distract from the brutish little war going on thousands of miles away.

John Lindsay was in his first year as mayor of New York. The tall, patrician politician urged the people to reclaim the city for themselves and led the way by staging happenings in Central Park. Cabdrivers took to calling him "Lindley."

Twiggy was *the* hot model. Teresa briefly considered trying to diet down to the preferred razor-thin shape and rejected the idea. To make it that far, she figured she'd have to sandpaper her hipbones. She did, however, have fun painting tiny flowers on her cheeks and wearing chunky plastic earrings in psychedelic colors.

It was hot that summer, the same wet, heavy heat that plagued New York every year. She spent some weekends at her parents' house, lying around the pool or going to the beach. But she didn't go as often as she might have. It was hard to sink back into the comfort of affluent suburbia when she was becoming aware of how little that had to do with the real world.

On a blistering August day, when not even the office air conditioner could cope with the leaden heat that pressed down on the city, she was sorting through a stack of files when she looked up suddenly to find Matthew watching her.

The shock of seeing him there held her momentarily speechless. She thought she might be imagining things until he came away from the door and walked toward her.

"Hi," he said softly, "how are you doing?"

"Fine . . . how about you?"

"Okay. I heard you were working here, so I thought I'd stop by."

He looked tired. His face was tanned but that didn't completely hide the shadows under his eyes. His hair was tousled, as though he'd been running his fingers through it. He wore a plain white cotton shirt with the collar open and the sleeves rolled up. His jeans were old but clean. She wondered what they thought of them at the *Times* but resisted the impulse to ask.

"Uh . . . that was nice of you," she said, stacking the files on her desk. What was she supposed to say to him? The lack of contact between them had hurt her. She had felt as though a dear friend had abandoned her.

Several times she had thought about calling him but hadn't been able to bring herself to do it. If he wanted to shut her out of his life, so be it. Except that now he was right in front of her, watching her with those quiet blue eyes and she had no idea what to do about it.

"You're looking well," he said gently. That was certainly true. Her hair hung halfway down her back like a fall of gleaming black silk. Since he'd seen her last, she'd taken to wearing a soft fringe of bangs that drew attention to her large, soft eyes. Her skin was faintly golden and she wore a trace of rose lip gloss on her full mouth. When he got closer to her, he could smell a light, citrus scent that made him breathe in deeply.

"Thanks. So are you." That was scintillating. If she kept it up, she would overwhelm him with such clever conversation.

"Do you have to stay much later?" he asked, his eyes focused vaguely over her left shoulder.

"No . . . I'm through. I was just about to leave."

"Want to get a bite?"

Was he asking her to have dinner with him? It sounded like it, but she couldn't be sure. He was being so casual about it, just showing up on the off chance she might be free. Tempted to tell him she had a date, she said instead, "That would be nice."

They went to a Ukrainian restaurant on the lower East Side. It had become popular since the release of *Doctor Zhivago* the year before, and they had to wait a few minutes for a table. "It's funny about places like this," Matthew said when they were seated, "they catch on for a while, do a boom business, then someplace else comes along and the crowd moves on. I wonder sometimes what effect it has on the people left behind."

"If they're smart, they enjoy it while they can and don't let it go to their heads."

"I suppose. Anyway, I'm glad we had a chance to get together." Their eyes met across the table. "It's been a while."

"You've been busy." It was an excuse, graciously offered, but he didn't take it.

"I've thought about you a lot," he said. "Your dad told me how well you were doing at school. That's great."

"What about you?" she asked, fiddling with her fork. "I see your articles occasionally."

He grimaced and reached for the bread basket, offering it to her before breaking off a chunk of dark, rich pumpernickel for himself. "Very occasionally. I don't get into print too often."

"Why is that?"

"Creative differences. That's the polite term for it. Let's just say that the editor and I don't see eye to eye on too many things."

"You don't have to stay there."

He shrugged. "It's the *Times*."

"What's that supposed to mean?"

"For a newspaperman, there's no place better."

"Then, since you don't seem to fit in very well there, maybe you aren't meant to be a newspaperman." It was harsh, but she couldn't help it. Seeing him fighting the same battles he had been a year before, still without any success, both hurt and angered her.

He looked surprised, as though of all the people he might have expected to say such a thing to him, she was the last. "You think I should just give up?" he asked finally.

"No, I'm not suggesting that. But I think you should ask yourself what it is you're trying to accomplish and whether or not you're going about it in the right way."

"That's very. . . pragmatic."

She picked up the menu and began to study it. "I suppose I'm a pragmatic person. That doesn't mean I don't have ideals, too."

"I wasn't about to suggest that it did. I was just surprised, that's all."

"Why surprised?"

He looked away, uncomfortable. When she remained silent, he finally said, "Because of the way you grew up. People from very privileged backgrounds don't tend to be practical. They've had no reason to be."

"You're talking as though you didn't have the same sort of upbringing," she protested, "when you did."

"It wasn't always like that. Remember, until I was five, I lived with my mother and then after she died, Dad was trying to get IBS started and things were pretty tight." He smiled faintly as he went on, "You came home from the hospital to a trailer parked in a potato field. You've heard about that but you don't really have any idea of what it was like. How could you when by the time you were old enough to start noticing much of anything, we'd moved up quite a bit in the world?''

"All right, so you had it tougher than me at the beginning. But that doesn't mean that because I got a few breaks, they made me into some kind of fairy-tale princess locked in an ivory tower."

"No," he said slowly, "I can see they didn't. You're intelligent and strong . . . and beautiful." He laughed a little shakily. "That's a powerful combination."

Teresa barely heard the last part. She was stuck on the bit about her being beautiful. Before she could stop herself, she asked, "Do you really think so?"

"Think what? About you being the way I said? Of course I do."

"I'm not beautiful."

"Where did you get that idea?"

"I mean it. I stick out in the wrong places and my eyes are too big and . . ." She had to stop. It sounded as though she were fishing for compliments in the most desperate way.

Matthew sat back in his chair and regarded her solemnly. He loved the way her thick lashes hid her eyes and how her cheeks were flushed. She had bitten her lower lip and it pouted softly. He had thought that staying away from her would somehow help, but it hadn't. Far from it.

Throughout the rest of the meal they stayed with carefully neutral topics. The weather had cooled off somewhat by the time they left the restaurant and it was almost pleasant in the bus they took uptown to her apartment.

"You don't have to do this," she had said, knowing it was taking him far out of his way. He had insisted nonetheless.

At her door, he smiled and said, "Seems we've played this scene before."

She thought about how she would feel not to see him alone again for another year. "It's early yet. Would you like to come in?"

"No . . . I'd better not. I've got work to do."

"It was just a thought. We could have coffee."

He hesitated, arguing with himself, trying to be strong and sensible—not having much luck. "I guess I could do with a cup, if it isn't too much trouble."

She assured him it wasn't and unlocked the door. The apartment was tidier than usual, for which she was thankful. One of her roommates was away for the summer and the other was so involved with her boyfriend that she was hardly ever there. Having grown up in a house with two brothers who thought the proper place for discarded clothes was on the floor or the back of a chair, Teresa tended to be neat. She scooped a rumpled newspaper off the cocktail table as she said, "Please sit down. The coffee won't take long."

Matthew did as she said, lowering himself onto the sagging couch, and glanced around. The apartment was typical of what he'd seen of student housing in New York, old, dilapidated, yet not unpleasant. The furniture was an eclectic mix obviously donated by assorted parents and other relatives.

Besides the couch, there were two worn easy chairs, an ornately carved cocktail table and what looked like a good, if battered dining room set. The rug was Oriental, faded and threadbare in patches but still lovely. Sheer lace curtains fluttered at the open windows where the wooden venetian blinds had been pulled up.

Sounds typical of a summer night in the city filtered in: cars honking, people talking, children at play. He heard the far-off ring of the ice cream truck's bells and remembered when that had been the signal to immediately run inside and plead for fifteen cents. Funny how that was. The truck came at the same time every evening, but kids never thought to get the money ready ahead of time. Maybe that would have ruined the fun.

"Penny for them," Teresa said softly. She had come back into the room to find him gazing absently out the window, his thoughts obviously far away.

He turned around to her and shook his head. "You'll have to make it fifteen cents, at least."

She set the tray with the coffee and cups on the table in front of him. "Why's that?"

"Never mind. I was just being . . . silly."

The bells rang again. She heard them and understood. A look he remembered very well from her childhood crept over her face, sweet but mischievous. "Come on," she said. "Forget the coffee. If we hurry, we can catch the ice cream man."

"You're kidding? You don't really want to . . ."

"I do." She was already hurrying to the door, leaving him with no choice but to follow. They dashed down the stairs and out onto the sidewalk, startling several matronly women relaxing on the stoop. "There it is," Teresa said, "at the corner."

Matthew grabbed her hand and together they ran down the block, arriving breathless and laughing. Several children were in line ahead of them. They waited while selections were made until finally it was their turn.

"What'll it be?" Matthew asked with a grand sweep of his arm, encompassing the entire illustrated list of selections on the side of the truck. "The sky's the limit."

"Hmmm . . . they all look so good. It's hard to choose but I think I'll have a . . . tutti-frutti sundae with extra nuts and pineapple topping."

"Good choice. I'll have the banana boat with chocolate ripple, strawberry sauce, whipped cream and hold the cherry."

As their selections were made up, he grinned down at her and added, "You realize that if there is any justice in this world, we are both going to be sick as dogs?"

"Not a bit. I'll have you know I could eat this stuff every day."

"Yeah, but if you did, you wouldn't be human anymore."

Laughing, they wandered back down the street. It was beginning to get dark and the ladies of the stoop had gone inside. Teresa and Matthew took their places, sitting close together on the hard stone step. Neither spoke until the cardboard containers of ice cream were almost empty.

"Ugh," Teresa said, scraping up the last of her sundae, "that was really awful."

"Mine, too. Disgusting." He tilted the cup and peered into it, confirming that nothing was left. "Too bad our tastes haven't improved any since we were kids."

"Do you remember when you got hold of that watermelon, put a hole in it and poured in almost a whole bottle of gin? Remember how sick we got?"

"Don't remind me. I also couldn't sit down for a week."

She chuckled softly at the memory. "Didn't Dad read you the riot act for leading me astray?"

"Yeah, I didn't have the heart to tell him it had been your idea."

"You didn't have to go along."

"Have you ever seen your face when you have your heart set on something?"

"Effective, is it?"

"Devastating. I never learned to say no."

"Why," she asked softly, giving him the full benefit of a doe-eyed stare, "would you want to?"

Why indeed? When it was so much easier to just give in. He moved closer, staring at the moist fullness of her mouth. There was a trace of chocolate sauce in one corner. He hesitated, bent his head and kissed it away.

As kisses went, this was modest. No straining bodies, no thrusting tongues. Just a sweet, gentle pressing of the lips that went on...and on...and on. Matthew's hand curled around the empty ice cream cup, crushing it without noticing. He was crazy to be doing this, absolutely certifiable. But it felt so good. Just this once, he promised himself. Then he would find the strength to stay away from her. Somehow.

Chapter Three

MATTHEW DID NOT KEEP his promise to himself. Throughout the rest of that year and into the next he saw Tessa regularly. He also kissed her, more than he thought proper. But he did not go any further, and that he counted as a victory. Sometimes they merely sat together in his apartment or hers, Teresa working on her course assignments while he wrote. Being together offered them some comfort from the turbulent events swirling around them.

In April, they marched together in the antiwar demonstration that brought hundreds of thousands of mostly young people to the Sheep Meadow in Central Park to hear Martin Luther King become the first civil rights leader to publicly condemn the war in Vietnam. Teresa found the experience exhilarating, but Matthew's reaction was more restrained. He thought it had about as much chance of making any real difference as the attempt by the newly formed Yippies, led by Abbie Hoffman and Jerry Rubin, to levitate the Pentagon. What they would do once they got it raised into the air they didn't say, but presumably it wouldn't have been anything good.

"We've started making fun of ourselves and what we stand for," he said one evening. "We've begun pretending that nothing is really very serious. And we're doing it because we've realized we're not going to be able to change anything.''

"Of course we can," Teresa insisted. An Aretha Franklin record was playing on the stereo. They had just come back from seeing Dustin Hoffman in *The Graduate* for the second time. Teresa loved the scene where the middle-aged man confides that the future lies in plastics. It fit so perfectly. Matthew thought it was a nice line, but mainly he liked looking at Anne Bancroft.

"There's an election next year," she reminded him. "It could change everything."

He shrugged, unimpressed. "Johnson will run again and win. He'll be president until 1972, God help us."

"He's in an awful lot of trouble, here and abroad. Maybe he'll decide it isn't worth it and go back to the ranch."

"Maybe, but then who will we get? Humphrey, Nixon, somebody like that? You think they can do any better?"

"They aren't the only choices. What about Robert Kennedy?"

Matthew got up to refill their coffee cups form the pot on the white Lucite table. He had never really gotten around to furnishing the apartment, instead just picking up things as they occurred to him. There was beige wall-to-wall carpeting left by the previous tenant, a couch covered in serviceable brown corduroy and Scandinavian-style bookshelves overflowing with the accumulated clobber of his profession. He still had the battered old desk he'd gotten in college, but it was all but invisible under the load of papers, books, files and typewriter spread over it. The bedroom wasn't much different, and the bath and kitchen were strictly functional. He'd hung a few pop-art posters on the walls and considered the place done.

When he sat down again, he said, "Kennedy would have to be crazy to run after what happened to his brother."

"There's absolutely no way anything like that could happen again."

Matthew really didn't think so either, but he doubted Robert Kennedy's ability to win. Granted, he had managed to get elected to the senate from New York, but that was mainly on the basis of liberal city voters. The country as a whole was a lot more conservative. Though it was getting a little hard to be sure about that.

Even the staid old *Times* had discovered the "counterculture" and was busy running articles explaining the differences between acid and speed, exploring life in the communes of the East Village and Haight-Ashbury, even describing the fashions of the flower children. He was writing more than ever these days—and getting published—but he couldn't say he was happy. A grim sense of something going very wrong kept him tense and worried.

Teresa helped. Being with her gave him perspective. She was at once a reminder of the far more secure and simple years of their childhood and a hint that the future might, despite all evidence to the contrary, be worthwhile. It was a scant hope to hold on to, but it was all he had.

"I've got to go see my parents this weekend," he said. "Want to come with me?"

Teresa nodded. She would have gone whether she really wanted to or not, knowing as she did that relations were strained just now between Matthew and his father. Matthew's continued refusal to join IBS angered James. He saw it as a repudiation of everything he had worked for. Alexis tried to be a buffer between them, but Teresa was sure she wouldn't mind having some help.

Matthew picked her up shortly after 11:00 A.M. the following Saturday. She had dressed for the occasion in a simple ivory linen sheath from Bergdorf's, part of her "other" wardrobe as distinct from the casual clothes she wore to class. With it she wore flat-heeled pumps that matched her good leather bag, sheer stockings and the pearl earrings she had received for her eighteenth birthday. Her hair was neatly brushed and secured with a black velvet ribbon at the nape of her neck. She looked young, lovely and sophisticated.

Or at least Matthew thought so. Accustomed as he was to seeing her in the plain, even drab clothes of a college student, he was frankly astounded by the transformation. She was always beautiful but now she was also something more: cool, self-possessed, serene in a way he could not help but envy.

"You look great," he said without exaggeration.

"You're not so bad yourself. Was it very hard getting into a suit?"

Catching the teasing gleam in her hazel eyes, he laughed. "Not as much as I expected." But then the suit he was wearing hadn't exactly come from Brooks Brothers. The flared jacket and form-fitting slacks were Savile Row with a dash of Carnaby Street, as was the dark-blue shirt and the vibrant splash of a red silk tie. He looked elegant, assured and virile. A combination she didn't want to think too much about.

They took a cab to his parents' town house. Going from Morningside Heights to the East Side was a transition between two worlds. At the beginning was the bedraggled, dingy neighborhood shared by students and old-time residents who hadn't been lucky enough to move up and out. At the other end was the sleek, glittering world of wealth and privilege.

Teresa felt the same disorientation that she experienced when she visited her own parents, and recognized its cause. She was trying to live in two worlds, as different from each other as it was possible to be, with often opposing values and expectations.

In this she was hardly alone; most of her classmates at both Barnard and Columbia were also from affluent families and had the same problem. Many of them solved it by arbitrarily rejecting everything their parents believed in while embracing anything they opposed. She couldn't take that easy way out, suspecting as she did that there was good and bad in both worlds. Somehow they would have to be reconciled, but she had no idea how that might be done, not when the gap between them seemed so huge.

The butler opened the door when Matthew rang. He was an older man with thin gray hair wearing a plain white apron over his well-cut black wool slacks and starched white shirt. To all intents and purposes, he ran the household, leaving Alexis free to concentrate on her job and family.

"Good morning, sir," he said, inclining his head slightly to Matthew. Teresa got a small smile. "Nice to see you again, miss."

"Thank you, Thompson," she said softly as she stepped into the foyer that was easily the size of an average living room. Directly to the right of the door stood a Sheraton breakfront with a Louis XV gilded mirror above it. A silver bowl containing a simple arrangement of anemones was reflected in the glass. Other fine antiques and oil paintings were scattered about, illuminated by a crystal chandelier that might have been taken from Versailles. The floor was black and white marble, as was the staircase that curved up out of sight toward the second floor.

James and Alexis were in the living room. They rose as Teresa and Matthew entered. Looking coolly beautiful in a pearl-gray silk dress that matched her eyes, Alexis gave them each a light kiss on the cheek. "We're so glad you could come," she said in her faintly smoky voice.

"Thank you for having me," Teresa responded politely. She had known Alexis all her life but had never lost the instinct to treat her with a certain degree of formality. Matthew's stepmother was a kind and loving woman, but she was also no one to underestimate.

James shook hands with Matthew in the way of men who are resolved to try to get along, and nodded to Teresa. He was a big, solidly built man with riveting blue eyes and square-cut features. Even in the gray pin-striped suit he wore, he looked hard and somehow dangerous. She knew he had been her father's commanding officer during World War II, and had come home to claw his way to the top of an industry that was nothing short of cutthroat. Along the way he had undoubtedly made some enemies, but he had also found a woman who was in every way his equal.

If she was worried about how her stepson and husband were getting along, Alexis did not show it. She smiled warmly as she took Teresa's arm and guided her over to the couch. "James," she said over her shoulder, "be a dear and do the drinks."

He obliged, pouring sherry for Teresa, a very light highball for Alexis, a beer for Matthew and the same for himself. As he handed his son the glass, he asked, "How are things at the paper?"

Equally politely, Matthew told him a bit about a series of articles he was working on that had to do with the intricacies of city politics. "It's interesting enough," he concluded, "seeing how the various ethnic groups have carved out niches for themselves, but I'd still like to be doing something on the national level."

"Perhaps you'll get your chance next year," James suggested.

Matthew rather doubted it but he wasn't about to say so and give his father the opportunity to suggest yet again that he should go with IBS.

They settled on safer topics as they worked their way through the drinks and moved on to the dining room and lunch. Alexis humorously described their difficulties in putting together the fall schedule. "We're working on an adventure show that's being shot at a variety of exotic locations. The leading man may look like the all-American hero but his agent never bothered to mention that he's afraid of spiders, snakes and almost everything else."

"Including his own shadow," James added. "The guy bolted out of bed the other night in his trailer and woke up the entire crew swearing he'd heard a lion roar outside his window. Turned out it was the makeup girl's cat."

"That's not as bad as what's happening on the new variety hour," Alexis said. "The biggest problem there is that when the star is cold sober, he's as funny as the proverbial dead doornail. But if he gets too sloshed, he passes out. We have to hope he'll settle somewhere in between.''

Matthew smiled as he listened to them but his eyes were serious. As always when he was with them, he was struck by the depth of love and understanding between his father and stepmother. Whatever differences they might have—and with two such strongwilled people there had to be some—they still stood united against the world. Much as he hated to admit it, he envied them that.

''How are Mandy and Jim?'' he asked as the remnants of the main course were removed and the dishes for dessert replaced them.

Alexis and James exchanged a quick look. Softly, she said, ''We had hoped they'd be here today but they had other plans.''

Not surprising, Teresa thought. The twins were seventeen, an age when a quiet Saturday afternoon lunch at home with the folks did not have much appeal.

''Mandy's taken to hanging around in Washington Square Park,'' James said, ''and Jimmy goes with her. I can't say I'm pleased about it, but she seems pretty sensible.''

Teresa agreed with that. Mandy was a golden girl, accustomed to getting anything she wanted out of life. She was as beautiful as her mother and as toughminded. It didn't seem likely that she would jeopardize her privileged existence for a quick fling on the more sordid side of the generation gap. Jimmy, however, was another story. Depending on his sister to keep him out of trouble didn't strike her as very wise.

"How's Jim doing in school?" Matthew asked. Alone among the family, he refused to use the diminutive form of his half brother's name, guessing correctly that it was resented.

"The same as usual," James said. His younger son remained a mystery to him. He had never understood the quiet, moody boy who looked so much like his vivacious sister yet was so different. The few times he had made an effort to get closer to him, he had failed completely. After a while, he had given up trying.

Alexis had much more contact with her son, mainly because she worked at it doggedly. But even she had lately had the sense that he was slipping away, despite all her best efforts to hold him.

Jim was still on Matthew's mind when he and Teresa made their farewells and left the town house. It was midafternoon. The East Side streets were crowded with shoppers. They drifted along with them, glancing in the store windows, and talking quietly.

"I'm worried about Jim," Matthew said at length. "When I saw him about a month ago, he seemed really distracted and uptight. I wondered if he was using drugs."

"Do you think Mandy is?"

"A little pot, maybe. Not more than that. She's like Alexis, fastidious."

"Your father thinks she'll protect Jimmy."

"He wants to believe that, and I'm willing to bet that she'll try. But she's just a kid, after all, not a miracle worker."

"Is that what you think he needs, a miracle?"

"I don't know," Matthew admitted. "But I'm afraid there are some kids who are just going to end up lost. I don't want him to be one of them."

Teresa's hand tightened on his. He had taken off his jacket and slung it over his shoulder. His tie was stuffed into his shirt pocket. He looked so strong and masculine that it was tempting to think he was invulnerable. But she knew better. He was hurting inside from his worry over Jim, his conflict with his father, his inability to do much about either.

"I wish I could help," she said softly.

He glanced down, meeting her eyes. "You do. It helps just to talk with you." Before she could respond, he reached out and gently pulled off the velvet ribbon that had worked itself loose. Her ebony hair tumbled free. She smiled a little self-consciously as she pushed a strand of it away from her cheek. The desire to touch him was almost overwhelming but she resisted it. She did not want to be so in thrall to her needs when he seemed so readily able to control his.

The late spring air was soft against her skin. Recent rains and a steady breeze had washed the city clean. Instead of exhaust and moldering garbage, she could smell moist, fecund earth and the fragile perfume of trees bursting into bloom. In Central Park, the dogwood was in flower. She wanted to walk there with him, holding his hand, sharing smiles. And when they had walked enough, she wanted to go back with him to his apartment, his arms and his bed.

Should she be ashamed of that? He had once been like a brother to her and to a certain extent still was. She felt the same deep affection and trust that she always had. It would have been far easier if she could wipe the emotional slate clean and start over, but that was not to be. They were bound together by the strands of too many memories. Whatever future they might have together had to be built on the past, which their generation seemed so intent on repudiating, and on the present, which seemed more and more to be careening out of control.

Teresa worked for IBS news again that summer. It was a busy time. During the first weekend of July, the pressures of poverty and prejudice made unendurable by failed promises boiled over; rioting broke out in Los Angeles's black ghetto of Watts. It had happened before, two years before, but this time it was worse. The television cameras showed block after block of buildings in flames against a dark, smoke-filled sky. The fires casting eerie shadows over the running figures of looters and police. Snipers took to the roofs. Nervous newsmen spoke of open rebellion, and the pictures broadcast to the nation and the world backed them up.

Newark went next, exploding two weeks later in a replay of Watts that if anything was even more violent. Detroit followed. Then Wilmington, Toledo, Pontiac, New Haven and so on, a litany of violence and chaos stretching across the country. "Revolution" began to look like more than a political cliché.

"New York could be next," Winston said one evening when they were sitting around the newsroom after the evening broadcast. Most of the staff had been in since early morning, trying to keep up with the wildfire pace of events. They were all worn out but too tense to go home.

"Lindsay's kept the peace so far," an assistant producer said. He was young, Ivy League, and tended to identify with the mayor.

The middle-aged director did not. He shrugged and took a long slurp of coffee out of a cardboard container before he said, "Bread and circuses, that's all we've got here. Lindsay shows up in his shirt sleeves with the TV cameras, walks up and down the street a few times and everybody's supposed to believe he's actually accomplished something."

"Hasn't he?" the young man asked. "New York isn't burning."

"Neither is Los Angeles or Detroit or Newark, not really. What's burning are the black slums within those cities. All they're doing is hurting themselves."

"They're protesting the deeply rooted injustices of this society."

"They're playing into the hands of the bigots," the director insisted wearily. "Every time some black kid gets on TV throwing a Molotov cocktail or running off with a stereo, the white backlash gets that much worse. Sometimes I wonder what we're doing when we put it on the air."

"Are you saying we should be censoring ourselves?" Winston asked quietly. He was stretched out in his chair, his jacket off and his tie loosened. With the makeup gone, deep circles showed under his eyes. Like the others, he was exhausted, but he didn't want to be by himself. There was some comfort in sharing the craziness that threatened to engulf them all.

"It's a classic case of the Heisenberg principle from physics," Teresa interjected. "The theory is that the simple act of observing a phenomenon changes it. That's what's happening here."

At the startled looks from the men, she caught herself. A little apologetically, she said, "I read that somewhere."

"Uh . . . right . . ." the young assistant producer murmured, clearing his throat. "I think what Teresa means is that by being on the scene, we alter it, we become, in effect, part of the story."

"Just so long as we aren't becoming the reason for the story," Winston said. He lit another cigarette and went on, "For the youngsters—" his tired smile touched Teresa and the young producer "—let me add that we've been debating this topic since the earliest days of TV and we haven't resolved it yet. I doubt you will, either, even if you hang around as long as we have.''

''That's the truth,'' the director agreed. ''But it makes a nice problem to hold on to. Nothing like a fine old philosophical debate to take refuge in when all hell is breaking loose.''

Later, when Teresa was leaving, she arrived at the elevator at the same time as the young producer. They nodded to each other and stood for a moment in silence before he said, ''It's funny with those old guys, isn't it? They think we're just replaying what they've already been through.''

''Aren't we?'' she asked.

He looked genuinely surprised. ''Of course not. You know what Dylan says, 'the times, they are a changin'.' We're the beginning of something completely different.''

''Other generations have believed that.''

His gaze, which had been surreptitiously admiring, sharpened. ''I think you're missing the point.''

''Maybe,'' she allowed with a slight smile. ''It wouldn't be the first time. I'm just a little nervous about all the talk of building a new, better world. No one seems to have any real idea of how to do it, except that when we get done everything will be wonderful for everyone. That strikes me as unrealistic.''

"We have to at least try," he insisted. "If you aren't part of the solution, you're part of the problem."

Teresa's smile faded. She was tired of hearing complex situations trivialized into simplistic slogans. It was as though an entire generation had grown up expecting every human problem to be solved in thirty minutes or less with time left over for commercials. No wonder any idea that took more than a dozen words to express seemed to leave most people baffled. Didn't anyone read books these days?

Matthew did, and she wished, not for the first time, that he was on hand to talk things over with. The paper had sent him to San Francisco to do a piece on the "Summer of Love" unfolding in Haight-Ashbury. Unlike Teresa, his editor had no idea that he had a personal reason for wanting to be there, to find his half brother and convince him to come home.

Jim had been gone for a month now. Mandy was the last person to have seen him, and she could shed only partial light on why he had gone. "He was getting real uptight," she had said tearfully when confronted by her parents several days after Jim's disappearance. Matthew had also been there, along with Teresa and Anthony and Maggie. The two families had been so close for so long that it was only natural for them to face a crisis together.

"Nothing seemed to matter to him anymore," she went on. "He was convinced he was never going to amount to anything, so he didn't see any reason to keep trying.''

"He's only seventeen years old, for God's sake!'' James paced back and forth across the living room, unable to sit still. He couldn't believe this was happening and was at a loss as to how to deal with it. "He'll come back when he realizes he can't get along without money.''

"He has money,'' Mandy corrected quietly. "About five hundred dollars, I think.''

"Where did he get that from?'' Matthew asked.

She refused to meet his eyes. "Working, odd jobs, doing favors for people. Like that.''

"Jobs?'' Alexis repeated. "I had no idea Jimmy was working.''

"Maybe because he didn't want you to,'' Matthew said. He walked over to Mandy, put his hands on her shoulders and forced her to meet his eyes. "What kind of favors?''

"Nothing...really, just taking stuff places. Across town, like that. It's no big deal.''

"I don't understand,'' James said. "He got that money delivering packages?''

"Delivering drugs,'' Matthew corrected, too angry to try to soften the blow. Mandy winced but didn't argue. "The dealers figure that a first offender won't get more than a slap on the wrist.'' Before his father could reply, he turned back to Mandy. "How much is he using?''

Her eyes filled with tears. They trickled down her pale cheeks as she said, "Too much. I tried to tell him. A little grass is one thing, but he wouldn't stop there." Glancing fearfully at her mother and father who stood in shocked silence, she added, "I didn't know what to do. I couldn't handle it by myself."

"Why didn't you come to us?" James asked, his voice low and harsh. He had gone gray beneath his tan. Alexis moved to his side, touching his arm in a silent gesture of comfort.

"You knew he was in trouble," Mandy insisted. "What could I have told you that would have made any difference? All right, maybe I should have said something about the drugs, but he's my brother, I didn't want to rat on him. And now—" Her voice broke as she buried her face in her hands, sobbing.

Teresa went to her, putting her arms around the younger girl's slender shoulders. She had never been particularly close to Mandy but now she truly felt for her. She was, after all, only a child confronted by a responsibility few adults could have handled. Recriminations would do no good; what mattered was to find Jim.

Which was what Matthew had gone to do. Private detectives had traced the boy west from New York's Port Authority Bus Terminal, eventually losing his trail in San Francisco. They were sure he had joined the migration of young people drifting into the old, run-down neighborhood of Haight-Ashbury for the much advertised love-in.

"That's a hell of a name for it," Matthew had said just before he left. "Every two-bit hooker, con artist and pusher will be out to take them for everything they've got. What'll be left won't be worth putting out with the garbage."

"You'll find him," Teresa had insisted even though she was nowhere near that sure. Kids were disappearing every day into the seamier neighborhoods around the country. If they turned up at all, it was panhandling or pushing or selling themselves in some back alley. Too many showed up cold on mortuary slabs.

It had to end soon, she thought. The craziness was eating them up alive. Every day brought new horror stories. Kids dying in Vietnam and at home. Neighborhoods burning. Nothing to hold on to except the dim hope that things couldn't possibly get worse. And even that was fading fast.

Matthew had thought he was prepared for what he would find when he reached San Francisco, but he had been wrong. At twenty-seven, he simply hadn't lived long enough to know the true potential for brutality and depravity that lurked within human beings. His father could have warned him, or Anthony could have, but it hadn't occurred to either of them that the violence and insanity they had lived through more than twenty years before on steaming jungle islands they rightly called hell could also happen in 1967 in America to their children.

On the surface, it didn't look too bad. There were lots of kids—flower children, the media called them—gotten up in gypsy rags: cast-off uniforms, baggy overalls, dresses Grandma might have worn if she hadn't had much taste, that sort of thing. It was innocent really, even rather sweet. They sat around on street corners, singing, smiling, offering strangers flowers. The idea was that they looked out for each other. There were crash pads where beds could be had for a night or longer. People shared food—and drugs. The smell of pot was heavy on the warm summer air. Matthew walked along, hands in his pockets, looking and listening. After a while, he began to see beneath the surface.

The guys selling the drugs weren't flower children, far from it. They'd let their hair grow long and had all the right moves, but they weren't the real thing. They were older, harder, had been there longer, and found it very funny that all these rich, dumb kids had landed in their backyard begging to get ripped off.

A girl, she couldn't have been more than Jim's age, came up to Matthew a couple of hours after dark when he was still wandering around trying to decide on a plan. He'd stopped briefly on a street corner and next thing he knew, a hand was touching his crotch. When he jumped back, he found himself staring into a pale, pinched face. Five bucks, she said, for anything he wanted. He looked at her filthy, emaciated body, at the needle tracks on her arms and the desperate light in her eyes and felt the urge to be sick. In the end, he gave her the money just to get her to go away because there was no way to help and at least it would buy her a few more hours of oblivion.

Hashbury, as the inhabitants called it, got worse as the night wore on. Sporadic screams and sobs drifted down from the old Victorian row houses long since broken up into cold-water flats. They mingled with the hard-driving rock blaring from windows— Beatles, Stones, Doors, Hendrix—all with the same message: The world was lousy; drugs and sex made it hurt less.

Nobody seemed to sleep or go home. People wandered up and down the streets all night, looking for a handout, a fix, something undefinable and never to be found. Matthew was exhausted, hungry, dazed. He wanted to get a few hours' rest but could not bring himself to do so. His brother was out there somewhere and he meant to find him.

Toward dawn he did, in a crash pad a girl had directed him to. As he had with dozens of other young people he stopped, he'd shown her Jim's picture, explained that his hair was probably longer now but he otherwise might look pretty much the same. Had she seen him?

"Don't know," she murmured, her gaze going back and forth from the picture to Matthew as her jaw worked a wad of gum. "What's he to you?"

"My brother."

"Yeah, thas nice, havin' a brother. Whatta you want him for?"

"I want to make sure he's all right." No sense mentioning he was there to take him home.

"Sure wish I had someone thinking about me like that." Her eyes shifted again. They were small and bloodshot, set in her old-young face. He figured she was about sixteen, going on eighty. "Uh…listen…I could use a little help myself." Her voice took on a whining edge as though she expected to have to plead her case.

Experienced now, he held up the five dollar bill. "Have you seen him?"

"Yeah, sure I have, lots of times."

"What's his name?"

"Name? How would I know? Hey, if he's your brother, you gotta know his name."

He waited, holding the money in front of her. The hours in Hashbury had toughened him. She wasn't getting it unless she had what he wanted.

She wet her cracked lips, eyes on the bill. "Lemme think a sec'. I did hear his name, a while ago, a couple of days at least. Sam . . . no, that's a biker hangs out around here. Somethin' else . . . Jim. That's it, Jim."

"Where is he?"

"Callie's place, number fifty-seven on Haight, top floor." Triumph in her eyes as he handed her the bill, and a parting shot before she strolled away. "Better get there quick, honey. He's not doin' so good."

Matthew took the steps three at a time. A thin, pasty-faced boy tried to stop him on the second floor. "Hey," he demanded, "what are you doing here, man? You a pig or something?"

Matthew rammed him against the nearest wall and went on. "You can't do that," the boy cried shrilly. "This is private property."

It would have been funny except that Matthew seemed to have lost his sense of humor somewhere along the line. Somebody opened a door as he passed the third floor, and shut it again hastily. He went on, ignoring the stink of stale air, urine and vomit. On the top floor, it occurred to him that he didn't know which apartment was Callie's. He thought briefly of going back downstairs and wringing the information out of the pasty-faced young man but decided against it. Instead, he banged on the nearest door. There was scurrying behind it and finally a thin voice called out, "Who's there?"

"The landlord. Open up."

It was better than nothing, he figured. If he'd said the police, he'd have had to break the door down. Instead it opened a crack and a dark brown face peered out. "What'chu wan', man?"

"Where's Callie?"

"Who?"

"Callie. Where is she?"

"Not here, man. Last apartment on the left. *Sheet,* you not the landlord, else you know that."

He turned and walked back down the hallway, stepping over a pile of garbage before he reached the last door. When he knocked, there was no answer. He tried again, louder. The door swung open by itself. Inside, the apartment was dark. He could make out a single candle burning in what must have been the main room.

Advancing gingerly, he gave his eyes a chance to adjust to the dimness. When they did, he could make out the shapes of perhaps a dozen people slumped on the mattresses tossed on the floor. Sweet, pungent smoke filled the room. Several hash pipes were being passed around. Nearby, a candle, spoon, a length of rubber tubing and a syringe lay discarded.

A fumbling hand reached for his ankle. He eluded it and walked deeper into the room. On one mattress, a couple lay entangled, both naked. On another, a boy in a shirt and nothing else lay curled up in the fetal position. A girl with small, adolescent breasts slumped nearby.

He found Jim in a corner. His blond hair was thick and matted. Grime encrusted his face; his clothes were filthy and hung in tatters on his sticklike frame. He was unconscious and his skin was cold.

Matthew lifted him in his arms and held him tight for a moment before slinging him over his shoulder in a fireman's carry. He left the room, stepping over the bodies the same way he had come in, carefully not looking at them.

Outside no one tried to stop him or ask if he needed help. A group of kids, passing a wine bottle around in a doorway, laughed as he passed. They thought there was something funny about him and what he carried. He had to walk several blocks before he found a police cruiser.

"OD'd," the cop said after shining a flashlight in Jim's rolled-back eyes. "Any idea what he took?"

Matthew shook his head. "Could have been anything. Can we get him to a hospital?" It surprised him how calm he sounded as though all his emotions had been turned off. There was so much more he wanted to ask: Can you help him? Will he live? He's only seventeen, my brother, please don't let him die.

But he kept all of that inside him, all the way to the hospital, in the emergency room and then much later as he sat vigil beside Jim's bed. He'd been luckier than most, he was going to pull through. The doctors had even been guardedly optimistic. "From the look of his arms," said one, "he hasn't been using heroin long. If you can get him out of here, and keep him away, he might have a chance."

A chance. It wasn't much, no guarantees, but under the circumstances Matthew grabbed hold of it with both hands. He was past being tired though he felt very old. In the morning, he would call his parents and tell them what had happened. When Jim was well enough to travel, he would take him home. Then he would go to Teresa.

The thought of her sustained him through the long, dark night, but it could not keep the dampness from his cheeks or the despair from his soul.

Chapter Four

NOW IS THE WINTER *of our discontent*. That line from *Richard III* kept running through Matthew's mind in the months after his return from Haight-Ashbury. The advantages of a good education. At least he didn't go around quoting Hermann Hesse or some other profound thinker whose work he felt more rightly belonged inside a greeting card than between the covers of a book. Stark and simple, that was old Will. Even at his floweriest, he didn't hesitate to say what was on his mind.

Made glorious summer by this son of York. Good for them; they'd had heroes back then. Too bad they weren't still around. Or were they?

"Kennedy's got to run," he told Teresa shortly after New Year when they were all at her parent's house on Long Island. Jim was there, too, seemingly recovered since his stay at the expensive, discreet rest home where he'd detoxed. But he had little to say and seemed content to go from one day to the next without thought of the future.

"It wasn't so long ago that you said he'd be crazy to try," Teresa pointed out. They were sitting on the couch together after dinner. Since Jim—that was how they thought of it, not in any more specific terms—

the families had made an effort to be together more.
Even Mandy went along. She was there now, looking lovely as usual, laughing at something Anthony
had just said.

The pair on the couch were a little removed from
the rest of the gathering. That was deliberate. "Since
Jim" they had drawn closer together, forming something of a bulwark against the rest of the world.

Teresa remembered, too vividly, the night Matthew had come back. She had woken late to the sound
of banging on her door. Since the previous spring she
had lived alone in a better apartment Maggie had
found for her, into which Anthony had installed one
of every security device ever made. Teresa had tolerated that for the simple reason that she wasn't feeling any too safe these days. Besides, it didn't cost
anything to ease her parents' worries.

She had gotten out of bed hesitantly, uncertain
whether she should answer. There could have been
any kind of nut out there. Only the ragged sound of
Matthew's voice calling her name had sent her fumbling for the locks.

"Tessa," he had murmured, slipping back into the
way he had addressed her when she was little, "I
need to see you."

She had let him in, appalled by how exhausted and
ill he looked. He had staggered slightly, almost as
though he was drunk, though she didn't have to be
told that he was not. Her arm had gone around him
instinctively as he slumped against her. Without

thought, without hesitation, she had led him into the bedroom.

He had been asleep before she finished getting his shoes and belt off, his long body collapsed on the narrow bed, arms and legs askew. It had been difficult to find room for herself beside him, but she had managed, defiantly determined that was where she was going to be.

They had woken together in the morning, Matthew abashed and wary. Teresa had been deliberately matter-of-fact. She had gotten out of bed and put on her robe just as though it was any ordinary morning.

Over coffee and breakfast, she had coaxed from him the story of what had happened in San Francisco. Later, when he was leaving, he had tried to thank her but she would have none of it. It was enough that he had come to her; she would wait for the rest.

In the meantime, there was a great deal to keep her occupied. She had started working for Senator Eugene McCarthy, supporting the quixotic Wisconsin Democrat in his challenge against President Johnson. Contributions were few, but young volunteers poured in daily and there was a spirit of hopefulness about the campaign. At least they were doing something. When, on March 12, McCarthy won the New Hampshire presidential primary, Teresa was as shocked as everyone else. Suddenly the tilting at windmills had turned grimly serious.

The weekend after the primary, Robert Kennedy declared his own candidacy for president and Teresa and Matthew had their first real argument.

"You have to switch," he insisted. "McCarthy doesn't have a chance. He's Adlai Stevenson all over again. But Kennedy can win and that's what counts."

"He should have come in sooner, then I would have supported him. But he let McCarthy do the dirty work, and now he's trying to ride his coattails. I can't go for that."

"Then you don't really care what happens in November. Don't you realize it's going to be Nixon for the Republicans? Do you really think McCarthy can beat him?"

"I don't know," she admitted. "But he deserves the chance to try. He had the courage to act on his convictions when Kennedy was still sitting on the fence."

Matthew shook his head in disgust at what he considered to be her blind stubbornness. "Kennedy is a realist. Very harsh experience made him that way. He can beat Johnson *and* Nixon. McCarthy won't be able to do either."

"Like he couldn't win in New Hampshire?"

"Those were Kennedy's votes; they just had no place else to go."

"That's ridiculous! McCarthy won on his own merit."

"Whether he did or not doesn't really make any difference. Do you honestly think he would be a good president?"

Teresa hesitated. She wanted to say yes but couldn't quite manage it. In fact, she wasn't at all sure what kind of president the Wisconsin senator would be. All she believed for certain was that he couldn't be any worse than what they already had.

More than half a million Americans were fighting in Vietnam, a tenfold increase in five years. More than twenty thousand had been killed, and the end was nowhere in sight, General Westmoreland's claims not to the contrary. The U.S. had suffered a crushing moral defeat during the Tet lunar new year offensive when the Communists had effectively put the lie to claims that the hearts and minds of the Vietnamese people were being won. Westmoreland was replaced, but the damage was irreparable. For the first time in history, Americans were having to grapple with not simply the possibility but the probability that they would lose a war.

In that atmosphere of bewilderment and recrimination, the presidential campaign heated up. On the evening of Sunday, March 31, Teresa was at home studying. Johnson was due to speak to the nation on TV and radio, but she couldn't bring herself to listen to him. She preferred to immerse herself in the far more elegant butchery of seventeenth-century Europe, and was deep into an analysis of Louis XIV's economic motives when she was interrupted by cheers from out in the hall. She ignored them until they got louder, then stuck her head out the door to ask what was going on.

"Johnson's bowed out," a buoyant young woman told her. "He's thrown in the towel." When she still didn't seem to understand, the woman explained, "He isn't going to run for another term."

"How do you know?"

"He just said so, at the end of his speech. Isn't it fab? Now Kennedy will win for sure."

Teresa went back into the apartment and shut the door. The seventeenth century no longer seemed so attractive. Loyalty made her want to stick with McCarthy, but common sense told her otherwise. With Johnson out of the picture, the Democratic establishment would be maneuvering hard and fast to get one of their own the nomination.

Vice President Hubert Humphrey was the most likely choice. He was a New Deal liberal with impeccable labor and civil rights credentials whose recent role as apologist for Vietnam had to be viewed as an aberration in an otherwise outstanding career. Kennedy would have a hard time beating him; McCarthy might well not have a chance.

"Have you seen the light yet?" Matthew asked when he called the next day. He didn't want her mad at him, but he didn't want her deluding herself either.

"Have you?" she countered, buying time.

"Never mind; I get the picture. What do you say we forget about politics for a while and concentrate on something else?"

"Is there something else?" she asked with a faint laugh. "Everyone seems obsessed by it these days."

"True, but you know what they say about all work and no play. I happen to be looking at two tickets for orchestra seats to *Funny Girl* this Saturday. Want to come?"

Did she? The show starring Barbra Streisand was the hottest in town. Tickets were all but impossible to get. She didn't want to ask how Matthew had done so. "Let's just say," she murmured, "that I could be talked into it."

He laughed triumphantly. "Never let it be said that I won't stoop to bribery. I'll pick you up at six and we can have dinner before the show."

Teresa looked forward to it eagerly. The grim mood on campus was weighing her down. She wanted to forget it for at least some little time, put on pretty clothes and enjoy herself with Matthew. Was it so much to ask, really? A small break from the bleak routine?

Except that it was not to be. Her last class on Thursday was over at four, but she stayed on campus, reading in the library. The hours passed and it began to get dark. She was vaguely hungry and thought perhaps she should go and get something to eat. Getting up, she gathered her books and walked past the small, glass-walled cubicle where a librarian generally worked.

At this hour there was only another student there, a young man, filling out file cards. A radio played softly in the background. Teresa was almost past when she saw him suddenly sit bolt upright in his chair, his hands gripping the edge of the desk. The music had stopped.

A cold, eerie sense of déjà vu crept over Teresa. She had seen the same expression on a person's face only once before, when she was thirteen and a student at a private day school. A teacher had come into the room and whispered something to her teacher. The woman had looked just like the young man did now. They had been sent home early that day because a president had been shot.

She began to tremble and clasped her books more tightly. The young man turned slightly and caught sight of her. His eyes were wide and dark. Silently, through the glass wall, she saw his lips move as he shaped the words, "He's dead."

He. Who? Kennedy? Matthew's fear for the brother of the slain president echoed in her mind. Could it have happened already? She forced her legs to move, walking around the glass partition. Her throat was tight and her voice unnaturally high as she asked, "Who?"

The young man was shaking his head dazedly. "Martin Luther King. They shot him . . . in Memphis. He's dead."

King? The man whose words she could still remember hearing, rolling out over the sea of human-
ity gathered between the Lincoln Memorial and the
Washington Monument a scant five summers ago,
exorting the nation to be true to itself and fulfill its
promises to all its citizens.

King was dead? That gentle man who had
preached nonviolence even when some blacks turned
on him for it and called him an Uncle Tom? When
those who lived by the sword died by it, there was a
certain sense of rightness. But when a man of peace
was cut down there was only the sense that the worst
had prevailed at the cost of the best.

She walked back to her apartment with no real
sense of where she was or what she was doing. People were milling around in the streets, exchanging
what news they had, trying to make some sense of it.
She wanted none of that. There could be no sense,
and she had already grasped the situation well
enough to understand that what news came next
would be only bad.

By the following day there was rioting in Washington, D.C., Detroit, Chicago, Boston and elsewhere across the country. Soldiers with machine guns
stood on duty outside the Capitol. Once again, people died. Teresa sat in her apartment and listened to
the sounds of police sirens coming from Harlem.
There had been looting and arson there, but not as
much as might have been. Blacks on all sides of the
political spectrum—from the most conservative to the

most militant—were working together trying to keep the peace.

Americans, Robert Kennedy said that day, seemed to be growing inured to violence. Yet there were still people, among them himself, who refused to become numb, refused to give up, who continued to hold out for what they knew to be good and right.

On Saturday, Teresa and Matthew walked together in the long, somber march down Broadway to City Hall. Blacks and whites, young and old, had come together, as in previous marches. But this time it was different. There was a sense of a time passing, of a chance missed. The whites were for the most part young, the blacks weren't. Young blacks had stayed away, as had middle-aged whites. The two groups who needed most to talk to each other were now further apart than ever.

On Sunday, Martin Luther King was buried in Atlanta. Teresa watched the rites on television and tried to find some hope in the thought that now, at last, the outrage of decent people would make the death meaningful. She wanted to believe that but could not quite bring herself to do so. In a few days, she would be twenty-two, certainly old enough to gain some wisdom and maturity. She was learning both at a harsh price.

Three weeks after the King assassination, the riots and unrest that had plagued the country came home to Teresa. What had begun as a protest against Columbia University's plans to build a gym in a park used by neighborhood residents turned into a full-scale uprising that saw school officials taken hostage, offices ransacked and the university itself placed under siege.

In the middle of it all, Maggie called her daughter. "Are you all right?" she asked quietly.

Teresa was ashamed to admit that the strongest emotion she could muster was resignation. That was wrong; she should feel something more, especially when the police attacked student spectators with billy clubs. But she was so tired of it all, as though she was a soldier in a war somewhere who had been under fire too long. Her nerve endings had been rubbed raw and rather than feel the pain, she had withdrawn into herself.

"Do you want to come home?" Maggie asked.

"No . . . I don't think so." That would have been the final defeat. Somehow she had to rouse herself, throw off the deadening lethargy seeping over her and try, no matter how vainly, to do something. Graduation was scant weeks away. She should be exhilarated at the prospect of at last finishing school and striking out on her own. Instead she felt simply afraid.

Was there anything good out there? Anything at all? Of course, there had to be. People like her parents existed, with happy marriages and stable lives. But they were older, settled, survivors of their own *weltschmerz*, what the Germans so aptly called the melancholy disillusionment with life. They had been honed in depression and war but triumphed over both and in the process learned to have faith in themselves.

Where were the victories of her generation? It seemed to Teresa that they were learning not to believe in anything, lest it be snatched away in an instant of violence.

Could people exist in a vacuum without belief, without hope? She did not want to find out. Robert Kennedy offered an alternative. More and more, she listened to him, experiencing the keen edge of his rage, letting his vision of what could be seep over her, knowing that here at least was one man who refused to give up, who still had the courage to feel.

In May, without saying anything to Matthew, she stopped working for McCarthy and switched over to Kennedy. The change in loyalties disturbed her; she did not try to rationalize it away. She admired McCarthy for what he had done, but she did not see herself as part of the elite, academic intelligentsia that more and more he seemed to represent.

In the midst of blood and tears and flames, all that seemed blatantly irrelevant. It was the slender, almost fragile looking, gaunt-faced man in his shirt sleeves standing alone on a platform or in the midst of a crowd, his voice breaking with fatigue yet still strong, who seemed to her to be at once the symbol of a better world to come and the means to achieve it.

And then he, too, was gone.

The same scenes, the same words, the same questions. The circumstances barely mattered. Los Angeles, victory in the primary, growing confidence of victory in November, a corner turned, only to find a monster waiting on the other side. The monster that was them. Blood on the floor and a woman sobbing. As though fate had only one song to play and was determined to do so to the bitter end.

Teresa lay in Matthew's arms and cried. He had come to her soon after he heard the news, knowing that what was a shattering blow to him would be also for her. Perhaps because he was older, he was a little better able to bear it. Or maybe it was as simple as the instinct to take refuge in love rather than in hate.

He held her through the long night as she slipped in and out of exhausted sleep. The gray light of the television screen flickered over them. The sound was turned down low, but he could hear it clearly enough when, shortly before dawn, the announcement was made that Kennedy had died.

He carried her to bed then and covered her with a blanket before going over to the window. Standing there, stretching the kinks out of his back, he stared out at the shadowy darkness giving way slowly to a formless morning. He felt as he had when he found Jim, only worse. Because now, for the first time, he understood what had driven his half brother to seek oblivion, and he feared the same need within himself. Feared it, but would not give in to it.

The strength of his father helped him there, tempered by the harsher experiences of his own early childhood. Odd how he felt lucky about that now, glad that he hadn't had it too easy. How much worse to only be awakening now to the fact that the world was a savage place. The longing to protect Teresa made him ache inside, even as he knew he could not. He could only help her get through it, hour by hour and day by day.

Later in the morning, they went out for breakfast at a small coffee shop near her apartment. She hadn't wanted to go, saying she wasn't hungry, but he had persuaded her. Though she pushed most of the food around on her plate, she did eat enough to satisfy him.

They held hands as they walked back. On a corner she saw someone she knew, a boy from one of her classes, going matter-of-factly about the business of buying dope. He was making no secret about it, any more than the pusher. Who had time for secrecy when there was a line waiting to buy?

"There'll be a lot of that," Matthew murmured. "They all just want to forget."

"I don't think Kennedy would appreciate it," she said shakily.

"No, but I'll bet he'd understand."

Her voice rose a notch. "How many of us are going to end up lost? Dead or the next thing to it? We're the future. Someday this country is going to have to depend on us. What will happen if we aren't here?''

Matthew had no answers. He knew her fears were justified. A generation was being destroyed. No nation could afford to do that and expect to survive. Sometime soon the older people in the country were going to have to really wake up to what was happening to their children and do something about it or reap the terrible results.

In June, Teresa graduated from Barnard near the top of her class. It was a joyous occasion for her family, despite all the sorrow that had gone before. Among the Garganos, she was a marvel, the first woman to go to college. At the party following the ceremony, her grandfather Joseph ceremoniously presented her with a beautiful gold watch bought to mark the event.

Her parents' gift was more discreet but in its own way no less symbolic of their feelings. Maggie and Anthony had set up a trust fund for their only daughter, containing a quarter of a million dollars. To her surprise, they had given her the right to manage the money herself. Which made it impossible to refuse. In effect, they were saying to her, here, it's yours, do what you think right with it. It was a gesture of faith that permeated even the shroud of numbness hanging over her and made her think that it might, after all, be worth trying to get on with life.

She moved downtown and took an apartment near IBS headquarters, where she went to work full time as Winston's assistant producer. The young man who had had the job had quit and gone off to live on a commune outside of Denver. Teresa remembered what he had said about being part of the problem or part of the solution and hoped he would find some happier middle ground.

She knew herself to be qualified for the job by virtue of her summer experience on the news team. But she also knew that it would have been very difficult to justify giving it to her if she had not been Anthony Gargano's daughter. When she accepted the position, realizing all that, she understood fully what it meant. Any urge she might have felt to prove her independence through rebellion was over. She would prove it through professionalism.

As the political season swung into high gear, she worked harder than she ever had in her life. In work she found a refuge from the pain of her raw emotions. Late in July, she went to Miami with Winston and suffered through the terminally bland Republican convention whose outcome was a foregone conclusion. Richard Nixon rode to victory on the first ballot and named Spiro Agnew as his running mate. Spiro *Who* quickly became a very tired joke.

Chicago and the Democrats lay ahead. They promised to be more interesting. The convention about to unfold under the ghostly shadow of what might have been faced innumerable problems.

"The Yippies are calling it theater," Winston said on the plane going out from New York. "They're talking about demonstrations throughout the city. But Daley is determined to maintain order.'' The old-line boss mayor of Chicago had made it clear he considered himself personally responsible for seeing that everything went well. He would not tolerate the slightest disruption.

The Yippies wanted to sleep in Lincoln Park. He said no. They wanted to bring a truck in to use as a bandstand. He said no. They wanted to hold a non-violent march. He said no.

They marched anyway. As they marched, they chanted ''Oink, oink'' at the police who had apparently forgotten the children's song about sticks and stones may break my bones, but names will never hurt me. Forgot it, or didn't buy the basic principle. They responded to the catcalls with their sticks and beat the marchers bloody.

Of course it was on television. Teresa was in the IBS convention control room when one of the technicians pointed to a monitor and said, ''Hey, take a look at what's happening outside.''

It looked like a war. People were screaming and running around frantically, trying to escape the police. A cameraman was knocked down by a policeman on a horse. Tear gas was released. The frenzy grew. A well-dressed, middle-aged woman coming out of the Hilton Hotel where the candidates were staying was grabbed by police and hauled off to a paddy wagon. The police then charged the hotel itself.

Teresa was on the phone, trying to reach the mobile unit. "Do they have a warrant?" she shouted. "Does anyone know if they're cleared to go in there?"

"They're cleared to do anything they damn well please," a harassed cameraman yelled back. "Daley's turned them loose and to hell with law and order."

"The whole world is watching!" the Yippies chanted, and they were. Journalists from France, England, Japan and elsewhere were roughed up right along with their domestic counterparts. Their reaction was, if anything, more profound. America was not only betraying itself, it was betraying them.

The night turned very long and grim. Down on the convention floor, delegates were screaming obscenities at each other. Up on the podium, speakers began by pleading for calm, ended by expressing their outrage. Daley sat stoically through it all, arms crossed over his stout chest, his bulldog face impassive. It was his city and his party at his convention where his candidate was going to be nominated. That he was doing Hubert Humphrey mortal damage apparently did not occur to him.

The fury fed by the pictures flickering across the television screens fed on itself, and out of it came a new target, the reporters themselves. *They* were the ones really doing the damage, making the city and the party look bad. It was their fault and they were going to pay for it.

"Stay with it!" Winston ordered. He was down in the midst of the chaos, trying to fight off a policeman who had decided for some unknown reason to stop him from broadcasting. Shouting into the microphone, his eyes pinned on the camera high above him, he yelled, "Whatever happens, don't lose the picture! People have to see this."

"My God," Teresa whispered, "he's going to be hurt." More guards had surrounded Winston, swinging billy clubs. He was still fighting but his knees had begun to buckle. Beside him, slightly out of focus but still recognizable, another face swam into view. "Matthew!"

He was on the convention floor as part of the team sent by the *Times*, a very junior part, admittedly, but still with full credentials and every right to be where he was. And if he had that right, how much greater was Winston's, the man whom millions of Americans turned to nightly to make sense out of whatever had happened that day. Seeing the older man's predicament, Matthew reacted first with disbelief, then with fury. Without pausing to think, he forced his way through the frightened, milling crowd and got to his side.

"Cut it out," he shouted at the policeman who was trying to get an arm free to bring his club down on Winston's distinguished head. "You bastard, cut it out!"

The policeman's face was a livid mask of fury. All the resentment and bewilderment he had felt for years were pouring out of him. He could no more restrain it than he could stop breathing. Muttering an obscenity, he wrenched his arm loose and swung the club in a high, lethal arc.

In the second before it hit, Matthew had time only to push Winston out of the way. He saw him land on the floor and get up partially, saw his face blank with disbelief giving way to concern. Everything seemed to be happening in slow motion. The screams and shouts of the crowd had faded away. The lights were growing dimmer. He was aware only of a blinding pain in his right temple and the stickiness of blood on fingers that were rapidly turning numb. Then he knew nothing at all.

Teresa screamed when she saw Matthew go down beneath the policeman's club. She fought her way toward where she had last seen him. Other reporters had formed a cordon, preventing the police from taking him away. A man from the *Times* was administering first aid.

Winston was on his feet, broadcasting a moment-to-moment report of what was happening. High above, the whirling camera moved in for a close-up of the bloodied young man lying unconscious on the floor. In the control rooms of the other networks, orders were given. Other cameras shifted to the scene. Rivalries were temporarily forgotten in shared outrage and disgust.

"Is this America?" Winston demanded, speaking quietly and clearly into the microphone. "Is this what our country has come to? This isn't democracy. When people can't gather peacefully, can't express their views, when the press isn't free, the most fundamental liberties of our nation have been taken from us.'' With compelling dignity, he went on, ''I cry for America tonight, for what's happening to us and to our children. This isn't what we've fought for and believed in. It's a travesty and we will live with the shame of it for a long, long time.''

In the silence that followed his words, an image flickered across the television screens of America: a young woman kneeling beside a bleeding young man, holding his head in her lap, her long black hair trailing over him like the veil of a weeping madonna.

Chapter Five

MATTHEW WAS HOSPITALIZED in Chicago with a fractured skull and a concussion. His doctors wanted him to stay there for at least a week, but James would have none of it. He sent a plane to pick Matthew up and bring him home.

Father and son met in the private room at Lenox Hill Hospital on the East Side, to which Matthew had been brought. James stood at the foot of the bed, his hands clasped behind his back. A pulse beat in his jaw. His eyes were little more than slits through which the clear blue irises gleamed dangerously.

"I was watching when it happened," he said. His gaze flicked over the pale face of his son, almost as white as the bandages swathing his head.

"Must have been quite a show," Matthew murmured. "How were the ratings?"

"High, of course. You made the prime time news on all the networks. Switchboards at our affiliates across the country were deluged with calls expressing support for Winston and you. If it's any consolation, you made quite an impact."

Matthew winced. "Did you have to use that word?" He grinned crookedly as he studied his father. Lying in the hospital bed, he had come to some

basic decisions about himself, facilitated no doubt by
the confrontation with his own mortality. During the
first moments of regaining consciousness in the Chicago hospital, he had been surprised to find himself
alive. Compared to the alternative, nothing else
seemed quite as serious or insurmountable as it once
had.

He was able to admit now, if only privately, that in
his admiration for his father, he had always been
afraid to compete with him. That was the root cause
of his refusal to join IBS television. He had not
wanted to have to prove himself in the same arena
where James shone so brilliantly. Now he knew that
however justified his fears might have been, he could
cope with them. They were father and son, cut from
the same cloth, meant to be not adversaries but al-
lies.

"When I get out of here," he said quietly, "I'd like
to come to your office and talk."

James nodded once, then left. When he was gone,
Teresa asked, "Did that mean what it sounded like?"

She had been with him almost constantly since he
came to in the hospital in Chicago. The best efforts
to get her to rest and eat had been only minimally
successful. It had been easier in the end to give in to
her. A cot had been set up down the hall from Matthew's room, where she went for brief periods when
he was sleeping.

He smiled at her gently. "It's time I quit fooling
myself. The only reason I stayed away from televi-

sion was because I thought of it as my father's turf. Now I think maybe we'd better learn to share it.''

Teresa was careful not to show her elation. If it had taken that crack on the head to bring him to his senses, maybe it was worth it. At least now he would be where he belonged. ''You won't regret it.''

''We'll see.'' His hand tightened on hers, his thumb rubbing softly against her palm. ''As long as I'm admitting what I really want, I might as well go all the way.'' His other hand came up to gently cup the back of her neck as he urged her toward him. Teresa had a moment to be surprised and to worry that this might not be good for him in his condition. Then she thought of nothing at all.

A long time later, she said, ''I think we can get in trouble for using a hospital bed for immoral purposes.''

''If anyone complains, I'll tell them you were restoring my will to live.''

She glanced up at him through her lashes. ''Have I?''

''Oh, yes,'' he assured her huskily, ''at the very least until I can finish what we've started here.'' Nice as it was to have something besides his head hurt, he didn't want the condition to continue forever.

''Promise?''

''Cross my heart and hope to . . .''

''Don't say it that way. Just say on my honor.''

He met her eyes, understanding. There had been too many deaths. Solemnly, he said, ''On my honor.''

It was perhaps a strange way to approach what was finally going to happen between them, but he thought it appropriate. He meant to behave honorably in all respects, to protect her from pain and fear just as he had when she was small. Above all, he did not want to disappoint her.

A week later, after he had gotten out of the hospital, he called and rather formally invited her to dinner. Just as formally, Teresa accepted. Although she could not have explained it fully, she felt the need for a certain level of ritual so that what happened was not allowed to be unimportant in any way.

When he called for her that Saturday night, he brought a bouquet of roses. She accepted it with a smile that told him she knew exactly what was going through his mind. They made appropriate small talk while she put the flowers in water.

Her movements were innately graceful, and he thought he had never seen her look lovelier. The simple green silk dress she wore emphasized the unusual clarity of her hazel eyes. She had left her hair down, as he liked it best, and had brushed it to an ebony sheen. Standing close to her in the small kitchen, he caught the scent of a slightly musky perfume that made his already taut body tighten further.

Teresa was trying very hard not to look at him. Beneath her outward calm, she was as nervous as the proverbial cat. Although she had absolutely no doubts about what they were going to do, she was still afraid of how well she would be able to carry it off. Above all, she didn't want to appear clumsy or foolish. It might have been easier if he hadn't looked quite so devastatingly attractive.

His thick, brown-gold hair was long enough to brush the collar of his white dinner jacket, but not so long as to look sloppy. The bandages had been removed and the only remaining evidence of his injury was a bruise on his right temple. The pallor of his days in the hospital was being quickly replaced by his usual healthy tan.

For some years now he had been as tall as his father, but only more recently had he grown into James's size and shape. His shoulders were unusually broad, as was his chest; by contrast his waist and hips appeared narrow. There was a physical presence about him many other men seemed to lack. It made Teresa very aware of herself as a woman.

They had dinner at a small restaurant on the East Side that seemed to appeal mainly to a clientele older than themselves. There was a dance floor and a good combo that played slow tunes. Teresa had been through the usual dance lessons inflicted on most children of affluent parents, but she'd had little opportunity to practice. In Matthew's arms, she found that she danced well. Her body moved with his naturally and without restraint.

He had ordered champagne with dinner. She laughed at him with her eyes but enjoyed it nonetheless. They had ripe, plump strawberries for dessert. By that time most of the champagne was gone and she did not hesitate to feed him berries from between her fingers. The white glint of his teeth as he took them from her made her briefly forget to breathe.

The waiters saw them out with tolerant smiles. "Now I know why you picked a French restaurant," Teresa said, giggling. It was a warm night and they had decided to walk back to her place. She hugged his arm to her, feeling the power of his muscles through the dinner jacket and her thin dress.

"Why's that?" he asked gently.

"Because they're supposed to be tolerant of lovers. Isn't that true?"

"Yes, I suppose it is." He smiled down at her, thinking that she looked even better now that she was more relaxed. The champagne had been an inspiration. It hadn't done him any harm either.

The fact was, he couldn't remember ever being so anxious about a woman. Not that he had been with that many; he'd never thought much of the current fashion for jumping in and out of bed with strangers destined to forever remain so. But he was hardly a virgin either. Which brought him to an interesting question: was Teresa?

He told himself that it mattered only because if she was, he wanted to be particularly careful with her. But he suspected that in fact more was involved. He found the thought of her with another man peculiarly painful. It took him a while to recognize what he was feeling as sexual jealousy, an emotion he had never had any reason before to encounter.

The curtains were drawn in her apartment and she had left a lamp on in the living room. It cast a warm glow over what was beginning to look less like a college girl's home and more like that of a career woman. The furniture was mostly new and more traditional than he might have expected; pieces she had picked out herself at W & J Sloane on Fifth Avenue. There were several good prints on the walls and a scattering of plants. Bookshelves had been built beneath the large windows looking out over a quiet street. Books were already spilling over onto the parquet floor.

"Would you like a drink?" she asked, a little nervously, he thought.

"Brandy would be nice, if you have it."

She did, thankfully. Yesterday she had gone out and bought one of all the most popular after-dinner drinks in the liquor store. What the man who had waited on her had thought she couldn't imagine, any more than she knew why she had done it. All she was sure of was that she didn't want to appear unsophisticated to Matthew or disappoint him even in so seemingly inconsequential a thing as not having what he wanted to drink.

As long as she was pouring, she decided to join him, but only very moderately. The champagne had not exactly gone to her head, but it had affected her, and she didn't want to add to it too much. While she was busy in the kitchen, Matthew put an Otis Redding album on the hi-fi. "Try a Little Tenderness" had been a hit song a year or so before the singer's death. It was still one of Matthew's favorites.

When Teresa came back, he had loosened his tie and was sitting on the couch, one booted foot resting on his knee. It was the first time she had noticed that he was wearing boots with an evening suit and the discovery made her laugh. "Here I thought you'd really cleaned up your act."

"You wouldn't want me to go too far, would you?" he teased, holding out a hand to her.

She took it and sat down beside him. "Oh, I don't know about that. It might not be so bad."

He took a sip of the brandy and regarded her steadily over the rim of the glass. She seemed very sure of what she was doing but he still had his doubts. Gently he reached out and touched the back of his hand to the smoothness of her cheek. She tensed ever so slightly.

"You're very beautiful."

"I'm glad you think so." The way she said it made him wonder if she still didn't really believe it herself.

"It's true. You've been pretty all your life, but as you've grown up, you've become beautiful." He smiled lightly. "At the rate you're going, you'll be a dynamite old lady."

She didn't know whether or not to take him seriously and was surprised that he might be joking at such a time. Yet it eased the tension that had been building in her, at least a little.

As though he sensed that, he set his brandy glass down and reached for her, cupping her face with both hands. Softly, he asked, "Are you sure about this?"

Her eyes locked with his; she nodded.

His mouth was warm and gentle and tasted faintly of brandy. He parted her lips softly and let his tongue slide in without aggression. Slowly, coaxingly, he drew hers into play. They had kissed like this before, but never with so clear an intent. The knowledge that they were not going to stop this time but would instead let the hunger flowing between them come to its natural conclusion, made every sensation vastly sharper and more powerful.

Teresa moaned softly when he finally drew away from her. Her fingers were tangled in his thick hair and one of her legs had eased over his. He stroked her thigh through the thin silk and took a deep breath. "I don't want this to get out of hand too fast."

Not quite sure what he meant, knowing only that she could not bear to stop, she tried to draw him back to her. "Not here," he murmured and stood up, lifting her with him until she was cradled in his arms.

Startled, she said the first thing that came into her head. "You're being very romantic."

He shot her a quizzical smile. "I should hope so. I'm trying hard enough."

In the bedroom, he set her down very gently on her feet. She had a moment to notice that his hands were trembling. Then they were reaching for her again, and she knew only the warmth of his big, hard body and the deep rumble of his voice as he said, "I want to do this right, sweetheart, but you'll have to help me."

"Anything," she said honestly. "Just tell me what to do."

He stiffened slightly as his suspicions surged once more to the fore. "Teresa...I don't want to get too personal, but..." He heard himself and broke off, laughing. "Listen to me. I don't want to get too personal when what we're about to do is as personal as two people can be."

Cupping her chin lightly, he said, "Sweetheart, if you haven't done this before, now would be a good time to tell me."

Mindful of the pressures on young women to become sexually experienced at the earliest possible opportunity, he had thought she might be a little embarrassed. But she met his gaze calmly. "I'm a virgin, if that's what you're asking."

"Uh...I thought you might be...."

The smile she gave him was startlingly mischievous. "You know, of course, that virgins are a severely endangered species. As a matter of fact, I may have been the oldest one at Barnard, outside of certain members of the faculty.''

He cleared his throat with some difficulty. "Yes...that might be the case. Uh, would you mind telling me why it is that you never—"

"Went to bed with anyone before? Oh, that's simple. I wanted it to be with you."

For some reason he didn't care to examine too closely, that excited him enormously. Enough so that he forgot, at least briefly, his resolve to go slowly and instead pulled her back into his arms with a quick, hard shudder. "Teresa," he murmured into the fragrant mass of her hair, "I hope you know what you're asking for."

"If I don't," she said with a soft laugh, "I'm sure you'll show me."

He growled something she couldn't quite decipher but didn't need to. A sudden rush of cool air at her back told her he had unzipped her dress. The swiftness with which he had done so made her think for an instant of the other women he had been with. A soft pout shaped her lips as she took a step away from him and let the dress slide away from her, revealing the swell of her breasts above the half-cup bra she wore. That and narrow bikini panties were her only remaining garments when she had stepped out of her high-heeled sandals. Doing so made her suddenly shrink several inches, which in turn made her more aware than ever of his height. She came just to his shoulders, forcing her to tilt her head back to look at him.

"It's not fair," she whispered.

"What?"

"Me being like this and you still having all your clothes on." As she spoke, she was moving to remedy that situation. Swiftly she eased his jacket from his broad shoulders and laid it carefully over the back of a nearby chair. His tie went next before she turned her attention to the buttons of his shirt. The matter-of-factness with which she was undressing him piqued Matthew. While he certainly did not want her to be frightened, he didn't think she should be too complacent either. Especially not if she was, as she said, a virgin.

When his shirt had fallen open and her hands were on his bare chest, he grasped her hips and drew her against him, letting her feel the full extent of his desire. She gasped softly but did not try to pull away. "Go on," he urged, "finish it."

When she did not immediately seem to understand what he meant, he grasped her hands in one of his and drew them down to the buckle of his belt. Color stained her cheeks. Relenting, he softened his grip. "It's okay, honey, I'll do it."

"This time," she retorted, putting him on notice that she did not intend to always be a novice. He grinned and sat down on a chair to pull off his boots. That done, he stood again and quickly removed his trousers and shirt. Left in only his briefs, he placed his hands lightly on her arms, stroking them gently. The sudden flash of apprehension in her eyes when she saw the evidence of his erection had not escaped him.

For the first time, he found himself really thinking about what intercourse meant to a woman. How would he feel if another person—bigger and stronger than himself—wanted to penetrate his body? While by no means ignorant about the prevalence of homosexuality, he had never been directly approached by a man, perhaps because he exuded such an implacable sense of masculinity that anyone who might have been so inclined had been warned off in advance. But the fact that he had never had to confront even the hypothetical possibility of such intimacy, did not mean that he could not imagine its consequences.

How did women cope, he wondered as he drew her closer. Were they simply conditioned to accept their biological role, or did they have to overcome fear and even resentment to be intimate with a man? He suspected it was the latter and could not blame them. But for the fact that he knew he could make this very good for Teresa, he might have stopped.

As it was, he gently unhooked her bra and took it from her. She started to raise her hands, as though to cover her breasts, then stopped and let them fall back to her sides. Under his scrutiny, she flushed slightly but did not flinch as she slipped out of her panties.

He doubted he had ever seen breasts as lovely as hers. They were high and full with dark rose nipples that turned upward. Beneath them, her rib cage tapered downward to her slender waist and slim hips. Her thighs were long and firm, separated by a nest of curls as dark as the ebony hair that spilled down her back.

Whatever thoughts he had still had about her as a child vanished at that instant. He saw her as she truly was, a woman, his to possess, to love, to cherish. His eyes were drawn to the pulse beating in the arched line of her throat. Compelled by a need now far beyond his ability to understand or control, he pressed his lips there and felt her tremble.

It was only a matter of a few steps to the bed. He took them quickly with her in his arms. Setting her down again, he smiled reassuringly as he pulled back the covers, then gently urged her down onto the mattress. She went obediently, watching him as he stripped off his briefs. Whatever she thought at that moment, he did not know. Perhaps he did not want to. It was enough to feel the compliance of her body and know that she would not deny him.

Always before he had thought of sexual release as being both the motivation and reward of lovemaking. But now he discovered nothing was so simple. The sheer pleasure he got from simply touching Teresa was beyond anything he had ever known. And the fierce delight that coursed through him when he heard her first soft cries of pleasure lifted his concept of joy to unparalleled heights.

He could not get enough of her. Every inch of her body from the top of her silken hair to the tips of her small toes enthralled him. He loved the satiny feel of her skin, the smell and taste of her, even the slight pain of her nails digging into him as she began to lose control.

Every new intimacy was a victory he diligently pursued. Before he at last eased between her legs, he had made her come twice and found in that a level of satisfaction beyond which his own pleasure seemed to pale into insignificance. Yet when it was at last upon him, nothing could have been more intense. In its wake, he was left shattered and reborn.

DESPITE HER OUTWARD ASSURANCE, Teresa had approached making love with Matthew anything but calmly. Beneath her natural fear of a new and strange experience, she had dreaded the possibility that her expectations were too high and that the actual event would therefore prove anticlimactic, a potentially all-too-appropriate term.

When instead the exact reverse occurred, she was both immensely relieved and exhilarated. Beyond the physical pleasure she found with Matthew, the sense of being truly close to him in the most intimate way possible was a vindication of her stubborn refusal to settle for anything less. She gloried in their intimacy and found every possible opportunity to be with him.

That was easier than it might have been now that Matthew was also working at IBS. Most of the people there had been surprised when he turned down a job in the news division and instead went with sports. Teresa was not; she understood that the events in Chicago had robbed him of the objectivity that was the journalist's most essential qualification. Unless and until it could be restored, he would not attempt to pretend otherwise.

Sports was ideally suited to his needs at that time, and vice versa. Run by his Uncle Dominick, a former hitter for the Brooklyn Dodgers, it was easily the most aggressive and fastest growing division at the network. Among other things, it had the largest technical staff whose sole job was to dream up new ways to film players in action.

Beyond the usual baseball and football schedules, they covered hockey, basketball, wrestling, skiing, gymnastics and even more esoteric sports. Dom was routinely accused of crossing the line between true athletic endeavor and pure entertainment. That didn't bother him. "Sports *is* entertainment," he said and went right on his way controlling more airtime each season, drawing in more viewers, and not incidentally reshaping the way the games themselves were played.

Matthew's first love had been baseball; some of his most cherished memories involved lazy summer afternoons at Ebbets Field in Brooklyn, watching his uncle crack a long, high one over the backfield fences. Naturally well coordinated himself, he had played soccer at school and later crewed at Princeton. He liked the very personal sense of achievement that came from doing a little better, going a little further, trying a little harder. Most of all, he liked to write about it.

Dom put him on the air at the end of each Sunday's regular sports wrap-up. "Just talk," he said. "Tell them what's on your mind." With some trepidation, Matthew did. He was a little awkward at first, but quickly enough his natural charm and humor asserted themselves.

Each week he picked a topic frankly intended to make people think, then presented it lightly but without equivocation. How did events on the football field relate to events in Vietnam? Was baseball with its slow pace and old-fashioned uniforms a harkening back to a simpler way of life? Was it wrong to want to win? Was it wrong not to?

The mail he got was mixed. Some viewers wrote to complain that his three minutes were a waste and he should be off the air. Others wrote to argue with particular viewpoints he had taken. More scribbled a line or two to say they liked him. He was called a commie, a hippie, an all right guy and a nice young man, this last from a little old lady in Monterey, California, who wrote in regularly and claimed to never miss one of his shows.

"Don't worry about whether the mail's good or bad," Dom advised. "What matters is that people are listening to you. Your Q score's way up."

"My what?"

"Q score. It's a measure of how many people recognize you. Frankly, if it goes much higher, I'm going to have to pay you more."

Matthew shook his head wryly. He was making a good salary already, vastly more than he had made at the *Times*, and he really hadn't expected to do better. But he was discovering that on top of all his other unfashionable ideas, he liked making money, so if Dom wanted to give him a raise, it was okay with him.

James was delighted by his success. It helped to compensate for his continued worries about James, Jr. His younger son would be nineteen in December. Efforts to interest him in going to college the following year had not been met with any enthusiasm. Mandy said he was better, and certainly there had been no repetition of the drug taking that had almost killed him. But he still seemed withdrawn and unnaturally passive, as though the world was simply too much for him to cope with.

His father was not completely unsympathetic to that attitude. He viewed the Democrats' defeat in November with sour vindication. Richard Nixon was not his idea of a president, but at least the sullen, suspicious side of his nature seemed offset by a certain iconoclastic brilliance that led him to try things other politicians would not have attempted.

He was almost like a man walking closer and closer to the edge of a cliff, daring it to crumble beneath him. The whole country seemed to be doing that, which might mean that Nixon's long-awaited time had finally come. Hadn't someone said that a leader finds out where his people want to go, then takes them there?

Teresa tried not to think too much about where the country was going. She could not ignore it, by any means, thanks to her work in the news division. But when she left the office at night, she did her best to put it out of her mind. There were far more pleasant things to concentrate on, all of them having to do with Matthew.

Not that there weren't problems. To begin with, there was the whole issue of marriage. He seemed to think that perhaps they should do something about that. Teresa didn't. Much as she loved him, she wasn't ready to get married. For the first time, she felt free and in charge of her own life. She wasn't about to relinquish that, not even for him.

Which brought them to the subject of birth control. If they weren't going to get married, and even if they had been, they certainly didn't want any little surprises. Scant weeks after their affair began, Pope Paul VI issued his encyclical on human life, in which he absolutely forbade all means of artificial birth control. By that time, Teresa was already swallowing one of the little white tablets every morning. She kept right on doing so, but she also regretfully stopped going to church.

It would have been a simple enough matter to continue; from what she heard the average penance for disobeying the papal edict was running at about five Hail Marys and a handful of Our Fathers. If she had wanted to, she could even have continued to take communion. She just couldn't bring herself to do so.

"Is it really that important to you?" Matthew asked softly one night as they were lying in bed together in her apartment. They had gone out to dinner, then come back and made love. He was pleasantly tired and could have slipped into sleep, but he sensed that she needed to talk.

"It's hard to explain," she murmured against his chest. "I never thought of myself as extremely religious or anything like that, but I'm used to going to church. It's a habit I had no reason to want to break."

"And now you do?"

She nodded sadly. "It isn't that I feel guilty about using birth control; I'm convinced the Pope is wrong. But if he's wrong about this, what else is he wrong about? How much of what we've grown up believing is really true?"

"I don't know," he said gently. "I never thought that much about it, but I guess now maybe I'd better." He turned slightly so that he could look at her.

"You know this isn't only your problem. We share it."

She nodded, her hand stroking his cheek. "That does make it easier."

He leaned back against the pillows, carrying her with him. Outside it was snowing. New York was in for a rare white Christmas. They would spend it visiting both their families, but they would also have a private celebration alone. Just as if they were a family themselves.

"I don't have anything against kids," he said, feeling the need to clarify that. "It's just that these are early days yet." Looking down at her, he asked, "Aren't they?"

"Very early," she agreed, relieved that he also thought so. More softly she added, "And very unsettled. I'm not sure about bringing children into this world."

That was a convenient excuse, but it also held an element of truth. Every generation wanted to believe that its experiences were unique, but she could see now that for people of her age and Matthew's there was some justification in that. They were coming of age in a time of almost unparalleled upheaval when all the most fundamental beliefs and values were being questioned and discarded. Until something new came along to take their place, there was very little to hold on to. Except each other.

It was hard enough for those who had at least taken the first, most crucial steps toward building their own lives. For those a few years younger, still on the cusp between childhood and maturity, the times were all the more terrifying.

Some, like Mandy, found refuge in a blithe refusal to take anything very seriously. As far as Teresa could tell, she let nothing get to her except her worries over her brother, and even there she kept insisting that everything would be all right. Until the early weeks of 1969, when Teresa got a phone call from her that made it clear how very wrong they all had been.

"I'm sorry to bother you," Mandy said softly. Her voice was light and high, retaining the quality of a very young girl's. "Is Matt there?"

Teresa didn't ask why she would expect to find him in her apartment. While they were hardly broadcasting their new relationship, they weren't trying to make a secret of it either. "No, he isn't. Have you tried his place?" Matthew had left half an hour before to drop by his apartment before going on to work. It was possible that Mandy might catch him there.

"There wasn't any answer...maybe I should wait and call his office . . ."

"He should be there soon." Teresa hesitated. She didn't know why but something about the way Mandy sounded worried her. Gently, she asked, "Are you all right?"

"Me? Sure. When am I not?" She laughed a little nervously.

"Never mind. Listen, it's been a while since we saw each other. How about getting together one day for lunch and some heavy-duty shopping?"

Mandy had a wide assortment of friends her own age, but she had always liked an occasional day out with someone older. That hadn't changed. "Yeah, that would be great." She was silent for a moment, then said, "I guess I may as well tell you since Matt will anyway. Jim told the folks last night that he's decided to join the army."

"W-what . . . ?"

"The army. He wanted to make it the marines, like Dad and Uncle Anthony, but they wouldn't take him 'cause of the drug thing."

"I'm not sure I'm getting this right. I thought he was still thinking about college."

"He was, but I guess he decided against it." Her voice cracked and she had to stop briefly before going on. "Dad's absolutely livid and Mom's trying not to cry. They both want him to get out of it, but for once Jim's standing pat. So I thought maybe if Matt talked to him . . ."

Teresa could see what she was getting at. There had always been a special relationship between Matthew and his half brother, but it had been especially strong since Haight-Ashbury. "He'll certainly want to try. Look, I'll be at the office myself in a few minutes and I'll try to find him. All right?"

"That'd be great. I'm sorry to dump this on him, but I don't know what else to do. The army. . ." All her horror and bewilderment were implicit in that single word. None of them knew anyone who joined the army voluntarily. Young men liable for the draft went to the most extreme lengths to keep their deferments or gain exemptions. Cases of rigid fasting to get below minimum weight limits, or pretended homosexuality, or even deliberately induced drug addiction were not unheard of. Anything was better than the army because rightly or wrongly that meant only one thing: Vietnam.

"It'll be okay. Whatever Jim's thinking of, Matthew will straighten him out." Teresa hung up a short while later, wishing she was really so sure of that. He would do his best, but whether or not he would succeed remained to be seen.

Matthew was thinking much the same thing. He had heard the news within a few minutes of arriving at work. Dom had called him into his office, shut the door and said quietly, "There's a problem." He told him, then waited while Matthew sat slumped in the chair across from him, trying to get his thoughts in order.

He'd worried a lot about Jim, and envisioned a lot of bad things happening to him but not this. What terrible combination of desperation and courage had driven him to take such an outlandish step?

A few hours later he was asking Jim directly. He had taken off from work and gone looking for his half brother, finding him at the East Village Shelter for kids where he'd been working several days a week.

Jim was in the kitchen, his sleeves rolled up and a worn apron covering his front. He was helping to make spaghetti sauce for the midday meal.

Matthew stood for a moment at the door watching him. Light blond hair was pulled neatly back in a ponytail. His face no longer looked gaunt, and his gray eyes were clear. He was smiling at something a young girl was saying. Then he looked up and saw Matthew and the smile faded. "Hi," he said softly, "I thought you might drop by."

"Then you know what brings me?"

Jim nodded, smiled again reassuringly at the girl and introduced Matthew. "This is Ginny," he explained, "about the best cook we've got." The girl blushed but looked pleased. "That means I don't burn water," she said. They talked a few moments longer before she excused herself and politely left them alone.

Matthew propped himself on a stool and watched as Jim stirred the sauce. After a time, he said, "I thought you liked working here."

"I do. It's just that it's time to move on to other things."

"The army?" He couldn't keep the sarcasm out of his voice. "Instead of helping to save kids, you'd rather be killing them?"

Instead of getting mad, as Matthew had hoped, Jim merely shook his head gently. "That isn't fair. It's also beneath you. Okay, so you aren't a real reporter anymore, but you should still know better."

"What do you mean, not a real reporter?"

"Hey, it's not an insult. But you used to cover politics and now you do sports. I like what you have to say, but it isn't the same."

"Maybe I had a reason for switching."

"And maybe I've got a reason, too."

Matthew got off the stool and walked over to the grimy window looking out over an alley. He stood with his shoulders hunched for a moment before he said, "I know what my reason was. What's yours?"

Jim sighed softly. "It's hard to explain. I tried last night with Mom and Dad. That didn't work out too well."

"Why don't you try again now, with me?"

"All right . . ." He wiped his hands on his apron and looked at Matthew squarely. "What it comes down to is that I'm sick of being a confused kid. I want to grow up, to be a man, to have a place in the world."

"That's fine, but the army—"

"Let me finish. I know I've got a lot of problems to work out. For one thing, I need to learn to think better of myself." He smiled apologetically. "I've depended on Mandy too long, expecting her to be the leader with me just following along. That wasn't fair. Any more than it was fair to close myself off from Dad because I thought I could never live up to his standards. I can, and I'm going to prove it."

"Did you tell him that?"

Jim frowned. "Yeah, he didn't go for it too well."

"Because of the way you're doing it. He wants you to have it better than he did, not to go through the same kind of hell."

"I've come to the conclusion that nothing easy is worthwhile."

"That's some kind of line. Maybe I should write it down so I won't forget it."

Jim flushed but still refused to lose his temper. "Sarcasm isn't going to do us any good. I know you're worried, and I appreciate that, but I'm convinced I'm doing what's right."

"I would really like to hear how you figure that."

"It's not that hard. I look at men like Dad and Uncle Anthony, and I ask myself how they got to be the way they are: so confident about what they want from the world. Oh, I know it's easy to make fun of some of them, to say they've sold out, but I'm not sure how right we are about that. The fact is that most older people I know seem pretty damn satisfied with their lives. Not with their kids, maybe, but with themselves."

"So?" Matthew asked, not taking his eyes off Jim. He was hearing echoes of himself in what his half brother was saying and he did not like them, but he could not pretend they weren't there.

"So I ask myself how they got that way. What made them different from us. Is it simply that they're older? I don't think that's it. I think it's because they never had the luxury of all the soul-searching, philosophizing bullshit we're wallowing in. They had a war to fight and then a world to rebuild. They didn't have time to just think of themselves.''

"And that's what you want? Something bigger than yourself?"

"Yeah, I guess I do. I want to stop just thinking about me.''

"Then why,'' Matthew demanded with deadly calm, "are you being so damned selfish?"

Jim did not pretend to misunderstand him. "I know what I'm doing is hurting Mom and Dad and other people who care about me. But I don't know any other way to go about it. Nothing else will work.''

"There's college, a job, the Peace Corps, all kinds of alternatives.''

"And meanwhile other men my age—whose families aren't rich—are going to Vietnam. I'm the same as them, don't you see? I don't have anything special to contribute. I'm an ordinary guy, and I want to be treated like one.''

"You have no idea what that means,'' Matthew protested. "I can't claim that I really do either, but at least I've got a few clues. It's *hell* over there. Don't you understand that? It was hell for our fathers but at least they had something to hold on to. They believed what they were doing was right. You won't even have that.''

"It can be right. We can make it that way.''

Matthew shut his eyes in despair. He could not cope with such remorseless idealism. Jim actually believed that even the murderous folly of blindly arrogant men could be redeemed, given meaning and purpose, by the faith of the young.

How could he dispute him? He had no experience of his own in war. He had only the terrible, gnawing conviction that they were all of them together, young and old, black and white, rich and poor, rapidly passing beyond even the hope of redemption.

Chapter Six

"YOUR DESK IS THE ONE in the corner," Teresa said quietly. "If there's anything you need, just let me know."

Matthew nodded and headed in the direction she had indicated, carrying the cardboard box he had packed upstairs in the sports department. His progress was surreptitiously observed by the other members of Winston's staff, all of whom had found one reason or another to be present in the newsroom just then.

Teresa couldn't blame them for being curious; it wasn't every day that the network president's son joined the team. But she hoped they wouldn't make things difficult for him. His decision to leave the sports division had been tough enough.

She didn't know exactly what had caused it but she had the idea that it was somehow related to Jim's departure. He had left for boot camp a couple of weeks before. His letters were determinedly cheerful, but they could only hope that he was really all right.

One of the secretaries glanced up as she walked by and grinned. "Our very own Callahan isn't too hard to look at, is he?"

"He's okay, I guess."

"Okay? Honey, you better get your eyes checked. He is a whole lot more than that."

Teresa laughed gently. If Debbie wanted to harbor fantasies about Matthew, that was fine with her. At least as long as she was the one he woke up next to every morning.

Later in the day, after the regular meeting to plan which stories would make the evening broadcast, he caught up with her in the corridor. They walked along together toward the coffee machine. "Seems like a good group," he said.

"The best in the business. Winston wouldn't have it any other way." She smiled as she added, "I suppose you know he's thrilled you decided to come on board."

"I hope he stays that way. It's not going to be so easy convincing people who are used to seeing me talk about baseball that I know much about hard news."

"You'll convince them," she assured him quietly. "Just like you'll convince the rest of the staff that you belong here."

"They figure I got the job because I'm the boss's son?"

"Some of them may think that. Does it matter?"

"No, I suppose not." On a lighter note, he asked, "Any rules against fraternization between staff members?"

Her eyebrows rose expressively. "Isn't it a little late to worry about that?"

"Not really. If there were rules, I'm fully prepared to ignore them."

"As it happens, there aren't. But," she added hastily, as he grinned and took a step toward her, "we should still be discreet."

"That's my middle name."

"Really? How very odd. Imagine giving a little kid a name like that."

"Tessa..."

"Teresa."

"Someday you're going to be Tessa again."

"Maybe...but right now it's Ms Gargano to you, buddy, and don't forget it."

He sighed dramatically. "God protect me from the liberated female."

"You didn't mind my being liberated last night."

"Did you have to mention that now—" he glanced at his watch "—with five hours still to quitting time?"

"It'll give you something to think about while you're waiting to go on the air." Tossing a smile over her shoulder, she added, "I wouldn't want you to get nervous."

Surprisingly, he wasn't. If anything, reporting the news was easier than what he had been doing. Whereas before he had always tried to look relaxed on camera, now a bit of tension was more than appropriate. Watching him on the monitor, Teresa was struck by how serious and confident he looked. In many ways, he was the perfect balance to Winston, the younger man with a fresh perspective but no less intelligence or sensitivity.

For some time now there had been dissatisfaction with the replacements who filled in for Winston when he was away. Because of that, the anchorman was pressured not to go into the field to cover stories himself, something he wanted very much to do. She wouldn't have put it past him to already be seeing Matthew as a potential solution to his problem.

But in the meantime, until he proved himself, it would be Matthew who went into the field to get the big stories. None was bigger than Vietnam. He and Jim arrived there in the same week early in March, Matthew on a press plane, Jim in the bowels of a C-15 shuttling new troops in and exhausted veterans out.

They did not meet, and Jim was in fact not even aware of the coincidence of fate that brought them both there at the same time. Matthew was not so fortunate. He thought constantly of his half brother as he followed the press officers around on their carefully planned tours of ''pacified'' villages and listened to them tell him how the war was being won.

At night, in the back alleys of Saigon, he heard a very different story. Among his contacts was a young man with links to the Vietcong. He told Matthew bluntly that the Americans could never win. ''We have fought to free our country for centuries, first from the Chinese, then from the French, now from you. Do you really think it matters to us any longer how many people die when so many have already? One day, Vietnam will be free and whole. Whether I live to see it, or for that matter whether you do, is inconsequential.''

That view of individual lives as meaningless dogged Matthew as he continued to put together his story. He remembered hearing James talk about the incredible fierceness of Japanese soldiers whose code of bushido prescribed death in battle as the greatest of glories. What was happening in Vietnam was different—there was no search for personal glory—but the effect seemed much the same. During his first broadcast, he talked about the gulf between Western and Eastern culture, and how that, as much as anything else, was the focus of the war.

''Do you think he's right?'' Mandy asked one evening about halfway through his trip when she and Teresa were having dinner. She was in her sophomore year at Vassar and had come down for the weekend. College was pretty much what she had expected, but then most things were. There had been very few surprises in her life to date, the only really important one being Jim and what she hadn't been able to do for him.

''I don't know,'' Teresa said as she tossed the Caesar salad they would be sharing. ''It makes a certain amount of sense, and if the phone calls that came in right after the broadcast are anything to go by, he definitely touched a nerve.'' She smiled faintly. ''But then Matthew has a habit of doing that.''

Mandy nodded, her cool gray eyes serious. "I've always thought it was really interesting the way he'll peel the layers off something until he gets right down to the core. Most people just look at the surface."

"That's why he's a good writer."

"It could get him in trouble though. There are people around these days who don't want anyone looking too closely at what's going on."

Teresa couldn't disagree with that. She knew from conversations with her father that the media was beginning to feel pressure from the administration to change the way it reported the news. Since television and radio stations were all licensed by the Federal Communications Commission, they were particularly vulnerable. James was determined not to give an inch, and Alexis took the same position at UBC, but both expected the pressure to continue.

"You miss him a lot, don't you?" Mandy asked when they sat down to dinner. She had let her hair grow recently and it hung in a silver cloud to her shoulders. Her skin had the flawless perfection of a baby's; she had somehow escaped all the usual adolescent problems. Tall and slender like her mother, she was easily the most beautiful young girl Teresa had ever seen. With very little effort, she could have been unbearable. What saved her was her refusal to take herself any more seriously than she did anything else.

"Miss who?" Teresa asked as she poured them each a glass of wine.

Mandy laughed softly. "That's pretty good. Who, indeed? How many guys are you seeing?"

"Only one," she admitted reluctantly.

"That must be who I mean then. Don't worry, Matthew will be home soon."

"I don't really think something will happen to him," Teresa said, the possibility having occurred to her only a hundred or so times since he left. "After all, he's only there for a week. What really bothers me is that I feel so at loose ends without him."

"What's wrong with that? The two of you have a good thing going."

"I suppose . . . I just didn't figure on it taking up my whole life." She wasn't sure why she was telling this to Mandy, except that she needed to talk about it and the younger girl was a sympathetic listener. "It's hard to explain," she went on slowly, "I love my job, I've got a nice apartment, friends, no money problems, I'm doing so much better than a lot of other people. But Matthew goes away for a few days and it all becomes meaningless. That's scary."

"Maybe that's just being in love," Mandy suggested gently. "I can't claim it's ever happened to me, but I sure wouldn't mind. It sounds great."

"It isn't. I'm too dependent on him. You know he still calls me Tessa sometimes. It's kind of a joke between us, only it isn't really funny. I'm glad I've grown up; I don't want to go back to being a child."

Though she spoke softly, her words rang with conviction. Mandy sat back in her chair and regarded her intently. "This is really bugging you. I didn't realize that at first. From the outside, you seem to have everything together."

Teresa laughed a little shakily. "Is that how it looks? I don't feel that way. Look, maybe I shouldn't be so frank with you, but the fact is I wanted Matthew for a long time before anything happened between us. If I'd had my way, we would have been lovers years ago. I know he waited because he wanted to protect me, but I wonder sometimes if he didn't also want to make sure that I would never be able to take him for granted."

"Can you blame him? He cares for you, Teresa, honestly he does. I've seen that just in the way he looks at you. Why shouldn't he want you to care as much?"

"I do, it's just that . . . I have the feeling that unless I'm careful, I could get completely caught up in him, even to the extent of living through him instead of through myself. I've seen it happen to other people. My mother fought against it the whole time I was growing up. I think that's why she went back to nursing as soon as her kids were old enough and why she's worked ever since."

"I think Dad wanted Mom to stay home with Jim and me," Mandy said thoughtfully, "but she wouldn't do it."

"Do you think you were harmed by that?"

"No, not me. But as for Jim..." She broke off, her eyes thoughtful. "I don't blame her for a thing, but I'm afraid she sometimes blames herself."

"There is that danger, if you aren't a full-time mother, you worry that anything that goes wrong is your fault. But I think the alternative is just as bad. If you really resent being with your kids all the time, how can you do them any good?"

"You can't," Mandy said. "You won't get any argument from me on that score. I think women's liberation is great; I just can't figure out what took us so long to wise up."

Despite herself, Teresa smiled. "It's a little more complicated than it may seem at first glance. Burning your bra doesn't make you liberated. I've seen plenty of women at school and now at work who are still depending on men for their own sense of identity. That's what I'm determined to avoid."

"You mean you don't want to be 'Matthew's girl' instead of being yourself?"

"That's it exactly, but missing him as much as I do, I'm starting to think that maybe I've become that without even realizing it was happening."

"Well..." Mandy said as she finished her salad, "it seems to me that if you're worried about being too hung up on Matthew, the solution is obvious."

"What's that?"

"Go out with other guys."

"But I don't want to," Teresa protested, genuinely taken aback by the suggestion. She had dated frequently in the past and had never met anyone she thought could hold a candle to Matthew. The thought of starting that whole process over dismayed her. "Besides," she murmured, "I think he'd really be hurt if I did that."

Mandy shrugged lightly. "Then don't tell him."

"That's dishonest."

"No, it isn't; it's practical and even kind." She propped her elbows on the table and cupped her face in her hands. "Look, you're worried about whether or not you're getting too dependent on Matthew. If you keep thinking that, it's going to have a bad effect on your relationship. So for his sake as much as yours, you have to do something about it."

"I don't see how going out with other men would help."

"It would if it made you feel more independent." Cool gray eyes glittered provokingly. "It might also make you appreciate Matthew more."

"*That* I don't need. It seems to me I'd only be exchanging one kind of dependency for another."

"Suit yourself, but most women your age are dating pretty actively. If you aren't going to end up believing you've missed something, maybe you should give it a try."

Much as Teresa hated to admit it, she thought there might be something to what Mandy was say-

ing. The fact was she had never really given any other
man a fair chance. For as long as she could remember, she had wanted only Matthew. Perhaps she
should at least consider alternatives.

"I suppose you have a plan in mind. . . ."

"Nothing terrible," Mandy assured her with a
laugh. "I've been wanting to try one of those new
singles bars. Why don't we go together?"

Teresa could think of few things that appealed to
her less but even so she agreed. With Matthew away,
it was as good a time as ever to decide if there was
anyone out there worth bothering about.

At the very least, going to a singles bar with
Mandy should be a very interesting experience, not
unlike opening a huge bag of candy in a roomful of
children and then trying not to get trampled in the
stampede.

Friday's, on New York's Upper East Side, was
crowded with several hundred young men and
women, all fairly well dressed with the men in jackets and the women in skirts. Almost without exception, they were holding drinks and doing their best to
look at ease. The noise level was ear shattering; Teresa instantly suspected that it was deliberately kept
that way to avoid the awkwardness of quiet.

Barely had she and Mandy stepped into the bar
than a ripple effect seemed to pass through everyone
in their immediate vicinity. One after another, the
women glanced toward the door, frowned and looked

away. The men went through much the same process, only they didn't frown and without exception when they realized what they had seen, they swiveled their heads back to gape at Mandy. At least Teresa presumed that was whom they were looking at; so unaccustomed was she to trying to attract the attention of any man other than Matthew she didn't notice that more than a few of the stares were coming her way.

"Oh, lord," Mandy murmured under her breath, "would you get a load of this place. It's like a zoo."

"We don't have to stay."

"Ah, let's. It'll be fun." Without waiting for an answer, she waded into the crowd and was quickly lost in a circle of admiring men.

Teresa sighed, elbowed her way to the bar and tried to catch the waiter's eye. She wasn't having much luck when a voice beside her said, "Been here before?"

Turning, she found herself beside a tall, dark-haired young man in a business suit. He looked about twenty-five, with the carefully styled hair and smooth cheeks of a junior account executive or possibly an assistant loan officer. "No," she said faintly, "this is my first time."

"You'll love it. Friday's is the place to be."

"You . . . uh . . . come here often?"

"At least two or three times a week. Wouldn't miss it." He smiled broadly. "After all, this is where the action is, and I'm certainly in favor of that. How about you?''

"What? Oh, action...sure, that's fine. You didn't happen to notice where my friend went, did you?''

"The blonde? Don't expect to see her again. She won't get out of here alone.''

"Oh, no?'' Teresa shot him a closer look, noticing that his narrow eyes were focused squarely on the swell of her breasts. Her mouth tightened in annoyance.

"Honey,'' he drawled, "that friend of yours is hot stuff.'' He moved a little closer. "But you aren't anything to sniff at yourself, so what do you say we ditch this place and go somewhere a little...friendlier?''

Knowing she was going to regret it but driven to play the charade through to the end, she asked, "Where did you have in mind?''

"Well...I've got a roommate, so what do you say we use your place, unless you've got the same problem?''

"No, I haven't got any problem. Would you mind telling me something?''

His hand touched her arm; the tips of his fingers were damp. "What's that, sweetheart?''

"I thought the idea of these places was that people got together, talked a little, found out if they liked each other, that sort of thing. Instead, you seem to think I should jump right into bed with you.''

"Hey, don't knock it. This is the age of sexual liberation. Women have as much right to getting their needs fulfilled as men. . . ."

"Bull. You're no more interested in fulfilling my 'needs' than I am in yours. All you're looking for is another notch on the old bedpost."

His hand fell away. He stepped back quickly as though she had struck him, or perhaps more correctly, as though she had suddenly blown her nose on her sleeve or made some other equally gauche social gaffe. "Look, honey, if you've got some kind of hang-up . . ."

Teresa sighed deeply. She really had no right to take out after him. He was, after all, playing the game by the rules whereas she was very much an interloper. "Look," she said after a moment, "let's forget it, okay? I just came here out of curiosity and that's getting satisfied very quickly."

His mouth twisted into a sneer that turned his whole face ugly. "Curiosity? Who do you think you're kidding? You came to keep an eye on that friend of yours. Maybe you're scared she'll go off with a guy and find out what she really likes."

It took Teresa a moment to understand what he meant. When she did, she was momentarily taken aback. His defense of his wounded masculinity was crude, but it was also so utterly predictable that she couldn't help but find it funny. If anyone had suggested such a thing to her a few years before, she would have been mortified. As it was, secure in the enjoyment of her femininity, she could afford to pity him.

"If it makes you feel better to think that," she said softly, "go right ahead. Now, if you'll excuse me, I could stand a drink." And while she was getting that, maybe Mandy would reappear.

She didn't, but Teresa found that after a couple of glasses of cheap—in taste, not price—white wine, she actually started to enjoy herself. Not all the men there were creeps; quite a few seemed more lonely than horny, an emotion she could identify with. She chatted with an engineer who worked for IBM, a writer for the *Daily News* and a stockbroker. She liked them all, but she did not give her phone number to any of them.

"So what did you think of the place?" Mandy asked when they were finally leaving toward midnight. Standing at the curb, oblivious of the regretful stares of males departing alone, they were trying to flag down a cab.

"It was all right," Teresa allowed.

"Did you meet anyone you wanted to see again?"

"No."

"That's all, just no?"

Teresa lifted her shoulders apologetically. "I guess this isn't the way for me to establish my independence."

"Oh, well, it was just a thought. Listen, have you thought about taking up judo or something like that? It would probably impress the hell out of Matthew if you could throw him down on the floor and have your wicked way with him.''

''I'm not sure 'impress' is the right word.''

''No? Maybe you're right. What if you started wearing glasses and put your hair up in a bun? That would make it look like you really didn't care whether or not he found you attractive.''

A cab screeched to a halt in front of them. As they got into the back seat, Teresa asked, ''Why am I getting the feeling that you aren't taking my problem seriously?''

''Because I'm not,'' Mandy admitted cheerfully. ''If it's any consolation to you, I'm probably too young and shallow to appreciate your predicament. In a few years, being in love with a wonderful man will probably make me miserable, too.''

''And you'll deserve it,'' Teresa assured her sternly even as her lips twitched. Finding out that a nineteen-year-old had more common sense than she did was unsettling, to say the least. ''Do I gather that your advice is to simply sit back and enjoy myself?''

''Nope,'' Mandy told her archly, ''my advice is to lie back.''

Teresa winced and groaned in mock dismay. ''Stepped right into that one, didn't I?''

''You'd think someone of my background would have more restraint.'' Mandy sighed, not at all apologetically.

No, actually Teresa wouldn't have thought that. The better she got to know Mandy, the more she re-

alized how much she resembled her parents. Both
James and Alexis were strong-willed, passionate
people. They knew what they wanted from life and
did not hesitate to reach out to take it.

To be fair, her own parents weren't very much
different. Certainly her father had never let anything stand in his way, and her mother had, in a
quieter manner, also fulfilled her own goals. She
wondered if any of them had ever felt the vague, disquieting anxieties that plagued her. As Mandy had
so adroitly pointed out, she had everything in the
world to be happy about. So why wasn't she?

A remembered phrase from her childhood darted
through her mind. Maybe she was just "going
through a stage." How many times had she heard
Maggie or Anthony say that when one of their darling children insisted on doing something particularly tiresome? Once Joey had managed to get
himself covered with red paint while trying to refur-
bish the doghouse and had solemnly told his cha-
grined parents not to worry, he was merely "going
through a stage."

If that was her problem, she could wait it out. But
somehow she feared it might go a little deeper.

Matthew came home a few days later. He was very
quiet and had little to say about his experiences. Teresa did not press him. She sensed that his horror at
what he had seen, and his fear for Jim, were too great
to be talked about. Though he clearly did not want to
discuss them with her, that prohibition apparently

did not extend to everyone. He spent hours closeted with Winston, going over film he had shot. The results were an hour-long program about Vietnam that pulled no punches and brought the wrath of the White House down squarely on IBS.

"I got a call from a gentleman at the FCC today," James said laconically when he had summoned the news team to an emergency meeting. "Suggestions were made that we may not have an easy time getting license renewals for our affiliates."

"He actually said that?" Teresa asked, not able to hide her shock. She would have expected the threat to be cloaked in at least a little subtlety.

James disabused her of that notion. "Came right out with it," he confirmed. "Not only that, he suggested that UBC would get the same treatment."

"I'm terrified," Alexis muttered. She had been asked to attend the meeting precisely because her own stations would be affected. Teresa had never had much opportunity to see Matthew's mother in a business situation and she was curious as to how she would handle herself. Certain things were already apparent: she did not lose her temper or scare easily, she did not defer to her husband but clearly respected his opinion, and she was more than prepared to fight for what she believed was right.

James shot her a quick grin before he said, "Word of this is bound to get out, so I thought it best to clear the air right off the bat. Both IBS and UBC have every reason to be extremely proud of their news coverage. I believe they both equal the best newspapers in the country when it comes to objectivity. That will be maintained, the administration and everyone in it will be treated with rigorous fairness. We are not going to stoop to the level of those people; however we are also not going to give them an inch. We will report the news, plain and simple." He paused for a moment, then added more softly, "It is my belief that, given enough rope, we can count on this administration to hang itself."

"It's a nice thought," Winston said, "but—"

"I mean that," James interrupted, stressing his point. "I've had a funny feeling about Nixon from the beginning and lately it's stronger than ever. You know there are rumors he keeps a so-called enemies list? In my opinion, there should be only one name on it, his own. He's a prime candidate for self-destruction."

"Do you realize what a terrifying thing that is to contemplate?" Winston asked. "It's his finger on the button. If he goes, he could take all of us with him."

"There won't be anything like that," James said confidently. "As contradictory as this may sound, underneath it all I think he's really a very decent man. He just has a fatal flaw that shows up in the people he keeps around him."

"You're being too charitable."

"Maybe, but that's how I feel. He's the president and he will be treated with all the respect his office merits. There will be no potshots taken. Not," he added hastily, "that any have been tried in the past."

"At least," said Alexis, "we aren't in the same boat as the other networks, trying to do instant analysis after his speeches or press conferences. Some commentators have revealed personal biases then, which opened the way to these attacks on the media in general."

James had always resisted the idea of commentators explaining to the public what the president had said within minutes of his having done so. With Winston's full support, that had never been a feature of IBS news coverage. Alexis had maintained the same policy at UBC.

"All right," James said summing up, "we go on as before but with extra vigilance. Any questions?"

"Only one," Matthew murmured. "What about the license renewals?"

His father smiled, a slow, teeth-baring smile that had all the gentleness of a wolf contemplating its prey. Very quietly, he said, "Leave those to me."

Teresa was more than happy to do so. As they left his father's office she had seen the cold light of understanding and approval in Matthew's eyes. He was no longer resisting the urge to model himself on James; in fact, since returning from Vietnam he seemed to be more set on that than ever.

It was as though he no longer saw the world as anything but a savage place where only the strong could survive. His father had done that and more, he had triumphed where other men had been destroyed. Matthew wanted to do the same; the surest way was to follow a route he already knew led to success. He would do as his father had done, and he would begin by binding the woman he wanted to him with every chain he could devise.

"I think," he announced one night shortly after his return, "that we should get married."

Teresa turned over slowly in the bed and looked at him. It was very late. They had come home from work, had dinner at her apartment and made love. She had been almost asleep. "Why," she asked slowly, "do you think that?"

He laughed faintly in the darkness. "You sound surprised. We've certainly known each other long enough."

"If you start from the time we became lovers, and in this context I think you should, it's been less than a year."

"Time enough to be sure. Besides, I'm twenty-nine. I'd like to be married." He propped himself up on an elbow and smiled down at her. "Aren't you getting a little tired of this musical beds routine? One night at your place, the next at mine? It's silly. We should settle down."

"Maybe we could live together. . . ." she ventured hesitantly.

"Why bother when we already know each other so well?" A frown drew his brows together. "Teresa . . . don't you want to get married?"

"I don't know," she admitted, sitting up and drawing the sheet with her to tuck around her breasts. She stared off into space. "It's such a huge step."

"Plenty of people do it all the time."

"And for plenty of them it doesn't work. I don't want to rush into anything." She was glad that she couldn't see his expression, sure that she wouldn't have liked it.

"What you seem to be saying is that you don't trust your feelings for me or mine for you."

Stung by the coldness in his tone, she shook her head. "That isn't true. I love you and I believe you love me, but I don't think that's all there is to it. I'm not ready for marriage."

He laughed rather harshly. "That's supposed to be the man's line."

She dared a glance at him over her shoulder. "In case you haven't noticed, times have changed."

He stared at her for a long moment as though fighting an inner battle with himself. She waited, wondering if he would become angry, almost hoping that he would. Much as she hated to admit it, she wouldn't have minded so much if he had tried to make the decision for her.

But instead he merely lay back against the pillows, looked up at the ceiling and said, "Yeah, I guess they have."

Chapter Seven

MATTHEW DID NOT MENTION marriage again, nor did Teresa's refusal seem to bother him much. Throughout the second half of 1969, they went on more or less as before, the only difference being that both were aware of a barrier between them.

Teresa tried once or twice to explain why she did not yet feel ready to make so serious a commitment, but she did not succeed. Matthew heard her out courteously enough, but his blank, unreceptive manner made her stumble over her words. She gave up before she had gotten very far.

Deep inside, she was angry at him for pushing her into a corner. He owed it to her to be more sensitive to her feelings and needs. Instead, he seemed to be telling her that she was not, after all, very important to him. That, more than anything else, hurt.

She had the terrifying sense that the failure of honesty in their relationship was costing them more than either could imagine. More and more they seemed like two people simply going through the motions of being together.

And that they were doing with increasing rarity. Teresa had taken over assistant producer duties for the hour-long news shows Winston did at intervals throughout the year. That, added to her regular duties on the nightly broadcast, kept her on the run.

Matthew was also moving up fast. After his trip to Vietnam, he made a swing through the South to report on the progress of civil rights there, toured the northern cities for a series on urban poverty and visited Israel.

He was away in July when the first moon landing occurred and again in August when several hundred thousand young people flocked to Woodstock, New York. Those two events—added to the murderous spree of Charles Manson and his followers in California the same month—seemed to Teresa to be saying something about the age in which they lived. Extraordinary technological achievement existed cheek by jowl with hedonistic disaffection and soulless violence.

In the back of her mind, she caught a hint of why Matthew might have felt driven to try to achieve some kind of permanency in his life, something that would offer protection from the remorseless barrage of events that seemed intent on engulfing them. She could even, upon reflection, feel more sympathetic to his motives. But now, when she might have been able to talk with him, he was not there.

At least the long nights alone gave her the chance to do something that had been on her mind for quite a while now. In high school and college she had written short stories, at first as class assignments and later simply because she enjoyed the experience. It satisfied some deeply seated need in her. She had never told anyone how important writing fiction was to her; the closest she had ever gotten was simply saying she wanted to be a writer. She supposed that people like Matthew presumed she meant a reporter, but in fact she did not. She wanted to write a novel.

The mere thought of trying to do so made her head ache. She literally had no idea where to begin, yet she determined to persevere. Night after night when Matthew was out of town or simply busy, she worked at the battered typewriter on the kitchen table. Wrapped in an old bathrobe with the hi-fi playing softly in the background, she struggled to capture the essence of people and scenes that were so vivid in her mind yet so stubbornly recalcitrant about getting down on paper.

At least ninety percent of what she wrote she threw away. The rest she hid. She labored under the burden of doing something that felt at once self-indulgent, arrogant and somehow shameful. Yet she couldn't stop herself.

Her preoccupation did not go unnoticed. One day early in November, as they were leaving a staff meeting, Winston gave her an assessing look and said, ''You seem to be burning the candle at both ends these days. Any particular reason why?''

Teresa flushed. She knew she had lost weight and there were shadows under her eyes, but with the proper clothes and makeup she hadn't thought anyone would notice. Apparently, she'd been wrong.

"I've just had a lot on my mind," she hedged, hoping he would let it go at that.

Winston continued to study her with the same thoroughness he turned on anything that aroused his interest but also with a degree of tenderness born of their long friendship. "Matthew's been on the road a lot."

She smiled faintly. "You should know; you send him."

"Do you resent that?"

"I . . . I think I'm a little envious of him having something that absorbs him so completely. I'd like to have something similar in my own life."

"Women frequently find that in a man."

Her eyebrows rose fractionally. "Is that what you'd recommend?"

He raised a hand in mock surrender. "Don't expect me to put my foot in that one. I was simply curious as to what you'd say."

Teresa sighed and shook her head. "It's true that I feel very deeply for Matthew. If I let it, that could block out everything else. But I don't think that would be good for either of us."

"Surely he doesn't disagree with you?"

They were alone in the corridor. She badly needed someone to confide in and thought the judgment of an older, more objective person might be of help. Hesitantly, she said, "He asked me to marry him."

"Don't tell me you were surprised?"

"No . . . not exactly. I just don't feel the time is right."

Winston ran a hand through his thick silver hair and regarded her gently. "Not for you, perhaps, but Matthew may well feel the need for a greater level of stability in his life."

"Do you think that's because he's older than me?"

"Partly, as we mature, the need to truly share ourselves seems to increase. But it may also be related to his recent experiences with his brother and in Vietnam."

Teresa hugged the papers she was carrying closer to her and stared off into the middle distance. "You're saying he needs something to hold on to."

Winston nodded gently. "Something good and decent that won't let him down. God knows, it's a common enough human craving."

"I don't want to deny him what he needs," she said softly. "I love him with all my heart and I think someday we could have a very good marriage. But I need more time before I take that step."

Winston shrugged, not unsympathetically. "Don't tell me. Tell Matthew."

She meant to; she really did, but before she could do so, events once again intervened.

Late in November, shortly after half a million people had marched on Washington to protest the war, word came that Jim had been wounded. For several days, that was all they knew. Finally, an IBS reporter stationed in Saigon was able to get them more details.

"He was hit during a firefight at Pleiku," James said grimly. "They helicoptered him out and he had emergency surgery at a medivac unit. Now he's on the way to a hospital in Japan."

"How soon can we get him here?" Matthew asked quietly. They were in the living room of the town house. Mandy had come down from school when she learned what had happened to her brother and sat curled up in a corner, having said barely a word. Matthew had returned home the day before from an assignment and had been at his apartment when his father called. He had picked up Teresa on his way over. It hadn't occurred to either of them that she should not be there. Knowing Jim as well as she did, and being so close to the family, she felt what had happened to him as keenly as any of them.

"I still can't believe this," Alexis murmured. Her face was ashen and she sat with her hands gripped tightly in her lap. "That stupid, impersonal telegram, telling us nothing really, and no one willing to say anything more." Her voice broke as her gray eyes flooded with tears.

James moved swiftly to her side. He bent over her, shielding her from the others, and spoke to her softly. Teresa saw his hand touch her cheek, stroking gently. After a moment, he stepped back but stayed near her.

"Thank God we have contacts of our own," Matthew said. "If we'd had to depend on the Pentagon, we still wouldn't know where Jim is or what had really happened.''

''I want him home,'' Alexis insisted, more steadily. ''And I don't care what it takes to get him here.''

James agreed. Just as he had with Matthew, he would move heaven and earth to get his son where he could have the best possible care, and he wasn't any too scrupulous about how he managed it.

''To hell with the formalities,'' Teresa heard him saying a short while later as he talked on the phone in his study. She had gone to the kitchen to ask Mr. Thompson for fresh coffee. All the members of the household staff were going out of their way to provide whatever help they could. Food was available at all hours, visitors and phone calls were screened even more scrupulously than usual, and every effort was made to discreetly but nonetheless clearly express their sympathy.

The study was down the corridor from the kitchen. Teresa had to pass it on her way back to the living room. Never one to eavesdrop, she was nonetheless riveted by the sheer, implacable determination in James's voice, a tone she had rarely heard from anyone and had certainly never had directed against herself. She stood frozen by the open door as he said, ''I'll have a plane in Tokyo in twelve hours with a fresh crew for immediate turnaround. I want Jim on it and back here by tomorrow.''

Whoever was on the other end must have been trying to point out the problems with that, but James would have none of it. "Screw the red tape. If I have to go get him myself, I will, and believe me nobody will enjoy that."

If he had been ranting and raving, it might have been possible to dismiss his demands. But in the force of such absolute determination, she could almost feel sorry for whoever he was talking to. Almost, but not quite. She shared James's conviction that the sooner Jim got home, the better.

He did so a few days later, minus the leg amputated in the emergency medical tent near where he had been hit. Theoretically, he was lucky; the five other men with him on patrol had all died. Jim left no doubt that he would have preferred to join them.

His doctors assured Alexis and James that his attitude was not unusual under the circumstances. It might well pass in time, or it might not. In the meantime, he resisted either speaking or eating.

Teresa went to the hospital with Matthew to visit him. He was in a room by himself, watched over by one of the private nurses James had insisted on. He had even specified that the nurses be attractive; "no battle-axes" was the way he put it. Everything possible was being done to restore Jim to health, both physically and mentally. Only it didn't seem to be working.

The young, pretty nurse had shaved him. He was dressed in fresh pajamas, his short blond hair neatly brushed. His eyes were open as Matthew and Teresa came in. They flicked to them briefly and a gentle smile touched his mouth.

Teresa moved to his side, taking his hand in hers. "Hi, Jim," she said softly. "How are you doing?"

He said nothing but continued to smile.

"He's a little better this morning," the nurse said encouragingly. "He even ate some breakfast."

Matthew glanced down at the mostly full bowl of oatmeal waiting to be removed and grimaced. With forced cheerfulness, he said, "If that's what they're feeding you, I don't blame you for not wanting to eat. We'll have to get you some real food."

Silence, and the smile. Beneath the crisp white sheet, his body looked thin and wasted, even more so than it had that acid-etched night in Haight-Ashbury. On the left side, where a leg should have been, was only flatness.

Teresa blinked back tears. But for the slight return pressure of the hand she held, she might have been looking at a mannequin someone had mutilated.

Matthew reached out and took his other hand. His voice was husky as he said, "You're going to be all right, kid. Just hang in there."

The merest flicker of understanding seemed to dart through the fathomless gray eyes, or perhaps it was only an illusion born of desperation. After a moment, his lids drooped and he sighed deeply.

"I'm afraid Private Callahan tires very easily," the nurse said gently. "That's to be expected at this stage."

"Yeah," Matthew murmured, "I guess so." He was clearly reluctant to leave, but there was little choice. Jim was effectively shutting them out, as he was all the rest of the world.

"He needs time," Teresa said softly as they left the room and started back down the hospital corridor.

"He needs more than that," Matthew shot back, unable to hide his bitterness. "A whole body, for one thing, and a whole mind." He stopped abruptly, his hands jammed into the pockets of his jeans and his face tight with anguish. "He's just a kid, for God's sake. How the hell is he supposed to go on from this?"

"Others have," Teresa pointed out gently. She put a hand on his arm tentatively, not knowing if he would accept comfort or not. When he didn't shake it off, she dared to persevere. "He's getting the best of care. Everything that can be done is."

"I know," he murmured. "That's why I feel so damned helpless. If I could think of something more to do, I would. But I can't."

Teresa pressed against him lightly. She understood how deeply the sense of his own frustration must rankle. He was a man accustomed to being able to shape, and to a certain extent even control, his personal world. But he could not do that with Jim, any more than he had been able to do it with her.

"You have to be patient," she said quietly as they began to walk again toward the doors. "I know there aren't any guarantees that Jim will ever really recover, but if everyone's expectations are unreasonably high, he'll sense that and he won't be able to cope."

"He said something to me before he left," Matthew murmured, "about wanting to be treated like an ordinary guy. I got the feeling he resented always having to run to keep up with the rest of us, and then not making it anyway."

"You can't really blame him. He comes from a rather formidable family."

Matthew smiled wanly. "Is that how you see us?"

"Sometimes."

He cast her a quick, perceptive look. "You can be pretty formidable yourself."

That surprised her; she didn't think of herself in such terms. On the contrary, it had cost her a great deal to stand up to him even once.

They were silent during the cab ride back to her place. Matthew hadn't actually asked if he could come over, but they had both more or less assumed it. His latest trip had kept him on the road for two weeks; they were hungry for each other.

"I could fix us a bite to eat," Teresa offered halfheartedly.

He fixed her with a steady stare as he shucked off his jacket. "Maybe later."

Her throat felt suddenly dry. Since she had turned down his marriage proposal, their lovemaking had not been the same. They still satisfied each other physically, but something was missing emotionally. Perhaps this time it would be better.

Silently, she took his hand and led him into the bedroom. Driven by the need to give comfort, she put aside her own concerns and concentrated on his. As he watched, with a slightly quizzical smile, she undressed, carefully folding each garment as she removed it. Before she had finished, he had unbuttoned his shirt and pulled it out of his trousers while kicking off his shoes. ''I was going to be subtle about this,'' he said ruefully.

She walked toward him, naked, her skin glowing in the faint light filtering through the drawn blinds.

He didn't answer. To say that he resented his need for her and was trying to deny it would shatter the moment. Instead, he rapidly finished undressing and reached for her.

There was no gentleness in his touch, or in hers. They strained together, each desperate for the other, each struggling against the hunger that drove them. The harsh intake of his breath matched her own. She tasted the scent of his skin on the tip of her tongue and knew he was rapidly passing beyond control. Her back arched helplessly as he nuzzled the velvety smoothness between her breasts, his thumbs tormenting her swollen nipples. The straining pressure against her belly made her throb with emptiness deep inside.

Long, leisurely lovemaking was beyond either of them. There was no time for the slow pleasures of arousal and fulfillment. Caught in a flash fire of passions they could barely comprehend, they could think only of satiation.

Matthew groaned her name deep in his throat as he pressed her down onto the bed. For an instant, he paused, struck by the knowledge that this was Teresa, the woman he loved, the person who above all others on earth was special to him. But she was also the woman who could make him lie awake at night wondering if she meant to leave him, and whether the pain might be less if he left first.

He resented how vulnerable she made him feel— indeed, there were times when he almost hated her for it. Baffled by his own seemingly contradictory emotions, he did his best to deny them. And most of the time he succeeded. But now he could not. Now he was driven to imprint himself on her in the most profound way possible. To wrest from her, if only briefly, the admission that her need for him was as great as his for her.

Without further preliminaries, he parted her thighs and found the warm, moist center of her. Teresa moaned softly, with eagerness rather than fear. Her hips lifted, seeking. At the first probing touch, she reached down a hand, guiding him to her.

He had meant to hold back, to prove in the most intimate of embraces that he was really the stronger, the one in control. He had a moment to mock himself for the arrogance of that before the undulating coils of pleasure tightened around him and he gave himself up to her.

AFTERWARD THEY LAY in the tangle of sheets and touched each other gently. The release of so many passions—desire, anger, fear, love—had left them both dazed and shaken. They were silent for a long time, speaking only with looks and the soothing caress of fingertips against sweat-moistened skin. At length, Matthew smiled weakly. "I've got a terrible urge to ask you to marry me again."

She laughed softly, glad that he had put it that way instead of asking outright. His reluctance to risk another rejection saved her the burden of disappointing him. Quietly, she said, "After what we just shared, do you really think anything could make it better?"

"No," he admitted, "I suppose not." His smile deepened. "But I wouldn't mind trying."

Her eyes glowed tenderly. "I don't think I could survive that."

"You're stronger than you know."

She shivered slightly, feeling the slight coolness on her damp skin. Together they reached down and pulled the sheet over them. Snuggling closer to him, she said, "Perhaps that's the problem. It would be so easy for me to take shelter in you. Sometimes I'm so tempted to do that.''

He smoothed her hair away from her face so that he could see her more clearly. ''But you never do.''

''Don't I? What do you think happened tonight? I started out wanting to comfort you and I ended up taking everything I could in order to block out all my own fears and doubts.'' She was not proud of that; even though she knew that sometimes such release was necessary, she feared making a habit of it.

Matthew sighed and lay back against the pillow. His hand stayed on her cheek, stroking gently. ''You're very hard on yourself, Teresa. We love each other, so we help each other. There's nothing wrong with that.''

''Not if it's done equally,'' she agreed, ''but I'm afraid that wouldn't always be the case with us. I still tend too much to look up to you, like I did when I was a little girl, instead of seeing you as a partner. That isn't fair to either of us.''

As the silence stretched out between them, she imagined him preparing to contest what she had just said and wondered how she would support her case. She had enough trouble trying to understand it herself without explaining it as well. But if that was what he wanted, she would do her best.

At length he said solemnly, ''I think the problem is that I am simply too terrific a person.''

It took a moment for his words to sink in. When they did, she laughed out loud, relieved and grateful that he had chosen to make a joke of it. "That's you, all right, Mr. Terrific. Do you think maybe you should work on developing some bad habits?"

"How about nail biting?"

"That's a good start, but something more dramatic would help. Dog kicking?"

"I don't have a dog."

"Bad table manners?"

"I could slurp my soup."

"Hmmm . . ." Her eyelids began to flutter shut. "And walk around in a torn undershirt. No, on second thought, that wouldn't help. . . ." Her voice slurred, then trailed off.

Long after she had fallen asleep, Matthew lay awake holding her. The utter satiation of his body did not ease the unmistakable sensation of being caught on the horns of a dilemma. Teresa loved him because he was a good man, but because he was a good man, she was afraid to love him lest she lose herself in him. Somewhere in there was the explanation for why women so often seemed to be attracted to men he considered creeps; it even made a perverse kind of sense. Which did not help him at all.

More and more he was coming to believe that to have any true chance of keeping Teresa, he was going to first have to let her go.

MATTHEW WAS AWAY even more frequently in the next few months, covering stories that took him out of the city and the country. He seemed prepared to go anywhere at any time in pursuit of the news. Sometimes Teresa wondered if he wasn't a little too eager to stay on the road. She tried to ask Winston but found there was no subtle way to put it and wasn't prepared to be too direct. Instead, she told herself that perhaps it was for the best.

When he was gone, she concentrated on her writing and tried not to think about the long road she still had to travel to become even what she would consider adept at her craft. Meanwhile, Matthew's progress was much faster. The assignments he drew and what he made of them caused his career to skyrocket. Before he turned thirty, he was being spoken of as a likely successor for the man Americans claimed to trust more than any other.

Certainly they did not trust their president, however much they may have wanted to. True, Nixon had begun to withdraw troops from Vietnam and true, he had sent his representatives to the peace table in Paris. But men were still dying, almost forty-five thousand now, and no end was in sight. The president kept saying the country had to win the peace if not the war. He didn't say how, or why.

"Everybody's so tired of this," Mandy said one afternoon when she and Teresa met for lunch. It was the last week of April, normally a time when New York was at its best, but as they sat at a sidewalk table overlooking Central Park, neither was aware of the gentle beauty of spring. Other, far grimmer, events held their attention.

Mandy had just been to visit Jim. He was out of the hospital now, staying at his parents' town house, and getting physical therapy. It did not seem to be helping. The therapist said he lacked motivation and suggested psychiatric care, but in a rare show of spirit Jim absolutely refused. He would not discuss his experiences in Vietnam with anyone, not even his twin.

"Do you want a drink?" Teresa asked gently. Mandy rarely had anything alcoholic. She had turned against all such substances since seeing what they had done to her brother. But this time she was willing to make an exception.

"I could use one," she admitted reluctantly. "I've got to go back to school tomorrow and frankly I'm not looking forward to it. The mood there is so . . . I don't know what. Sad, maybe, and scared. I think we're all beginning to suspect that nothing is ever going to change, at least not for the better."

"We can't simply go on as we are," Teresa said. "The course we're on is too destructive to be endured much longer. Something will have to give."

"Any ideas what?"

Teresa didn't want to answer, not being anxious to make her friend feel any more depressed, but she still felt driven to honesty. "We have to give up our belief in extremes. Instead of believing either that everything is possible or nothing is, we're going to have to become a little more realistic, which in the long run will be good, but in the short run will be very painful."

Mandy smiled faintly. "It sounds as though all that history you studied made you a deep thinker."

The history and the writing, which was forcing her to take a step back and regard the world from a new perspective. She was tempted for a moment to tell Mandy about that but resisted, still too unsure to reveal so vital a part of herself.

"Tell me more about school," she encouraged. "You'll be a senior in a few months. Do you have any plans for after graduation?"

"Not really. I thought I might travel some, maybe live abroad for a while."

No mention of getting a job, but that wasn't unexpected. Girls like Mandy thought in terms of a career, and then only if it was congenial. Not for them the humdrum routine of nine-to-five and subservience to a paycheck. Teresa wondered absently how she had escaped that and thought perhaps it was because neither of her parents had been born to wealth.

Whether knowingly or not, Alexis had passed on to her daughter the presumption that she could deal with the world strictly on her own terms. It wasn't inconceivable that Mandy might one day succeed in doing so as brilliantly as her mother had. But in the meantime she had some difficult lessons to learn.

"It's tough these days being an American abroad," Teresa pointed out. "We're not very popular."

Mandy shrugged. "Money takes care of that, like so many other things."

Surprised by her cynicism, Teresa did not respond. The bleakness in the younger girl's eyes troubled her. With the single exception of Jim, Mandy had always seemed impervious to life's darker side. She was one of the very fortunate few on whom fate had truly smiled. Yet she was also part of a generation increasingly aware that it was fighting the wrong war. The real struggle was not to win the hearts and minds of people on the other side of the earth but to fulfill the promise of its own birthright.

"Generation gap" was such a hackneyed phrase, yet it had never seemed more accurate than during the first week of May, when the war everyone wanted to end was instead abruptly widened. The invasion of Cambodia sparked strikes on campuses across the country. For the most part they were peaceful, but a small minority of demonstrators introduced a new, previously unseen level of violence. It was promptly met in kind.

Teresa was in the newsroom when the first reports came in from Kent State University in Ohio. There had been trouble there for several days; after a demonstration against the Cambodian invasion got out of hand, National Guardsmen had been sent onto the campus. Many of them were no older than the students themselves. The young were being used to control the young. It didn't work very well.

The voice of the IBS reporter on the scene shook as he relayed the first report. "They've fired on the students. Several are hit. I'm trying to find out more.''

''Do you have film?'' Winston demanded. In his shirtsleeves with the half-finished script for that night's broadcast in his hand, he listened somberly. By the time he turned the phone over to his director, his face was pale.

Addressing the news team, which had instinctively gathered around him, he said quietly, ''We'll be going on the air immediately. We will report only what we know for sure; there will be no speculation and no inflammatory comments by anyone on camera. Is that clear?''

They all nodded, wondering even as they did so why he felt compelled to mention something so obvious. They were, after all, all professionals.

But they were also human and for the most part young, and in the hours that followed their objectivity was strained to the utmost. Four students were dead, nine others wounded, some severely. None of the students had had any weapons. They had been standing too far away from the National Guardsmen to endanger them in any way, but close enough to be gunned down by the M-1 rifles turned on them.

Late that night, after the 11:00 P.M. broadcast, Teresa went home. Matthew was in Washington and would not be back until the following day. She got into bed, pulled the covers over herself and turned her face into the pillow. Only then did she discover that she had lost even the ability to cry.

Chapter Eight

"I'VE READ YOUR MANUSCRIPT," the editor said over the phone, "and I think it has real possibilities. I'd like to get together with you."

"That would be very nice," Teresa replied. "When would you suggest?"

They made an appointment for lunch the following week, then chatted a few more minutes before hanging up. When Teresa put the phone down, her hands were shaking.

For the first time, she had found the courage to show her writing to someone. Deliberately, she had chosen a stranger, an anonymous editor in one of the larger publishing houses. After mailing off the bulky manuscript, she had done her best to put it out of her mind. By the time three months had gone by, she had almost succeeded. Until the phone call.

Despite her best efforts, she couldn't help but be excited. The call might not mean anything; the editor hadn't actually said she wanted to buy the book. On the other hand, she hadn't suggested it was fit only for fish wrapping either.

She glanced at the calendar and the date she had just circled in red. The time between now and then seemed to stretch out forever. She didn't want to spend it alone. Her parents had been urging her to come for a visit. She could stay with them and commute into town each morning with Anthony. He had finally stopped using the Long Island Railroad and switched to a limousine, which he grudgingly admitted was an improvement, ''Though I miss having someone to play cards with.''

It was good to be with her folks. Joey and Tony were both away at college and the house was very quiet. ''Too quiet,'' Maggie complained when she got home from the hospital to find both her husband and daughter on hand. ''I never thought I'd say that when those two hellions were still living here, but I miss them.''

''They'll be home for Easter in a few weeks,'' Anthony reminded her, ''and God only knows what they'll bring with them this time.''

''What do you mean?'' Teresa asked as she put her feet up on the hassock. ''They got past the snakes and spiders stage a long time ago.''

''I'm not sure I wouldn't prefer that,'' Maggie said as she accepted a drink from her husband and sat down on the couch. ''For a while, they were satisfied to bring home shaggy-haired friends who never seemed to get enough to eat. But last Christmas . . .'' She looked at her daughter. ''Surely you remember what happened then?''

Teresa did and couldn't help but smile. Joey had arrived home with a girl, not having bothered with any advance warning. He had introduced her as a "friend" but it had been perfectly obvious that the relationship was a good deal closer. Maggie had promptly instructed the maid to make up the guest room, which earned a grimace from her son and a tolerant grin from the girl. No one had been satisfied with the arrangement, and ever since Maggie and Anthony had been wondering how to handle the situation when it arose again, as it inevitably would.

"I suppose we should be glad we don't have any more daughters," Anthony said as he loosened his tie and sat down. "At least you're old enough to look out for yourself. And then, of course, there's Matthew...." His voice trailed off on a faint note of questioning.

Teresa smothered a sigh. She didn't really want to talk about Matthew with her parents, but she felt she owed them some explanation. They had known for quite a while that everything was not right but had been very careful not to intrude.

"Matthew and I aren't seeing much of each other these days," she said at length.

Maggie and Anthony exchanged a glance. After a moment, Maggie asked, "Would you like to tell us what happened?"

"Nothing really. We didn't have a big argument or anything like that. It's just that little by little we've drifted apart. You know he's been traveling so much...."

"He doesn't have to do that," Anthony said. "At least not to the extent he has."

"I think he does what he feels is necessary," Teresa put in gently. "In all fairness to him, I don't seem able to give him what he wants."

Maggie's eyes were dark with bewilderment. "We thought you two were so happy."

"We were, as far as it went. Some time ago Matthew asked me to marry him. I said no, that I wasn't ready. He never actually asked again, but if he had, the answer would have been the same. After a while, I guess he just got tired of waiting for me to change."

"We never knew he'd proposed," Anthony said thoughtfully. "If I had, I'd have guessed you would say yes."

"Oh, I was tempted. But it was…" She broke off, fumbling for the words that would make them understand.

"It's all right," her mother said, putting a hand over hers. "You don't have to explain. Marriage is the biggest step anyone can take; you have to be sure before you do it."

"Were you really so uncertain?" Anthony asked. He, for one, would have liked an explanation, though he wasn't about to push for it. With Teresa married to Matthew, he would have had no more worries about her. Despite what he'd said about her being able to look after herself, he still thought of her as his little girl. In an increasingly dangerous world, he longed to keep her safe. That was impossible, but Matthew might have been able to manage it.

"Please try to see it from my position," Teresa said, speaking more to him than to Maggie, who she already sensed understood. "I don't feel as though I've really grown into myself yet. There's still so much that I want to accomplish. I was afraid that if I married Matthew I would have an excuse not to even try."

"I don't see why marriage should be incompatible with your ambitions," Anthony protested. "Many wives work now." Didn't he have an example of that in his very own home? Maggie had insisted on going back to nursing as soon as the children were old enough, despite his firm objections. With hindsight, he could see that she had been right, but at the time it had caused a few problems.

"They work," Maggie agreed, "but they don't tend to build careers for themselves. There's always a feeling that they shouldn't try to go too far because they'll end up losing whatever they've gained anyway when they start a family."

Anthony regarded her thoughtfully. She looked very serious, yet he couldn't help but think she was blowing the problem out of proportion. "Is a career so important to you? More than a husband and children?" Before she could answer, he went on, "It isn't as though you had any money worries, at least not as far as I know." He didn't really think she could have gone through her trust fund so quickly, but perhaps he was wrong.

"No," she said, "I've got plenty of money. But there are other reasons for wanting a career."

"Of course there are, but I don't see how they stack up against a good family life."

"Maybe that's because you're used to having both," she reminded him gently.

He looked a bit taken aback by that, as though the tables were suddenly turned and now he had to explain himself. "I'm older," he said at last. "I've had time to put things together."

"That's what I need, time."

"Of course you do," Maggie agreed. Her support was completely with her daughter. If she had been Teresa's age, she would have felt exactly the same way. There were so many more opportunities now for women, but there were also many more problems. She couldn't help but be a little glad that she hadn't had to make such choices.

"Do you think Matthew will wait for you?" Anthony asked, not realizing how hard a question that was until his wife shot him a chiding glance.

"I don't know," Teresa admitted. The thought of Matthew with another woman was so painful that she could not contemplate it for more than a few seconds at a time. Yet she realized it was a very real possibility. At thirty, he could hardly be expected to live like a monk.

Which raised the question of whether or not she should be thinking about other men. After that one brief foray into the singles' world, she had never returned. Try though she did, she could muster no enthusiasm for doing so now. Her writing consumed every free moment and satisfied her in a way no man ever could.

Not that she didn't miss Matthew. She thought about him far more than she would have liked, and during those rare times when he was in the office, she seemed to be aware of him every instant. In their dealings with each other, they were scrupulously polite, two people tiptoeing around unfinished business as though it were a field strewn with mines. Just when she would think she couldn't stand it much longer, he would be gone again and the tension would ease at least a little until he returned.

But now there was something else to absorb her. Lunch with the editor had proved a very pleasant experience. For the first time, she discovered what it was like to be able to talk about her writing with someone who understood. Clare Danvers didn't think it at all odd for her to speak of her characters as though they were real people. On the contrary, she seemed to feel that was perfectly sane. Even more important, she encouraged Teresa to keep on writing.

"I have the feeling that you're one of those people who will write under any circumstances, simply because you feel driven to do so," Clare said as they shared a table at the Russian Tea Room. "But that doesn't mean you don't need encouragement. While there are rough spots in the manuscript that I want to work on with you, it is basically very good. So good, in fact, that I'm prepared to offer a contract.''

"You mean to publish it?''

To her credit, Clare smiled only faintly. She was a few years older than Teresa, a slim, pretty young woman drawn to publishing by a genuine love of the written word. She did a better than average job of spotting new talent and encouraging it. ''That's exactly what I mean. Do you have an agent I should talk with?''

"No . . . no agent.''

"I can recommend several if you'd like.'' When Teresa continued to stare at her dumbfounded, she explained, ''Some authors prefer an intermediary to handle the business discussions.''

"Yes . . . that might be a good idea.'' She laughed suddenly as the full meaning of what was happening finally reached her. ''Forgive me, I must be acting like an idiot. But I honestly never let myself think about being published.''

"That's all right,'' Clare assured her. ''I've seen enough writers go through this to have some understanding of what it feels like. I just hope it will be everything you imagine.''

"It will be,'' Teresa said with absolute certainty. ''I know there are bound to be problems ahead, but I'm sure I can face them. You see, what's happening here somehow . . . legitimizes me. It makes me feel as though I haven't been deluding myself all this time.''

"If this first book is anything to go by, you haven't. Just keep on with what you've been doing and the rest will fall into place."

Teresa believed her, but even if she hadn't, it wouldn't have mattered. At that moment she felt as though absolutely nothing was beyond her reach. For the first time in her life, she had a clear vision of what was possible.

That vision, that reason for having faith in a future that had once seemed only dark, sustained her through the next several months as she worked on the revisions for her book. She had known going in that for her at least rewriting was tougher than writing. That she had discovered in the very early stages of her attempts to get her thoughts down on paper.

The problem was that the first version came in a white heat of inspiration; what followed was cold and methodical. As she had learned to stand apart from the world and see it with the eye of an observer rather than a participant, now she had to learn to stand apart from her own work and view it with some measure of objectivity.

The task was nearly beyond her; she lost track of the long, painful hours she struggled to achieve the exact shade of meaning, the precise clarity of nuance that she sought. Clare helped as much as she could, but in the end the effort had to be Teresa's. She was fighting not only to expand the limits of her ability as a writer but also to overcome the fear of being judged. So long as the book was being revised, it would not be published. The day came when she had to let it go.

"We've scheduled it for next June," Clare told her. "I can't promise you a huge print run or a major publicity effort, but we will do our best."

"I'm sure you will." Teresa toyed with her salad. Instead of being happy with this news, she felt vaguely depressed, as though something vital had been removed from her life. The sensation was not very different from what she felt whenever she let herself think about Matthew.

"Do you have an idea for your next book?" Clare was asking.

"Idea, yes. A plan, no. I suppose I should get working on that."

"It might make you feel better." At Teresa's startled look, she laughed and said, "Postnovel depression is a pretty common disorder. It seems to consist of a feeling of being all at sea plus a fear that the first book was a fluke."

"Are you by any chance clairvoyant?"

The older woman laughed softly. "No, just an editor. I'm not going to lie to you; some authors really do have only one book in them. But I don't think that's the case with you. So when you're ready, I'd like to see an outline."

"Not a manuscript?"

"No, this time an outline will be enough."

Feeling as though she had very definitely arrived, Teresa headed back to work. She had still said nothing to anyone at work or in her family about the book, and she didn't intend to start now. June was still some nine months away. With that much time, she might come up with a way to be off the planet when the book came out.

MATTHEW RETURNED from his latest trip to Southeast Asia late in September. The war there was winding down, at least on the ground. In the air, bombers continued to attack Communist strongholds. Casualties had dropped dramatically, and the withdrawals of American troops continued. Meanwhile, the peace talks in Paris lumbered along. The general consensus was that Nixon would wait until after the forthcoming election, then make a quick deal to get out. But that meant at minimum another year of fighting, something a public weary with war did not seem willing to contemplate.

A distinguished member of congress had made the half-joking suggestion that the way to end the war was to declare victory and withdraw. Matthew thought the idea had some merit. It certainly seemed to be what the American public was doing. Any mention of Vietnam tended to be met with impatient weariness and a determination to change the subject.

There was a great deal else to think about. Inflation was rampant, with prices increasing at a rate that hadn't been seen in almost twenty years. Crime was doing the same. When a middle-aged man who lived in Matthew's building was beaten up and robbed, he reluctantly put better locks on his windows and started being more cautious about his own comings and goings. He also worried about Teresa.

She was so withdrawn from him these days that he had no idea how to approach her. Far from their relationship being helped by his absences, they seemed to be destroying it. He wanted to put an end to that and try to recover lost ground but didn't know where to start. Whenever he tried to talk to her, he could feel the barriers between them. She seemed to be hiding something; he feared it was another man.

The very possibility of that alternately made him want to lash out at her or stay as far away as possible. Over and over he told himself that he shouldn't feel jealous; she was a person, not a possession; she had a right to live her life as she chose. He believed that, in an intellectual sense. Emotionally, he couldn't accept it at all. Any more than he could accept the idea that some other woman could give him what Teresa had withheld. He wanted her, no one else, and as the months passed and the distance between them increased, he became ever more determined to have her.

Matthew's campaign to win back Teresa, and to do it on his own terms, was planned as carefully as any military offensive. Once he had decided what he wanted to do, he studied the objective with meticulous care. That was hardly difficult. She seemed more beautiful than ever to him, with a hint of sadness and vulnerability that made him long to smash through all the barriers between them and demand that she listen to him. But he did not. Instead, he bided his time and honed his strategy.

To begin with, he sharply curtailed his trips out of town. Winston had been urging him to do so, and in the fall of 1971, when he suggested that Matthew be named co-anchor with him of the nightly news, he made the offer so tempting it could not be turned down.

"You'll have considerable say in what gets on the air," he assured Matthew when they discussed the job change. "We'll split the broadcast time evenly, and you'll do half the interviews. I plan to be taking more time off in the future, so there will also be plenty of opportunities for you to run the show on your own."

"Are you sure you want to do this?" Matthew asked. They were sitting in Winston's office after the evening broadcast. Outside it was raining steadily. In a few days, it would be Thanksgiving. He planned to spend it with his parents but wished that Teresa could also be there.

"I've been at this post for a long time now," Winston said, "and frankly I'm beginning to find it a bit wearying. I'd like to be able to do more writing, to tackle issues in greater depth, but except for the handful of special programs we do each year, there's no chance of that. If I can share the load with someone else, maybe that will change."

"There aren't many men who would want to give up even part of the kind of power you have."

"I suppose that's true, but I pride myself on being a realist. At some point, power must pass from one generation to the next. If we try to hold on too long, we make the transference only that much more difficult."

"I'm flattered that you feel this way about me," Matthew said.

"Don't be. Flattery has nothing to do with it. I've watched you for several years now and I believe, quite simply, that you are a good reporter. You care about the truth, and you have the strength to put it first, above all else."

"Thank you," Matthew said. He was deeply touched by Winston's approval but knew that by itself, it would not be enough. "You realize, of course, that there will be problems with my taking over the anchor job?"

The older man smiled. "You are referring, I presume, to your father?"

"He's got other plans for me."

"Have you talked about them directly?"

"No . . . and maybe I'm presuming too much, but I don't think that's the case."

Winston nodded. "Neither do I. James wants you to succeed him as head of IBS."

Having never put that possibility so plainly even to himself, Matthew was a bit taken aback by such bluntness. Yet he could not pretend to disagree. "That does seem to be his intention."

"How do you feel about it?"

"It's hard to say. I've never thought of myself as an executive, but that doesn't mean I wouldn't make a good one."

"Would you enjoy it? Here we have only one responsibility: getting the facts. Up there—" Winston glanced toward the ceiling and by extension to the executive floors above "—you'd have to juggle many others."

Matthew nodded. He didn't underestimate for a moment what his father did. James was more successful than most at delegating authority, but in the final analysis everything that happened within IBS depended on him. He set the tone for the entire network. The decisions he made shaped what millions of Americans saw and heard. Ultimately, they influenced how those same people thought and acted.

Could he handle the same level of responsibility? Certainly not at the moment; he knew he wasn't ready for it. But someday? If he was honest, he would admit that he hoped so.

"Let me talk with him about what you're suggesting," Matthew said. "Whatever objections he may have, we'll work them out."

In fact, that proved easier than he would have expected. James was not surprised to hear that Winston considered his son to be a worthy successor for the anchor chair, he simply didn't want him to get too comfortable there.

"It will be good experience for you. Whoever anchors the nightly news is also expected to essentially run the department. That's how Winston's always done it and there's no reason to change. When he's away, you'll be responsible for allocating manpower, staying within budget, coping with the sponsors and so on. Think you can handle it?"

"There's only one way to find out," Matthew said. He was relieved that his father had raised no serious objections, though he had been prepared to answer them. Instead, James had confirmed that he wanted his son to have a much larger role than simply reporting the news. Yet he was not pressuring him to agree to any definite plan for eventually taking over the network. That was a far cry from his vehement efforts to get him to come with IBS in the first place. It signaled his acceptance of Matthew as a man in charge of his own destiny and introduced a new stage in their relationship where they could deal with each other on a more equal footing.

Shortly after Matthew's meeting with his father, Winston called the news team together to inform them that he would henceforth be sharing the anchor duties. He emphasized that the basic approach to the news would remain the same but made it clear that he expected Matthew to have his own way of doing things. If there was any resentment of this promotion for the boss's son, it didn't show. Matthew had earned his stripes in the toughest kind of reporting; no one was about to suggest he wasn't qualified for the job.

Teresa certainly believed he would do it well, but she was concerned about having to work even more closely with him. Since Matthew had stopped traveling so much, Winston had been something of a buffer between them. It had been him she went to for the day-to-day decisions that kept the show running smoothly. Now she and Matthew would have to be in much closer contact.

Barely had the new anchor arrangement been made public than Winston announced he was taking a vacation. "Nothing ever happens over Christmas," he assured Matthew. "You'll barely know I'm gone."

"Yeah, right. It'll be a piece of cake."

"If you need anything, just ask Teresa."

Winston had been gone a day when Matthew decided to take his advice. He found Teresa on the set making sure that a newly installed camera worked properly. She didn't see him at first, so he had a chance to watch her unobserved. The slim tweed skirt she wore with a matching jacket and simple silk blouse made her look at once very feminine and very professional. Her hair was arranged in a loose chignon at the nape of her neck, with a few stray wisps brushing her forehead. His fingers curled under as he remembered the weight and softness of her hair.

Her expression was pleasant but serious as she spoke with one of the cameramen. He must have been explaining some difficulty to her since she nodded several times and then smiled encouragingly. The man smiled back, apparently convinced that the problem would be settled. She made a note on her clipboard and went on, speaking quietly with several more people as Matthew watched. Besides the sheer pleasure of looking at her, he enjoyed seeing how she handled herself. Her manner was quiet, cordial, professional. The stage crew obviously respected her, as she did them.

Which didn't mean that they didn't know a good-looking woman when they saw one. Intercepting an especially appreciative grin from one of the gofers, Matthew scowled. He strode forward and said to Teresa, "I'd like to see you in my office."

Surprised, she nodded. "All right. I'll be finished here in a few minutes."

"It's urgent." Without pausing to think, he took hold of her arm and propelled her toward the door. "Come on."

They were outside in the corridor before Teresa could jerk herself free. "Just what do you think you're doing?" she demanded. "There's nothing going on that's so urgent you couldn't have waited a few minutes."

"You looked like you were going to be there all day," he insisted, irately punching the button for the elevator.

"I was only getting a few problems straightened out. That happens to be my job, in case you hadn't noticed."

"So is doing what the anchorman tells you," he shot back, "which in case you haven't noticed, is me." Knowing perfectly well that he was acting like an idiot, he still couldn't stop himself. The months of pent-up frustration were beginning to break loose. One way or another, they were going to have to clear the air.

Teresa looked more than prepared to do that as she preceded him into the elevator. "Oh, I've noticed, all right. But let me tell you something, getting to be co-anchor does not make you some kind of tinhorn dictator. The news team is just that, *a team*. I, for one, intend to keep it that way."

"That's fine with me," he said more softly. The warm flush of her cheeks and the brightness of her eyes distracted him. Only with an effort did he get his thoughts back on track. "You and Winston work very well together. I hope we'll be able to do the same."

"I don't see why not," she acknowledged grudgingly, "provided you don't make a habit of dragging me off by the hair."

"It was your arm, not your hair, and I wasn't dragging."

"Details. The point is I expect you to treat me as a professional. Whatever happened between us personally has nothing to do with what goes on here."

"Happened? You make it sound as though it's all in the past."

"Isn't it?"

The elevator stopped and a portly, middle-aged man got on. They rode the rest of the way in silence. As they stepped off at their floor, Matthew said, "This isn't the time or place, but I want to talk with you about that. Will you have dinner with me tonight?"

She had been planning to work on the outline of her new book and was tempted to say no. But the chance of seeing him again away from the office was too appealing. "All right. But in the meantime, what did you want to see me about?"

He was embarrassed to admit that it was a relatively minor mix-up with the film for that evening's broadcast, something he was perfectly capable of correcting on his own. Teresa could have called him to task about it, but instead she merely straightened everything out and then went on about her business.

What with one thing and another, it was after 9:00 P.M. before they were both free to leave. Fortunately, in New York eating dinner at that hour did not present a problem.

"What are you in the mood for?" Matthew asked as he held the lobby door open for her. The security guard nodded to them as they left.

"Truthfully, a hot tub and a cup of tea," she said. "This was definitely one of those days."

"We could do this some other time. . . ."

"No, I'd rather make it now." She finished buttoning her coat and glanced up at the slice of leaden sky visible through the buildings. "It looks like snow."

"Only a dusting, according to our crack meteorologist."

"That means get out the dogsleds."

They paused at a light. Matthew turned his collar up. He was hatless as usual, and the wind off the East River whipped at his hair. At least he was wearing a scarf, the one Teresa had given him two Christmases before.

"Did you have a good holiday?" she asked as the light changed and they crossed Madison.

"Fine, how about you?"

"It was good to spend some time with the folks, not to mention Joey and Tony. They're both growing up so fast."

"Didn't we all. Mandy's the same. She's got all kinds of ideas about what she'll be doing after she graduates next spring."

"Such as?"

"It seems she's torn between taking a world tour and becoming an actress. Or possibly going to law school."

"*Law school?* That's serious."

"At the moment. If Mandy gets her hands on it, the legal establishment will never be the same."

Teresa couldn't help but laugh. The idea of beautiful, pampered, lighthearted Mandy buckling down to anything as tough as law school was ridiculous. Or was it? "Do you think she might actually go?"

"She took the law boards and did extremely well. Her advisor at college is recommending that she apply to the top schools. He thinks she'll get in."

"What do your parents think?"

"Dad's past being surprised at anything she does, and Alexis is all for it."

"Has she said why she might want to be a lawyer?"

Matthew shook his head. "It's impossible to get a straight answer out of her; she responds to everything with a joke. But if I had to guess, I'd say it has something to do with Jim."

"How is he?"

"About the same. He doesn't do much except putter around the house. The latest prosthesis is the best he's had so far, but he seems to prefer the crutches."

"He's still refusing to see a therapist?"

"As vehemently as ever. He simply won't talk about Vietnam to anyone."

"I take it you've tried?"

"Of course, but not with any success. When I bring up the subject, he retreats back into himself. Nothing gets through to him."

"Perhaps if James tried . . ."

"He has, and so has Alexis. They went so far as to consult a therapist themselves for advice on how they might be able to help Jim. The upshot of it was that no one can, until he's willing to help himself.''

Though Matthew spoke matter-of-factly, Teresa did not mistake that for a lack of emotion. She knew Jim's condition troubled him deeply. In some ways, Matthew had felt as protective toward his half brother as he had toward her. She suspected he still did and was having a hard time coming to terms with his inability to be anyone's champion but his own.

Gently she touched his arm. ''You've done everything you can. It's up to Jim to do the rest.''

''What if he can't?''

''Then you live with it, as he does. This is a tough world; we all feel the pain of it to at least some extent.''

He looked at her for a moment before he said, ''We didn't decide where we're going to eat. How about O'Shaughnessy's?''

That was a small restaurant near her apartment where they had eaten several times before, usually leisurely brunches after a night of lovemaking. She wondered if he had suggested it deliberately to remind her of all they had once shared. If so, it was working.

Seated across from him at a small table in the back, she was struck by the sudden realization that if she had accepted his proposal, they would have been married for several years by now. She would be a very different person from what she had actually become. But how much of what she had feared would actually have come to pass? Quite a bit, she suspected. For one thing, she was certain she would not have completed a book and be starting another. Had Matthew been on hand to distract her, she would have found excuses to put off the solitary reckoning with her inner self that was the source of creativity.

Yet she would also have received much from him, and given in return. Proud though she was of her accomplishments so far, she did not deny that they had come at a heavy cost. She had missed a great deal.

Several people came into the restaurant. They noticed Matthew and murmured to each other, glancing at him surreptitiously as they were led to a table. He kept his eyes carefully averted until they were past, knowing that the slightest contact would be interpreted as an excuse to come over and get acquainted.

"The trials of being a celebrity," Teresa said when they were gone.

He flushed and looked embarrassed. "I don't mean to be ungrateful to the people who watch me, but I have to retain a little privacy. Nobody can be 'on' all the time."

"You don't think you can manage to be serious and insightful every moment of the day?" she teased.

"Only if I have on my serious and insightful tie," he said solemnly. "You know—the one with the blue background and the discreet red stripes I've been wearing on camera."

"I've been meaning to mention that to you. We've gotten some mail asking if you only own one tie. Several people have even offered to send you a new one."

He reached for a bread stick. "You're kidding?"

"Nope. You have to realize being an anchorman is very different from being a correspondent. When people see you in the same place night after night, they notice a lot more about you. Many of them take a personal interest."

"I'm not there to look good," he protested, "just to report the news."

"You know that isn't true. Looks matter a lot on television; it's such a visual medium. Winston has always believed that one of the primary reasons for his early success was that his hair went silver prematurely and enabled him to look distinguished when he was still relatively young."

"I am not doing anything to my hair."

"I wasn't suggesting you should. But you can't ignore the image you project. Do you know," she asked, picking up the menu the waiter had left, "that there are actually companies now specializing in designing images for television personalities, remaking them sometimes from the ground up so that they come across better on camera?"

He made a disgusted sound. "That figures. It's like the old Hollywood star system, and I'll be damned if I get caught up in it. We have to maintain a rigorous distinction between entertainment and

news, otherwise we'll have no credibility. Anyway,"
he added, "I'd just as soon not talk about business.
There are more important things on my mind."

She took a sip of her drink and asked, "Such as?"

"I miss you."

Such simple words, leaving no opportunity for
equivocation or denial. He had missed her, and he
had the courage to admit it. Did she have less?

"I miss you, too," she admitted softly. "I also
know I was largely responsible for our drifting
apart."

He raised his eyebrows. "Are you sure about that?
I had something to do with it, too."

"I know, but if I had agreed to marry you . . ."

"Do you think we'd be better off?"

"No," she admitted. "At least I wouldn't be.
There was something unfinished inside me, something I had to come to terms with before I could consider really sharing my life with another person." His
attentive silence encouraged her to go on. Hesitantly, but with growing confidence, she told him
about her book. As she finished, she said, "It's
coming out in June, and the editor is encouraging me
to write another."

For what seemed like a long time after she finished, Matthew simply looked at her. He didn't say
a word, only studied her so intently that she became
uncomfortable. "Sorry," he said when he realized,
"it's just that of all the things you might have said,
this is the least expected."

"I know I never told you as much as I should have about what I was feeling."

"We were both guilty of that, but I have to admit it never occurred to me that you had such drive and ambition. You've always been so quiet."

She laughed a little shakily. "You know what they say about still waters."

"Apparently it's true. I wish you had confided in me more, but in all honesty I'm not sure I would have understood. All things considered, perhaps you made the right decision."

"That's very generous of you."

"I can afford to be generous," he told her.

"Why?"

"Because I never intended to give you up, only to give you the time you said you needed. And that," he added with a smile, "has just run out."

Several possible replies occurred to her, some funny, some serious. She uttered none of them. Instead she merely returned his smile and said, "I think I'd like to order dinner now."

Chapter Nine

MATTHEW AND TERESA were married in a civil ceremony at her parents' home in June of 1972. Some three hundred guests attended the reception following the private exchange of vows. Because her first book was being published the same month, Teresa had little opportunity to help with the arrangements; Maggie and Alexis took care of them. The lavish party went on far into the night, with the last guests finally straggling home after dawn, long after the new couple had departed for a week-long honeymoon on Antigua.

They came back to set up housekeeping in a spacious co-op on Central Park West. That summer Teresa gave up her job at IBS and began to write fulltime. The first book—the story of a young woman's coming of age during the sixties and seventies—had gotten good reviews and enjoyed a slightly better than modest sale. She was ready to try another.

Life settled into a pleasant routine. During the day she wrote, except for a few hours when she ran errands and walked in the park with the terrier pup Matthew had given her. At 7:00 P.M. she settled in front of the TV to watch the nightly news. Sometimes she regretted no longer being part of it, but when she looked at the stack of manuscript growing on her desk, she did not doubt she had made the right choice.

Matthew was home by 9:00 P.M. and they had a late dinner together. It was all very ordinary, very reassuring. She thought she wouldn't mind if it went on like that forever.

Of course, it did not. Late in October, he went on the road again briefly to cover the final stages of the presidential election, returning in time to anchor IBS's election night coverage. As expected, Nixon won easily, sweeping every electoral vote except those of Massachusetts and the District of Columbia. In the aftermath of his overwhelming victory, pressure on the media increased. Matthew was called into long meetings with his father and the network lawyers, figuring out how to protect affiliate licenses without sacrificing journalistic integrity.

In January, James went to Washington to testify before an FCC hearing examining IBS's programming policies. The signing of a Vietnam peace pact expected to take place within a few days was not easing relations between the media and the administration. If anything, the ever-increasing coverage of the Watergate break-in and the mysteries surrounding it—mysteries that increasingly seemed to point to White House involvement—had worsened tensions.

"I've had it with those bastards," James said when he and Alexis came over to the apartment for dinner one evening shortly after his return. "Something is going to have to give."

"You said once that they'd hang themselves," Matthew reminded him. "I still think that's true."

"So do I, but it had better be soon. I'm not sure how much more of this the country can take."

Teresa frowned slightly as she looked at her father-in-law. This latest trip seemed to have taken a great deal out of him. Lines she hadn't noticed before were deeply etched around his mouth and eyes, and beneath his habitual tan his skin had a slightly gray tinge.

Later, as they were sitting down to dinner, Teresa found a moment alone with Alexis to ask if everything was all right. "Of course," her mother-in-law said automatically, then relented slightly. "Well, perhaps not completely right. This business with the FCC is a terrible annoyance, especially coming at a time when James has so many other demands on his time and energies."

Though Alexis was as beautiful as ever, her features were nonetheless a bit strained. She had lost weight recently, when she really did not need to. Teresa doubted it had been deliberate. "If there's anyway we can help . . ."

"You already have," Alexis assured her. "Your marriage was a wonderful boost for us. Frankly, it's what we always hoped for."

Teresa was genuinely grateful for her in-laws' approval. Having grown up knowing Alexis and James almost as well as she knew her own parents, she cared for them deeply. To an outsider, their lives must have looked perfect. They possessed what most people could only envy—love, wealth and power all in large measure. But none of that had protected them from sharing the fate of so many other, far less fortunate families.

Their grief for Jim was no less profound because he had not died. On the contrary, Teresa thought sometimes that it must be worse. Death at least brought with it prescribed rituals of mourning and recovery intended to help the survivors. To have to witness a young life slowly shrinking away into nothingness and be unable either to deny what was happening or stop it was anguishing in the extreme. Yet James and Alexis faced it with dignity. It was only when the pressures of the outside world became too much that the cracks in their perfect lives began to show.

After Alexis and James had left, she mentioned her concern to Matthew. They had stacked the dishes in the kitchen for the maid to take care of the next day. It was well after midnight. Embers glowed in the living room fireplace where before there had been a cheerful blaze. Matthew was sitting on the couch, his long legs stretched out in front of him, a snifter with an inch or so of brandy nearby.

Teresa was beside him. She had kicked off her shoes and tucked her feet under her. One arm was propped up on the back of the couch, her head resting against it. She was tired but not yet ready to sleep. There was too much going on in her mind. "Your father seems to be taking the situation with the FCC very seriously."

He turned slightly, looking at her. "It's not really them. I think he's just disheartened about things in general."

"He looks tired."

"That's not so strange. He's past fifty but he keeps going like a thirty-year-old."

She smiled faintly. Not so long ago Matthew would have said a twenty-year-old. "I thought he was giving you more responsibility?"

"Not really. Oh, he brings me into discussions and makes sure I know what's going on, but I don't kid myself that I'm making any of the decisions. The only person who has any influence with him as far as running IBS goes is Uncle Anthony and I don't see any chance of that changing."

His resentment did not escape Teresa. She sympathized with it even as she wondered if he wasn't perhaps expecting too much. "You have a great deal of authority within the news division," she reminded him gently.

"Only because of Winston. He's very different from my father in that he's willing to make room for a younger man." He took a sip of his brandy, then sighed. "I'm not being fair. Winston has less at stake, and besides that, Dad's having a rough time."

"Because of Jim?"

"That's a big part of it, but I think there's more involved. It can't be easy for him to contemplate turning over what he's worked so hard to build to another man, not even his son."

"But he wanted you to join the network."

"And I think he wants me to ultimately head it. But that doesn't make it any easier for him to let go."

The sadness in his voice hurt Teresa. She wanted to make everything all right for him, but knew that she could not. All she could do was offer some small measure of comfort. Rising, she held out a hand to him.

Later, lying awake after they had made love and Matthew had fallen asleep, she thought over what he had said about his father. His evaluation of the situation matched her own. She foresaw a difficult period ahead when two very strong men—so alike in many ways—must ultimately come into conflict.

In an ideal world the transition of responsibility from one generation to the next would be made smoothly, but in fact that rarely happened, especially not when such powerful personalities were involved. It was human nature to deny the inroads of age, the signposts of mortality. Just as it was to want to seize the bright day before it passed into darkness.

ON A NIGHT in mid February, James woke with a pain in his chest. He'd been having them on and off for the past few months and kept meaning to see a doctor. But somehow he never got around to it. Experience had taught him that if he simply waited, the pain would go away. It did, but in its aftermath, he was unable to fall back asleep.

Not wanting to disturb Alexis, who lay beside him, he slipped out of bed, found his slippers and put on a robe. It was in his mind to go down to the kitchen and have a glass of milk, but on his way there he was distracted by sounds from the den. The television was on. James hesitated a moment, then headed in that direction.

Jim was sitting on the couch across from the set. His crutches were propped nearby. As usual he wasn't using his artificial leg even though the therapist said he had learned to walk on it quite well. He hadn't bothered to shave in several days and his thick blond hair was typically unkempt.

James resisted the urge to chide him about his appearance, having learned long ago that any such efforts were futile. Jim merely tuned out anything and everything he didn't want to deal with. He did, however, glance up briefly when his father entered the room.

"I couldn't sleep," James explained.

Jim shrugged. His gaze returned to the television.

James sat down at the other end of the couch. There was a commercial on for the "One Hundred Hit Tunes of the Thirties and Forties."

"Relive the timeless pleasures of the swing era," the announcer was urging. "Recapture beautiful memories with Tommy Dorsey, Benny Goodman and so many more. Complete money-back guarantee. Call . . .''

"You watch too much of this stuff," James said.

Jim smiled faintly. "That's funny, coming from you."

"Just because I work in the business doesn't mean I think people should spend their lives in front of the TV."

"It's not a bad place to be. If you wait long enough, the whole world comes to you."

"That number again is . . ."

"Game shows, old movies and soap operas are hardly the world, at least not the real one."

"No loss."

"Don't delay. Supplies are running out fast."

James rubbed the back of his neck. The lack of rest was catching up with him. "It's stuffy in here."

"Open the window."

He got up to do so. Outside the night was cold and crisp. He thought he could smell snow. When he returned to the couch, the commercial was over. Over the titles of the movie that would normally have been on next, an announcer was saying, "All regularly scheduled programming is preempted to bring you this special report from CBS news."

James remembered then what this night was, and wondered how he had managed to put it out of his mind, even temporarily. "Mind if we switch to IBS?" he asked.

"Suit yourself."

Click. Winston appeared on the screen, seated at the desk from which he delivered the nightly news when Matthew wasn't filling in for him. He had just returned from a vacation in California and looked particularly tanned and fit. His voice was low and controlled, but with an underlying note of excitement appropriate to such a significant moment.

"The first American prisoners of war to be released by the North Vietnamese are expected to arrive at Clark Air Force Base in Manila within the next few minutes. Matthew Callahan is there."

The scene shifted to Matthew, standing on the edge of an airport runway with palm trees in the background. His hair blew slightly in the breeze as he spoke into the microphone he held. "This first stage of the POWs' homecoming is being kept as low-key as possible. Family members are not on hand; actual reunions won't take place until the former prisoners move on to San Diego, expected to be several days from now."

The camera panned the runway, showing a cluster of military officials gathered off to the side. "If our information is correct," Matthew went on, "the first C-141s carrying the freed men cleared North Vietnamese airspace without incident and should be arriving here in the next few minutes."

"Matt," Winston interjected, "can you hear me?"

Pressing a hand to the earpiece to hold it more firmly, he nodded. "You're coming through fine, Winston."

"Good. Do we have any information on the condition of the men?"

"Not directly. All we know for sure is that they're coming out in order of length of captivity, as opposed to rank. That means the first ones captured will be the first out."

"Some of those men have been incarcerated for upward of seven-eight years. A few even longer. Would you say it's likely they may be in a poor condition?"

"I don't want to speculate about that, Winston, but the fact is the Pentagon has decided to hold the men here for medical checks and debriefing before allowing them to meet their families or reporters. It stands to reason that there's some uncertainty about how they'll react to freedom. We know they've been kept under conditions outlawed by the Geneva Convention, so we have to be prepared for the likelihood that at least some of them may be in bad shape."

"*Some?*" Jim ran a hand nervously through his tangled hair. "What does he expect, for those guys to come bouncing off the planes like they've been on R&R?"

Though Jim spoke as if to himself, James felt drawn to answer. "Matthew's just trying to prepare people for what they're going to see. He knows most of them don't have a clear idea of what the POWs have been through."

"There's no excuse for that. Plenty's been written about it and talked about on TV."

"People haven't necessarily been paying attention."

Jim shook his head angrily. "Bastards, the whole bunch of them. They're the ones who should have had to go over there."

"Who's they?"

"You know who. The ones who stayed here, safe and sound, while a bunch of poor schnooks like me got our asses shot off. The ones who draped themselves in the flag *and* the ones who burned it. The ones who never bothered to try to understand anything because it might get in the way of their preconceived notions. They should damn well have to pay attention now."

Their gazes held for a moment before Jim glanced away. More softly, with an underlying note of weariness, he said, "What's the good of talking about it? It's too late to change anything."

"Mistakes were made. That doesn't mean they have to be again."

A harsh laugh broke from the younger man. His hand moved restlessly in the empty space where his leg should have been. "Mistakes? That's what you call them? Like when you pick the wrong program for a time slot or sign the wrong talent?" His hand closed into a fist, lacking anywhere to strike. "People my age lost everything—hope, illusions, ideals, life, everything. What kind of mistakes cause that?"

"Human ones, unfortunately." James looked at his son for a moment, seeing the pain, the rage, the bewilderment he had no trouble recognizing because he had felt them in himself. "Do you really think it was any better for my generation?" he asked quietly.

"Damn straight it was. You guys had it made."

"Like hell." He was getting mad now, even though he knew that was wrong. For the first time in longer than he could remember—maybe for the first time ever—he and Jim were really talking. He didn't want anything to stop that, but he couldn't let such a distortion of the truth go by unchallenged. "I lost plenty of good friends in World War II and not all because of the enemy. Too many died because of misjudgments on our side, the kind of thing that happens in any war."

"But you still won."

"Yeah, we won. It's better than losing, but it doesn't mean all your problems are solved, not by a long shot. All we really won was the right to start over again. You think that was easy?"

"I don't know what to think," Jim admitted more calmly. "I've done a lot of it in the past few years, trying to come to some conclusions in my own mind. Sometimes I catch a glimmer of light, but it never lasts long."

"If it's any consolation to you, I know the feeling."

"You? That doesn't seem possible."

"Why not?" James asked.

"Because...you've got it all put together. You beat life at its own game a long time ago."

"*Beat it?* Hell, all I did was come to terms with it."

"But...you got everything you wanted," Jim protested.

"Nobody gets everything. *Nobody.* I'll admit I've been a lot luckier than most, but some of that luck I made for myself just by being too bullheaded to give up when a smarter man might have."

"There's got to be more to it than that. Ever since I was a little kid, I've watched you, trying to figure out how you do it. Are you saying it's just a matter of being stubborn?" James sighed and leaned back against the couch. Matthew was still talking on the screen. The runway behind him remained empty. "No," he said at length, "there's more to it than that. A lot of it is knowing what you want. Most people don't. They just drift through life, kind of like corks bobbing along in a river. All of a sudden they get to the end and they don't know what hit them."

"Know what you want...stick to it...and everything will work out. That's what you're telling me?"

"No." James grimaced impatiently. "That's the kind of two-bit psychology garbage you hear on talk shows. What I'm trying to get across is that there's no easy answer, no one solution for everyone. It's a damn tough world; a lot goes wrong." He broke off, his gaze drawn unwillingly to the empty pajama leg pinned up out of the way. "I don't have to tell you that. You know it better than I do."

"You really believe that?"

"I never fought in a war people hated. I was never seriously wounded or forced to cope with a disability." He shook his head, as though in denial of what could not be denied. "What can I say to you? Of course, I wish none of it had ever happened, but I don't know how it could have been prevented."

"It was my choice to go," Jim reminded him. "You tried to talk me out of it."

"And you didn't listen. Maybe if I'd been a better father, you would have."

Silence, until Jim said, "I don't know if this is going to make any sense to you, but you don't have any right to feel guilty about what happened to me. It was my life; I decided what to do with it. Sure, I wanted you to be proud of me, but the main thing was I wanted something of my own. Doing what I did seemed like a way to get it."

James's chest hurt again but differently this time, the tightness coming from unshed tears. "Didn't work out quite the way you expected, did it?"

"How much ever does? I came back busted up, not coping too well with losing my leg, and I discovered that pretty much everybody in this country hated me for what I'd done. Oh, not you or anyone in the family, but outsiders were a different story. At the hospital, there were people who wouldn't talk to me after they found out I'd been in 'Nam."

His father's mouth tightened. "I never knew that."

"There was no point talking about it. It was like that all over, still is. When I saw how it was, I thought, What the hell, who needs this, and pulled back into myself. The leg just gave me an excuse."

"Did you . . . understand from the start why you were doing it?"

Jim laughed. "No way. Like I said, it's taken me years of thinking about it to even get a clue." His smile broadened, becoming rueful. "You gotta admit, I was never too quick to pick up on things."

"You did all right," James insisted defensively.

"Be honest. It bothered you that I wasn't the way you thought I should be."

"All right . . . that's true. I did worry . . . and maybe sometimes I came down on you too hard."

"You're doing it again—blaming yourself. Believe me, it won't work. I went through the whole scene of trying to pin what happened to me on anyone except myself. You know how I ended up feeling? Helpless, that's how. Like those corks you were talking about. Lately, I've been thinking there's got to be a better way."

The camera was panning across the runway again. A plane had come into view. It was making its final landing approach. The two men broke off and stared at the screen.

"Looks like they're coming," James said softly.

"Yeah . . . shouldn't be long now."

The plane taxied to a stop near the terminal. Stairs were pushed into place. There was a brief delay, then the door opened and a man began to walk down the steps. He was dressed in dark pants and a beige zippered jacket that couldn't disguise his thinness. Moving slowly, holding on to the railings, he negotiated the steps one by one. Another man followed, then another and another.

"Funny," James said, "I didn't believe until just now that this would really happen."

"Me, too. It was in the back of my mind that maybe it was a trick."

More men were coming off the plane. Some had to be helped, but even they made an effort to stand tall and erect. Many had the strained look of men old before their time. But there were others among them for whom age was not simply the result of abuse. These were men who had served in other wars, professional soldiers who had finally seen their luck run out. Men of James's generation.

"I didn't expect that," Jim said quietly. "I thought they'd all be young."

"So did I. Should have figured, though."

"The old guys look pretty good."

James winced. "They're not old, just...mature."

"Oh, yeah, sorry. Mature. Anyway, they look good. So do the others."

"It's a question of pride."

Jim shot him a glance. "There hasn't been much talk about that lately, has there?"

''Not a whole lot.''

The men were marching into buses to take them to the hospital. They were stiff backed, shoulders straight, even though the effort clearly cost them. Did they realize what they were going to, Jim wondered. Families that might or might not have survived the ordeal of separation. A country determined to forget as quickly as possible everything they had been through. A future that held only uncertainty.

The camera cut to Matthew. Quietly, he said, ''The first POWs to be released are safe on friendly soil. The rest are expected to follow shortly. What will happen to these men now that they have returned—how well they will put their lives back together—no one can say. The Vietnam war has left a bitter legacy that will be with us for a long time. It would not be accurate to say that this is the end of anything. But it can be a beginning.''

The transmission from Manila slowly dissolved. The two men sat in silence for a few minutes. Then James stood up and Jim reached for his crutches. Together, going slowly, they made their way up the stairs together.

MATTHEW RETURNED from Manila to plunge immediately into the fast-breaking events stemming from the Watergate break-in. What had seemed initially to be no more than a third-rate burglary perpetrated by buffoonish bunglers had evolved into a stark confrontation between pragmatism and idealism. At its heart lay the question of how the nation wished to see itself—and be seen by others—in the post-Vietnam era: as a people ruled by power or served by law.

The distinction was a very important one, as Matthew pointed out on the evening of Saturday, April 28, 1973, when IBS broadcast a two-hour special on Watergate and all its ramifications. Many people had contributed to the program, and many more appeared on it, but *Nation of Power or Nation of Law?* bore Matthew's stamp from beginning to end. Relentlessly he drove home the concept that democracy could not exist without respect for the laws that guaranteed essential freedoms, and that once those laws began to be ignored by the very people sworn to uphold them, liberty could not long survive.

"We're all enormously proud of him," Alexis said the following morning when she and Teresa spoke by phone. She was sounding more optimistic these days since Jim had taken a turn for the better. He was using the crutches less and venturing out of the house more. He had even taken a part-time job clerking at a neighborhood bookstore. With the improvements in her son, Alexis was better able to express her concern for Matthew. "There's no getting around the fact that he made many enemies last night."

"I know," Teresa said. "I'm ashamed to admit it but in the middle of the program I wished he would just stop and not go any further, even though I knew he couldn't."

"Somebody had to do it. Papers like the *Washington Post* and the *Times* have done a tremendous job of getting to the facts, but they still aren't reaching enough people. Only television can do that."

"It's such a complicated story. I'm not sure people will understand."

"Matthew went a long way toward assuring that," Alexis pointed out. "Whatever happens now, he's already accomplished a great deal."

"Does James feel that way?"

"Truthfully I think he's a little surprised Matthew could be that tough."

"He's his father's son."

Alexis laughed faintly. "That's certainly true. And since he is so much like James, we can't expect him to be satisfied with doing anything less than his best." There was a touch of regret in her voice, as though she almost wished Matthew could have been content with a more secondary role that would have kept him out of direct conflict with his father. But she was far too realistic to hope for that.

"I'm glad he has you," she told Teresa softly. "He shouldn't be alone, any more than you should be."

Was it merely coincidence that Alexis should say that now or had she perceived what Teresa was trying to keep so carefully hidden? As the first anniversary of her marriage approached, she was beginning to realize that there were problems she had not foreseen. Not that she had any doubts about loving

Matthew or his loving her. It was more a matter of an imbalance in the equation of giving and taking.

They did not share equally in what she thought of as the emotional life of their marriage. For her, it was only natural to want to know what Matthew was thinking and feeling; she coaxed him into telling her about his problems at the office, his hopes and concerns, even his dreams. That wasn't easy; his experience in early childhood had made him naturally reticent, yet she persevered.

Believing that such was the fabric of true intimacy, she longed for him to do the same and looked forward to sharing with him her private self. When he showed no interest in doing so, she was at first baffled, then hurt. Yet she clung to the conviction that he loved her, hearing it in the gentle touch of his voice, seeing it in the warmth of his eyes, feeling it in the eagerness with which he returned to her whether from a few hours apart or days.

The apparent contradiction bewildered her. In an effort to understand it, she began to look at other marriages more closely. Before long, she realized that the problems she faced with Matthew were so common as to be considered universal. If anything, they were far milder than what she saw in some relationships.

Even in the most loving marriages she knew besides her own—those of her parents, and Alexis and James—the conflict was there. The women were much more closely attuned to feelings, better able to understand and share them. The men stuck to what they regarded as realities.

She wondered if that was why Alexis and Maggie had worked so stubbornly to build lives apart from husband and family, even though the cost had been high and was paid mainly in the coin of their own emotions. The outside world, for all its problems, was their escape.

But she had chosen to live in the inner world of the mind and spirit. She needed to share that with Matthew, to have him understand what it was that she did, and why.

Sometimes sitting at her desk looking out over Central Park, she felt as though she were a woman of another place and time, sitting in front of a giant loom, weaving warp and woof together according to patterns set down so long ago that they were older than thought itself. The image was fanciful; it faintly embarrassed her, yet she believed it accurate nonetheless.

Still she said nothing of it to Matthew, letting herself believe that a better time for doing so would come.

Teresa's second book—about a family's experiences during the Vietnam war—was published early in the fall of 1973. Clare Danvers had been even more enthusiastic about it than the first one, saying it represented a significant step forward for her as a writer. The critics agreed, *The New York Times Book Review,* pinnacle of literary respectability, calling it "sensitive and perceptive." Another respected literary publication, *The Literary Quarterly*, had also praised it. The print run was a little larger this time around, and there was even talk of a possible paperback sale.

Shortly after the book came out, Teresa gave Matthew a copy. He said he was eager to read it, yet somehow days and then weeks slipped by without his finding the time to do so. The book collected dust on his bedside table until she put it away.

The excuse she made for him was that he was very busy, and that was true. For the first time in American history, a vice president had resigned. Spiro Agnew stepped down to avoid imprisonment on a charge of income tax evasion. The deal he had struck with the Justice Department kept him out of prison at the cost of his high office. Coming on top of the Watergate scandal—that had already brought down Nixon's top aides—the vice president's problems might have appeared redundant. Except that they seemed to presage more to come.

Barely had the smoke begun to settle, when the fires were relit by what quickly became known as "the Saturday Night Massacre." While the headlines screamed of a new war in the Middle East and United States forces were put on worldwide alert, the attorney general and his top assistant resigned rather than obey the president's order to fire the special Watergate prosecutor.

Suddenly impeachment was no longer unthinkable.

"I wish they'd just get it over with," Teresa muttered to herself one evening when she and Matthew were lying in bed. "I'm sick and tired of Watergate."

"What's a five-letter word for lizard beginning with a?" he asked, glancing up from the *Times* Sunday crossword puzzle that he never got to until the middle of the week. His black-framed reading glasses were perched on his nose and his hair was still damp from the shower he'd taken after dinner. The down-filled comforter was pulled up to his waist, revealing his bare chest. Winter or not, he refused to wear pajamas.

Folding her part of the paper to the inside where the story she had been reading was continued, she said, "Agama."

He checked the corresponding clues skeptically, only to discover that she was right. "How did you know that?"

"What do you mean, how did I know? I just did."

"Nobody just knows something like that. You don't even do crosswords."

"Waste of time."

"I can never finish these things." He tossed the puzzle aside and stretched out in the bed, eyeing her. She'd gotten her hair cut recently over his protests, but he had to admit it looked rather nice falling to her shoulders where it turned under gently. The blue silk nightgown she wore had thin straps that left her arms and shoulders bare. It was cut low to reveal the full curve of her breasts. Through the thin fabric, he could see the outlines of her nipples beginning to harden. "Going to read all night?"

"The light bothering you?"

"Uh-uh." He reached out under the covers, stroking her thigh.

Still studying the paper, she said, "Wholesale prices are up."

"So is something else."

She glanced at him chidingly. "Should I conclude you're not interested in a serious discussion about the economy?"

"One of the things I appreciate most about you," he said as he reached over to turn off the light, "is how you pick up on the subtlest signals."

Tossing the paper aside, she smiled. "Sweetheart, right now there is nothing the least bit subtle about you."

"Just a growing boy."

"Hmmm . . ." She snuggled against him, feeling the hardness of his body against her own. "Who's getting too big for his britches."

"Imagine," he murmured, nuzzling her throat, "if I couldn't go to work tomorrow because I couldn't get into my pants."

"*That* would stop you?"

"Well, maybe not, but you'll admit it would cause a lot of talk."

"Can't have that."

Their lovemaking was good, as always, but it left Teresa feeling vaguely unsatisfied. Not physically— Matthew had seen to that. But he seemed unaware that she had other needs. She didn't want to feel close to him only when he was deep inside her.

There had to be more, but she had no idea how to go about achieving it.

Chapter Ten

THE NOTE ON THE LETTERHEAD of *The Literary Quarterly* was brief and cordial. Penned in dark-blue ink by a firm hand, it said: "I greatly admire your work and would like to meet with you. Kindly call me at your convenience. Sincerely, Graham Brockton."

Teresa read it over twice, standing in the vestibule where she had stopped to get the mail after picking up some groceries. It had been snowing off and on for several days. The streets were littered with slush as gray as the late February sky. A chill wind blew off the river; it rattled the windowpanes in the vestibule and made the people hurrying by outside tuck their chins even further into their collars.

Finding the note in among the bills, magazines, a letter from her agent, an invitation to speak at an upcoming symposium of writers and other assorted correspondence surprised Teresa. She had never met Graham Brockton, but she thought she knew who he was.

A call to Winston confirmed it. "That's right," he said in response to her inquiry, "Graham is Alexis's brother, though the relationship is essentially meaningless. I don't imagine they've seen each other since her father died more than twenty years ago. Although . . .'' He paused for a moment, considering. ''Although they may have had some direct contact when she took over UBC from him.''

''The takeover was unfriendly, wasn't it?''

Winston's laughter was low and wry. ''That's putting it mildly. When Graham found out who had been buying up UBC stock secretly, he damn near had a heart attack. I think he would gladly have throttled her if he could have figured out how to get away with it.''

''Nice . . . didn't you tell me once that he was running a literary magazine?''

''*The Literary Quarterly.* To give the devil his due, he seems to be making a pretty good job of it. Maybe that's where he always belonged.''

''He's written to me asking to get together.''

''Are you going to?''

''I don't know. . . . On the one hand, from what you've told me, he doesn't sound like a very nice person. But on the other, I have to admit I'm curious about him.''

''More grist for the mill?''

''Perhaps, or at least I can use that for an excuse.''

''It sounds as though you've already made up your mind to see him.''

''I guess I have,'' she admitted.

''Be careful. He's not anyone I'd be in a hurry to trust.''

Teresa took the warning to heart, but it did not prevent her from calling the offices of *The Literary Quarterly* the following day and arranging to meet Graham for lunch later in the week. Matthew was out of town again, covering the grand jury proceedings looking into charges that key Nixon aides had conspired to cover up the Watergate scandal. He called home each evening as usual, but she did not mention Graham, guessing that Matthew would not approve and not wanting to listen to his cautioning.

On Friday, she took a cab across town to the East Side. Graham had suggested a small, unpretentious French restaurant in a brownstone near the river. He was waiting when she arrived. Her first impression of the tall, slender man who came forward to greet her was that she would have guessed he was Alexis's brother even if she hadn't known that in advance. Her second was that the similarities between brother and sister were equaled only by the differences.

Graham was only slightly older than Alexis, but whereas she wore her age gracefully, he was burdened by his. The silver-blond hair brushed back from his forehead was thin and dry. Webs of lines were etched around his gray eyes and on either side of his straight nose and narrow mouth. His shoulders were slightly stooped, and he walked with a faint hesitation that suggested he might be in some pain. What must once have been a strong, graceful body had taken on the appearance of a dry husk that not even the elegantly tailored suit could disguise.

Yet he smiled cordially as he offered her his hand and said, "I'm so pleased we could do this. It's been on my mind for quite some time."

"I enjoy your magazine," she replied carefully. "And, of course, I appreciate the kind reviews I've received."

"You deserve them," he told her as they followed the maître d' back to a table in the corner. "Frankly, I don't read even a fraction of the books that come in for review; that simply wouldn't be possible, given how many of them we get. But I have read both of yours and been very impressed. You have a rare gift for characterization and dialogue."

"Thank you," Teresa murmured as she took her seat.

The little ceremony of accepting menus and giving drink orders carried them through the next few minutes. When the waiter had left, Graham leaned back in his chair, smiled again and asked, "Are you working on something new?"

"Yes, but it's going slowly. I'm afraid of repeating myself."

"That's understandable. You strike me as the sort of writer who feels she has a great deal of distance to cover and is impatient with anything that slows her down."

Teresa stared at him. Rarely had anyone so astutely discerned her feelings. "Are you always so perceptive?"

He laughed and shook his head. "Not at all, but I have had some experience with creative people over the years, enough at least to be sympathetic to their difficulties. Will it help at all if I tell you what you're going through isn't particularly unusual?"

"Well . . . they do say misery loves company. Not that I'm really miserable," she added hastily, "only . . . disquieted."

He nodded. "You realize that is the price exacted for achievement? If you ever reach the point where you are completely satisfied with your work, it will be over."

The waiter arrived with their drinks. Teresa took a sip of hers before she asked, "Do you write?"

"Only the occasional article. Nor do I paint, sculpt, dance, compose, play an instrument or do anything else that could be construed as creative. I am, however, an observer of the arts in all their forms—I like to think a sympathetic one."

"What about your magazine?"

He grimaced slightly and shook his head. "It's a business, that's all. More congenial perhaps than some others, but still a business."

Looking at him, observing the slight tremor of his hand and the tightness of his mouth, Teresa suspected he had found it even more difficult than most to accept his own limitations. To test her theory, she said, "Some people believe running a business is very creative."

"It can be, under the right circumstances. If there's sufficient scope, vitality, potential."

"You once ran a much larger business, didn't you?"

He ducked his head slightly in a self-protective gesture. "Do I take it you are aware of my relationship to your family?"

"I know who you are, if that's what you mean. And I know that at one time you ran UBC, until Alexis took it over."

"Ah, yes, my dear sister. How is she these days?"

"About as always, I imagine. She doesn't change much from year to year."

"A rare blessing. Does she approve of your marriage?"

One for his side, Teresa thought wryly. If she wasn't going to beat around the bush, neither apparently was Graham. "Yes, she does. I couldn't ask for a nicer mother-in-law."

"You're very fortunate. There is a great deal to be said for being part of a closely knit family."

They paused briefly to decide on lunch, then resumed. "Are you married?" Teresa asked. She justified the question on the grounds that he was, after all, also a part of her family, if only in absentia.

Graham laughed faintly and shook his head. "No, that never appealed to me. Although I must admit there was a time when my father tried very hard to convince me otherwise."

"I know very little about him, but I have the impression that Charles Brockton was a very forceful man."

"That's putting it mildly. He was a steamroller, crushing anything that got in his way. Had he lived, there's no doubt I would have been a severe disappointment to him. Ironically enough, it's Alexis who has fulfilled his fondest hopes."

"Why ironically?"

"Because he never believed women were good for much outside the home. That's the only reason he left UBC to me instead of to her. Do you know," he added as he buttered a slice of bread, "I used to lie awake at night wondering what she was plotting. I was convinced she wouldn't just let it go, but I had no idea in the end of how utterly ruthless she could be."

"I'm very fond of Alexis."

"And won't hear her criticized? Believe me, I meant it as a compliment. Her tenacity and cleverness were nothing short of astonishing. It wasn't until years later that I found out, quite by chance, how she had managed it."

Despite herself, Teresa felt driven to follow up on his lead. "How did she?"

"By. . . brainwashing herself, if that's the right word. You see, she convinced herself that I was somehow involved in James's imprisonment in North Korea. I suppose you know about that?"

"I had heard of it," Teresa said, "but not from either of them. It happened early in 1951, right after

the twins were born. He was held for more than a
year, wasn't he, and an effort was made to force Alexis and my father to broadcast Communist propa-
ganda in return for his safety?''

"That's right. The rescue mission your father led
was nothing short of brilliant. It made headlines
around the world and turned both him and James
into popular heroes.''

"Don't you think they were?''

"Undeniably. I'm not about to disparage their
achievement. The point is for once in my life I was
innocent. Of course, I had done so many nasty things
to Alexis over the years without her being able to pay
me back that I suppose there was a certain justice in
her finally getting even.''

He seemed philosophically resigned to his loss, but
Teresa wondered. Alexis had proved herself to be remarkably tenacious in her quest for vengeance; was
her brother the same?

"Why did you arrange this meeting?'' she asked
quietly as the waiter set their lunches in front of
them. "Was it really because of my work or because
you want a way back into the family?''

Graham took a sip of his drink before he an-
swered. "Odd, in your writing you're so subtle. But
now you're being just the opposite.''

"That's the difference between being an observer
and a participant. When I write, I have to be subtle;
it's necessary to coax the reader into following where
I wish to lead. But here the initiative is yours not

mine, so I want to know exactly where you're heading.''

"You're presuming I know myself.''

"What is it you want me to do, Graham?''

He sighed deeply. "I would like you . . . to be patient. To get to know me as I am now, rather than as
I was. The objectivity I sense in your books makes me
hope you will be fair. That's all I ask. If, after a time,
you think it appropriate, then I would be grateful for
whatever help you might give me in reestablishing
contact with my sister. She is, after all, the only family I have.''

If there had been a shred of self-pity in his voice,
Teresa would have stiffened her spine against him.
But he spoke calmly, with dignity, simply asking her
help as one human being to another. Even as she resolved to go very carefully with him, she knew that
she at least had to give him a chance.

TERESA DID NOT MENTION her meeting with Graham to Matthew or anyone else in the family. She
couldn't have said exactly why she kept it to herself,
only that it seemed appropriate. Besides, there was a
great deal else going on.

In early spring, her grandfather, Joseph Gargano, was taken ill. He had always been a robust
man; even in his late seventies he had continued to be
involved in the restaurant business and had taken
pride in his garden where he spent many pleasant
hours. It was there that his wife, Maria, found him.

In the midst of planting tomato seedlings, he had lost consciousness and did not respond to her frantic cries.

Joseph was rushed to the hospital, where the doctors diagnosed a severe stroke. Maggie and Anthony hurried to be with him, as did his other children and grandchildren. On the third day after his attack, with his family gathered around him and without regaining consciousness, Joseph slipped away.

In the aftermath of her grandfather's death, Teresa spent far more time than usual at the house in Brooklyn where her father had been raised and where her grandmother continued to live. She went not out of any sense of obligation but because she genuinely wanted to be with Maria. The frail, white-haired old lady was a source of indomitable pride and courage. Despite her grief, she accepted her husband's death as the will of God, spoke lovingly of all their joyful years together, and clearly looked forward to reunion with him in the not too distant future.

Sitting in the kitchen with her, watching as her small, blue-veined hands rolled dough and peeled tomatoes just as they had for more than half a century, Teresa listened to the same stories over and over about how Maria and Joseph had met and married, the struggles they had faced together and the victories they had shared. She stored up the memories as though they were bits of gold, recognizing them as her grandmother's legacy to her, to be added to and eventually passed on in a link from one generation to the next.

Maggie was often there when Teresa arrived and the three spent pleasant hours together, the two older women doing most of the talking. As always, Teresa was struck by the frankness of the conversation when no male ears were listening. Words were spoken about pain and love and the intertwining nature of each, about the joy and anguish of children, and over all the pleasures and frustrations of womanhood.

The new book continued to go slowly. In writing about the relationship among several women of different generations, Teresa was examining issues very close to her heart that remained unresolved within her. That confusion was inevitably reflected in her characters, which made them very difficult for her to cope with.

To further complicate matters, she was increasingly absorbed in her problems with Matthew. He remained oblivious to her dissatisfaction, insisting that everything between them was fine. From his point of view, it undoubtedly was. But she had a very different perspective.

"It's hard for me to explain," she admitted one evening shortly after he had returned from yet another trip. They had eaten dinner almost in silence; afterward she had cleared up while he read the paper. When she was done, she had considered going directly to bed, but that would have meant putting off yet again what had already been postponed too often.

"I miss you a great deal when you're away, but when you come back, I don't feel as though you're really here."

Matthew hadn't wanted to talk; he was tired and preoccupied. Her insistence irked him. "You realize that makes no sense at all?"

"Don't say that. It makes sense to me, otherwise I wouldn't bring it up."

He sighed and made a visible effort at patience. "I know I'm traveling a lot, but it can't be helped. It's not only an important part of my job, it's also invaluable preparation for what I may do in the future. Besides, the fact is that I'm away less than many other men my age."

"I don't happen to be married to any of them. As far as I'm concerned, you're away far too often. But that's really the least of it. I wouldn't mind so much if I didn't feel that we're simply not in touch, no matter where you happen to be."

"We were damn well in touch last night."

Teresa's hands tightened in her lap. "*That's* different. Why can't you listen to what I'm saying? It isn't enough to make love with you. I need more. If you're honest, I think you do, too."

"Oh, I see, if I don't go along with what you're saying, I'm not being honest?"

"You're deliberately twisting my words. Do you really think everything is right between us?"

He didn't answer directly. Instead, he said, "I don't know what you expect. As far as I can see, we have a good marriage. What more do you want?"

"Nothing," she said quietly. "That's exactly what I want."

He stared at her for a long moment. "I see. Whatever it is you're trying to tell me, Teresa, I wish you'd just spit it out."

"I'm not trying to tell you anything. I'd just like us to talk about something besides work or the weather. We used to share our feelings about so many things."

"We were children then. Life was simpler."

"Was it? It seems to me that the only real difference is that we were more open and trusting with each other."

He looked away, concentrating on refolding the paper. Finally, he said, "I've always thought we were among the lucky ones. It has never occurred to me that there was anything wrong with our marriage."

The sad bewilderment in his eyes tempted her to weaken. For both their sakes she could not. "Not wrong so much as missing. It's as though our lives are broken down into a multitude of small pieces, each kept in a separate compartment so that it doesn't intrude on any of the others."

"What's wrong with that?" he insisted, genuinely baffled. "I don't want to bring my job home with me and have it constantly intruding on our life together, any more than I want you to do the same."

"Is that why we never talk about my writing?"

"We do. You keep me up to date on what's going on with your agent and editor."

"That's the business end. I'm talking about the actual writing."

"You wouldn't want me to tell you all the little details of what I do, would you?"

"Actually, I already know a great deal about it," she pointed out. "Whereas you know almost nothing about what I do."

"What difference does it make? You have your work and I have mine. Even though you used to be in television, I still don't expect you to understand everything I do, and you obviously don't or you wouldn't be upset about the traveling. So why isn't it fair for me to be the same way about what you do?"

"Because at least I'm interested. I care. You . . . seem to do your best to deny that there's anything more to me than what's right on the surface."

"I don't understand this," he said wearily. "You're clearly upset, but I'll be damned if I can figure out why. You're my wife; I love you. What more is there?"

"I'm not just your wife," she protested, trying to find the words that would get through to him. "I'm other things, too. I can accept what you are even when I don't always like the effects of that. Why can't you do the same with me?"

"You want to talk about your work with me, is that it?"

She shook her head, discouraged by how little progress they were making. "I want you to acknowledge that it exists; that's all."

Matthew took a deep breath. He stood up and walked over to the windows. His hands were jammed in his pockets and his shoulders were slightly hunched in an attitude she recognized all too well. "I'm going to say something you won't like," he said without looking at her. "I think the only thing that's bothering you is that you have too much time on your hands. You're free to do essentially as you please. You don't have to work for a living or take care of children or do any of the other things most other women your age are concerned with. Maybe if you did, you wouldn't be able to sit around worrying about why we don't communicate more."

"You think this whole thing is just some . . . self-indulgence on my part?"

He turned back to her, his expression unreadable. "I don't see what else I can think. You haven't given me one good reason to believe there's anything wrong here except in your own imagination." In an attempt to lighten his words, he smiled faintly. "Which you have to admit is pretty active."

She sat stiffly on the couch, not meeting his eyes. Softly, she said, "It's a shock to discover how patronizing you can be."

Matthew grimaced. He had tried his best; if he had failed, he wouldn't believe it was his fault. "Look," he said flatly, "I'm tired and I've got more than enough on my mind without adding anything more. If you want to fight, you'll have to do it alone."

"You can't shut me out like this," Teresa protested. "It isn't right."

"I don't know what's right or wrong, all I'm sure of is that this discussion is pointless. I'm going to bed."

Long after he did so, she stayed up, sitting on the couch and staring unseeing at the opposite wall. In her mind she went back over their conversation, thinking of all the things she should have said to him. She wasn't some spoiled, shallow woman seeing problems where there were none. Not only was she a competent adult, but she was also clearly more sensitive to the true realities of the situation than he. At least she wasn't afraid to admit everything wasn't perfect. If he had come to her with such a problem, she would have done her utmost to understand and help. Why couldn't he?

Only gradually—and reluctantly—did she begin to see his side of it. They clearly had very different expectations about what marriage should be. His were satisfied; hers weren't. While she might envy him his equanimity, she couldn't blame him entirely for her lack of contentment. To do so would be to claim that it was his responsibility to make her happy, when in fact it was her own.

So he didn't understand how she felt. Was that really his fault? Difficult though it was, she had to admit that she had given him very little chance to understand. That evening had been the first time she even admitted straight out that she believed they had a problem. It was easy to be angry at him for not responding more supportively, but that did not mean in time he wouldn't come to see her position more clearly.

Telling herself that—and managing to at least half believe it—she finally went to bed. Without turning the light on, she undressed and slipped into a nightgown. The sheets on her side were cold. She shivered faintly and wrapped her arms around herself.

Several moments passed before she heard a sigh from the other side of the bed. "You took long enough," Matthew murmured. "I thought I'd have to come and get you."

She didn't respond but he moved a little closer. He sighed again. "You haven't been crying, have you?"

That stung her to respond. "No, of course not."

"Good. I'll bet you're cold, though."

"I'm all right."

"You're always so stubborn." He reached out and took hold of her gently, drawing her to him. The warmth of his body enveloped her. With a faint sigh, she accepted it as enough for the moment.

JAMES BUTTONED HIS SHIRT and tucked it into his waistband. After putting his jacket on, he pushed the curtain aside and left the cubicle. "The doctor will see you in his office," a pretty young nurse said with a smile. He nodded and followed her directions down a short corridor to where Landis was waiting.

Hal Landis had been an acquaintance of his for several years, since they met at a cerebral palsy fund-raiser. Drawn together by their experiences as marines during World War II, they had similar attitudes toward politics, women and life in general. Once a month or so they got together for lunch or a drink. When James had called the week before and said he wanted to see him, Hal had presumed it was social. He'd been surprised to learn that James wanted to consult him professionally.

"Sit down," he said as James came into the office. The two men were similar in height and build, with Landis being the younger by less than a year. Photos of his wife and three children were clustered on his desk. Behind him was a vibrant Impressionist painting whose vivid colors seemed out of place in the otherwise plain office, but which James knew suited the doctor perfectly.

"Find anything interesting?" he asked laconically as he took a seat and propped a foot comfortably on his knee.

Landis looked up from the EKG printout he'd been studying. He peered at James over the top of his glasses. "Unfortunately, I did. I suppose you want it straight?"

James stiffened almost imperceptibly. "Of course."

"There's a flutter in your heart rate. It's not an uncommon condition, and it may or may not be serious. But it can be a warning sign of worse to come. I want you to have more tests."

"What for?"

"To determine exactly where we stand. Don't argue with me about this, James. You've put off doing something about it long enough; it's time to face up to the problem."

"I'm not arguing," he replied mildly. "If I weren't willing to take your advice, I wouldn't have come to see you. But I'm not going to follow along blindly either."

"All right. I think—stress on the *think*—that you may be headed for trouble. With the test results I have right now, I can't explain exactly why I feel that way. But I've been in this racket for a few years and I've learned to trust my instincts. I'll feel a whole lot better if I can get more information on what's going on inside you."

"Fair enough," James said. "When do you want to do this?"

"It shouldn't be put off." Landis flipped through the leather-bound calendar on his desk. "I'd like to schedule you for a stress test the end of this week. Okay?"

"I'll have my secretary call and confirm. Any instructions?"

"Yeah. Don't eat or drink for twelve hours beforehand, except water, bring clothes to work out in and don't worry."

James laughed faintly as he stood up. "I like the last part especially."

Landis shrugged. "I tell all my patients that and none of them ever listens, but the fact is worrying won't help a damn thing." He paused for a moment. "Are you going to tell Alexis?"

"There's no point."

"She'll have to be informed eventually."

"I'll work that out when I have to. First, I want to know myself what I'm dealing with."

"Fair enough. Just remember, you're not in this alone."

James thought about that as he left the office and started walking down Park Avenue. It was a clear, sunny day with temperatures in the sixties. Spring had settled in firmly and summer wasn't far off. Young girls in short skirts strolled by, their hair blowing in the breeze off the river. He heard their laughter as though from a great distance.

Despite his seemingly matter-of-fact reaction to Hal's news, he was shocked by it. In hindsight, he could recognize that his body had been giving him warning signals for a long time; he'd just never listened to it before. Not until Joseph Gargano died had he even considered the possibility that the good health he had always taken for granted might no longer be guaranteed.

The problem, he decided as he crossed Sixty-ninth Street and headed south, was that he had let himself get too damn comfortable. Back during the war, he'd never lost sight of the fact that he could be killed. But, paradoxical though it might sound, he'd never really thought of dying. If it happened at all, he figured it would be over in an instant and he would either know nothing about it or come to in some afterworld where, at the very least, people wouldn't be shooting at each other. Of the possibility that he might die slowly, he had thought not at all. That had always been beyond the limits of consideration. Yet now he was forced to confront it.

However serious his condition might or might not be, the fact remained that he was no longer young. His body was showing its age. He could not count on it to accept whatever he happened to feel like dishing out. Alien though the concept might be, he had to start taking care of himself.

Alexis had been after him for years to stop working so much, get more rest, cut down on the tension and let other, younger men carry more of the responsibility. By that she had, of course, meant Matthew. He had gone along to a point but had drawn the line at giving up ultimate authority for everything that happened within IBS. Perhaps it was time to at least consider doing so.

TERESA SAW GRAHAM several more times as spring turned to summer. She continued to be cautious of him but found she enjoyed his company. He knew so many people in the literary world that she had only observed from a distance. She found his stories fascinating, all the more so because of his sharp-eyed perception and ironic wit. Entertained though she was, she didn't fail to notice that he never spoke maliciously about anyone. Tolerance and sympathy underscored everything he told her.

"The problem with becoming a successful writer," he said one afternoon when they were having tea at the Algonquin, "is to define what one means by success. On the one hand, there is the acclaim of the literary critics, among whom I modestly include myself. On the other, there is the acclaim of the masses, which has a very healthy effect on one's bank account. Few writers manage to achieve both."

"It seems to me," Teresa said as she selected a scone and dabbed a bit of cream on it, "that any writer who becomes a best seller is automatically looked down on by the critics. It's as though they believe anything that lots of people enjoy has to be lousy."

"You'll admit the public is not known for its refined tastes?"

"True, but they aren't a bunch of cretins either. Every once in a while they go for something genuinely good."

"Give me an example."

"*Huckleberry Finn, David Copperfield, The Catcher in the Rye, The Grapes of Wrath,* all books that have been very popular as well as distinguished."

"Salinger has never appealed to me," Graham said, "but I'll go along with the others. Don't forget though, Steinbeck's had an awful time being taken seriously. How many critics have you read who claim he's really no more than a journalist? Hemingway hasn't had it all that much easier. Even someone like Mailer gets lambasted from time to time."

"Everyone we've mentioned so far is male. What do you suppose it takes for a woman to be considered an important writer?"

"Well . . ." Graham ventured with a smile, "it doesn't hurt to be absolutely outrageous. Like George Sand, for instance, or Virginia Woolf."

"A nice, normal home life doesn't make it?"

"'Fraid not. Which isn't to say, of course, that perceptions won't change."

"I'm not holding my breath. If it happens at all, it will only be as the result of a long, hard struggle."

"I sense a certain . . . loosening up," Graham said as he stirred his tea absently. "Perhaps I'm kidding myself, but people seem a bit more tolerant these days."

Teresa was glad to hear him say that; now that she knew him better, she understood the high price he had paid for refusing to conform to what others regarded as normal. It seemed the height of unfairness that he should be penalized all his life for simply being himself.

They spoke a while longer about books in general and Teresa's latest in particular. She was still having a hard time with it. Graham encouraged her to press on, confident the results would be worthwhile. She found it easy to talk him about her writing, and she appreciated his reassurances.

Eventually the conversation turned to other matters. "I heard the other day that the FCC is looking into the possibility of charging UBC and IBS with restraint of trade," Graham said.

"That's come up before, but this time it looks serious."

"It's Nixon's doing, of course. His or the people close to him."

"Maybe," Teresa ventured, "but the fact is when Alexis bought UBC, neither it nor IBS were anywhere near as powerful as they both are today. Much as I hate to admit it, I think the government may have a case."

"How does that opinion go over at home?"

"I haven't tried to find out," she admitted.

He leaned back in the leather armchair, his legs crossed and the teacup balanced on his knee. "There are several ways to cope with the problem. I'm sure it will be solved before very long."

"What approach would you take?" She was curious to hear what he would say since with his background he was in a better position than almost anyone else to judge the situation, provided he could bring himself to be fair.

"Me? That's hard to say. It's been so long since I was involved in anything like that." He thought for a moment, then said, "I suppose I would move to undermine the government's case, perhaps by selling off less profitable affiliates and consolidating the rest."

"You mean merging the two networks?"

"Yes, that's what I'd be aiming for eventually. Of course, there would be all sorts of problems to overcome, but I think it could be done, particularly if there is a change of administration."

"Do you think that's likely?" Teresa asked.

"I'd say it's imminent. If the House votes for impeachment, everything will be over except the shouting."

"There will still be the actual trial by the Senate, and Nixon could win that."

Graham shook his head. "I don't think it will go that far. My guess is he will resign."

She hadn't considered that possibility and didn't know what to make of it. Each evening all the network news shows were filled with details of the evidence being presented to the House Judiciary Committee. It was up to the thirty-eight men and women on that committee to decide whether or not to recommend that the president be impeached. All the commentators devoted considerable time to explaining exactly what that involved, spelling out over and over that impeachment was the equivalent of an indictment rather than a guilty verdict. The president would still have his day in court with the right to refute all charges against him, if he could.

Late in July, as expected, the committee voted to recommend impeachment on the grounds that the president had obstructed justice by attempting to cover up White House involvement in the Watergate break-in. Two very tense weeks passed amid mounting discussion of whether or not the country could trust its safety to a president operating under such profound stress. What that translated to was fear that the man whose finger rested on the proverbial button might, under such extraordinary circumstances, do something irrevocable.

"I'll be staying late," Matthew said when he called from the office the first Thursday in August. "It looks as though there's going to be a major break, but no one's sure what."

Teresa balanced the phone in the crook of her shoulder. She was sitting at her desk, a fresh sheet of paper in the typewriter in front of her. Normally when she was working, she left the answering machine on. But the way things were going, a distraction was welcome. She had been looking forward to having Matthew home that evening and was disappointed he would be delayed. Still she kept her voice carefully neutral as she said, "All right. Do you want me to hold dinner?"

"No, don't bother, I may be staying really late."

He hung up a short while later, leaving her to stare absently at the empty page. In the months since she had tried to express her concerns to him, little had changed in their marriage. The easiest explanation for that was that they were both so busy, but she suspected more was involved. It was as though they had made a tacit pact not to rock the boat, at least not for the moment.

Matthew did not get home that night at all. He stayed at the office putting together a program to run in the event of Nixon's resignation, now seen as increasingly likely. The president's admission that he had ordered a halt to the Watergate investigation scant days after the break-in was seen as a death blow to his chances for acquittal. The only question that remained was whether or not he would put himself—and the country—through the torture of a trial. Rumors floating out of Washington strongly suggested he would not.

Even so the members of the news team who gathered around the television monitors the following evening were tense with excitement. The president had requested time from all the networks to address the nation and, as always, they had obliged.

The speech was brief and to the point. Matthew considered it one of Nixon's finest. The president spoke with consummate dignity as he announced he would resign his office effective at noon the following day. A few of the people watching cheered, but most remained silent. There was no pleasure in the president's downfall and little feeling of vindication; only the leaden sense that Watergate was simply one more in the relentless barrage of shocks that had pummeled the country for more than a decade.

"It has to end sometime," Winston said as he and Matthew were leaving the building late that evening after the president's speech. "The country's becoming numb."

"We've all had too much to cope with," Matthew said as he draped his suit jacket over his shoulder. It was a warm night, though not unpleasantly so. "People like me, in our thirties and younger, have never even known a time when the world seemed essentially stable."

"I've got news for you, kid," Winston said as they stood on the corner. "It was no picnic for my generation either. We had a couple of little upsets called the Depression and the War. You have to go back to the last century before things start to look peaceful, and that's little more than an illusion."

"You're saying it's always been like this?"

"No...that I wouldn't claim. The pace of change is much faster than ever before. That's what's exhausting people."

Matthew thought he might be right. Time was a man could count on at least a few things in life. No matter what else happened, he was reasonably sure of his own place in the scheme of things and the places of those closest to him. But no more. Everything was up for grabs and no one seemed to have any idea of how it would all turn out.

Certainly he didn't. And that, more than anything else, was what scared him.

Chapter Eleven

WHEN TERESA TYPED the last page of her new book she felt as though she had come to the end of a long battle whose outcome had been in doubt until that very moment. It was all she could do to read the final paragraphs over one more time before stuffing the manuscript into an envelope and sending it off to Clare. For once she was not anxious to hear from her editor. All she really wanted to do was put writing and everything associated with it out of her mind for at least a while.

Yet despite the mental and physical weariness gripping her, that proved unexpectedly difficult to do. Without the routine of spending hours each day in front of the typewriter, she felt at loose ends. There were only so many places she cared to go by herself, so many books she wanted to read, so many people she enjoyed talking with. Before very long, she was ill at ease with her self-imposed leisure and anxious to find some way to end it.

It was then that she began to notice children.

They had never played any large part in her scheme of things. While she was certainly aware of them, she had given them scant attention. Growing up with two younger brothers had robbed small human beings of much of their mystique, at least so far as she was concerned. Always before she had considered them no more than vaguely annoying creatures, in perpetual need of attention, around whom it was impossible to lead a normal life.

Now, quite without warning, they seemed a great deal more appealing.

It might, of course, be related to her age. She would be twenty-nine that spring, a year away from what was supposed to be the make-or-break thirties. If she was going to have a child—perhaps even children—this might be a good time to consider doing something about it.

Several things stopped her from taking the plunge immediately. To begin with, there was the awesome responsibility involved in bringing a new life into the world. At times the mere thought of doing so overwhelmed her. Yet she kept remembering that her mother, who must certainly have had many of the same concerns, had not been stopped by them. Nor had a multitude of other women who had borne children and raised them, often in the face of enormous odds.

The question that increasingly absorbed her was whether or not she was capable of doing the same. For a while she took comfort in the fact that she wouldn't be taking it on alone; any baby she had would have a father as well as a mother. But how much difference would that really make? Matthew was away more than he was home. The day-to-day burden of child rearing would undoubtedly fall on her. Could she accept that and make it work, without losing herself in the bargain?

Looking within herself for the answers to her concerns, she found only more questions. Why, exactly, did she want a baby? Out of loneliness or some deluded notion of perpetuating herself in another human being? Or was it that a great, untapped font of love existed within her that she was afraid of seeing grow dry and empty over the years?

She thought about the other women she knew best and realized with some surprise that they were few in number and, with the single exception of Mandy, all older than herself. Her own generation had always been so large and unruly, so boisterous and demanding as to intimidate her. She had preferred to keep her distance, more often observing from a safe position on the sidelines rather than participating.

Even when she had passed through the same rites of passage that marked the transformation from child to adult, she had done so with an old sense of impartiality, as though nothing was quite happening to her directly. Only once had she allowed herself to become fully involved—with her marriage—and that was not working out at all as she had expected.

Would motherhood prove equally fraught with surprises and disappointments? There seemed only one way to find out: by experiencing it for herself. But before she fully made up her mind to do so, she could at least catch a glimpse of what the future might hold through the experiences of the women who had gone before her.

Maggie was pleased when Teresa called her and suggested they get together for lunch. "I can hardly believe how long it's been since we spent any time alone," she said when she arrived at her daughter's apartment one afternoon several days later. "Since you were married, we always see you with Matthew."

"He's in Washington this week," Teresa said as she poured them each a glass of white wine, then found a vase for the flowers her mother had brought. They lent a note of color to a day still teetering on the promise of spring. "But he'll be back Friday."

"He seems to be taking over more and more for Winston," Maggie said as she seated herself on the couch. From there she could see the table in the dining area, set with a linen cloth, matching napkins and pretty blue and white china. That seemed a lot of trouble to go to when they could just as easily have eaten out.

"I suppose you've heard about Winston beginning semi-retirement later this year," Teresa said. She smoothed her skirt with one hand as she sat down, then raised her glass to her lips and took a small sip.

Maggie nodded. "That surprised me, until I realized he was past sixty-five."

"Somehow one never thinks of Winston as being old."

The lines around Maggie's hazel eyes deepened as she smiled. "I'm afraid none of us is getting any younger."

"You'll never be old," Teresa insisted, "or Dad either. I can't imagine that happening to either of you."

Her mother shook her head slightly. Her hair was almost entirely silver now and elegantly styled. "It's odd, but age doesn't have the same meaning to me that it once did. I don't view it as an enemy anymore."

Teresa shifted on the couch, realizing that she had been sitting very stiffly so that the muscles in her back were beginning to cramp. "I guess what I mean is that some people, as they get older, seem to dry up inside. They become estranged from the world, alone and afraid, condemning everything around them. That's what I think must be truly terrible."

"I agree, but I don't believe it's anything you have to worry about."

"No one ever has any guarantees."

"That's certainly true." Maggie laughed faintly. "My, how did we get on to such a serious topic?"

"Do you mind talking about serious things?"

"No . . . not if I know the reason for them."

Teresa put her glass down and looked at her hands. "I suppose this will sound a little strange since I'm almost thirty, but I feel in particular need of a mother just now."

Maggie sat back against the couch. Her gaze focused on her daughter, not without sympathy but also not without the clinical detachment that had made her such a good nurse. "Is it something to do with Matthew?"

"No . . . yes . . . I'm not sure." She shrugged apologetically. "That isn't very helpful, is it?"

"At least it tells me you aren't on the verge of a separation . . . or divorce."

"No, of course not." Teresa met her mother's eyes warily. "Did you think we would be?"

"Nowadays one never knows. You and Matthew seem happy enough, but appearances can be very deceptive."

"We love each other. I'm sure of that."

"But you've found out loving doesn't solve everything? Is that it?"

A thread had worked its way loose on Teresa's skirt. She plucked at it absently. "How deflating to realize that I've simply discovered something the rest of the world already knew."

"Not the entire world," Maggie said gently. "But it is something people tend to realize as they get older. Which is not to say that love is in any way deceptive. While it doesn't solve problems, it does provide a reason for coping with them."

She was silent for a moment, looking into her wine before going on. "That sounds rather profound, doesn't it? I wish I had great gobs of similarly wise things to give you, but I don't. In fact, when you said you needed a mother, I was taken aback to realize that's a part I can't play anymore.''

''But . . . you are my mother.''

Maggie sighed and stared off into space. ''How to explain this to you? I was a little girl's mother—a baby's, a child's, an adolescent's. At each stage, I encountered difficulties, but I think in the end I managed fairly well. The problem is that I don't have any experience being a mother to a grown woman. I wouldn't know where to begin.'' Softly, she suggested, ''Perhaps you could accept me as a friend, instead?''

''I've always thought of you that way.''

''Have you? When you were small and fell down and hurt yourself, it wasn't a friend you turned to. When you woke up in the night afraid, or found a particularly lovely flower, or had a really important secret you wanted to share, you didn't go to a friend. You needed a mother then, and I was happy to be that for you. But Band-Aids, hugs and lullabies-aren't going to solve what you're facing now. I only wish they could.''

Teresa swallowed against the tightness of her throat. Maggie might not have any easy solutions, but she did have something far more precious, wisdom. ''I think I understand what you're saying. Motherhood isn't a permanent condition. You take it up at a certain point in your life, have it for a while and then let it go.''

"And cherish the memories," Maggie added quietly. "Above all that. I wouldn't have wanted to miss them for anything."

"I'm glad to hear it," Teresa said with a smile, "though there must have been times when we drove you nuts."

The two women laughed together before Maggie said, "Let me help you get lunch on the table and I'll tell you all about it."

Over quiche, salad and more wine, they continued to talk. "You have to realize," Maggie said, "that in some ways things were simpler back then. At the end of the war, almost every woman I knew—including myself—felt a tremendous urge to create something good out of all the desolation that had gone before. Our first instinct was to get pregnant, which we did in enormous numbers."

"You never had any doubts?" Teresa asked.

"Not that first time. The second I did waver a bit, but when I saw your brother, I felt it was all worthwhile. And the third... well, you know the circumstances of that."

"When Dad was going to Korea to try to get Uncle James out?"

Maggie nodded. "There was a very real possibility he wouldn't come back. I suppose I responded as women have for centuries, wanting to keep something of him with me."

"Didn't you ever... feel trapped?"

"More times than I can remember." When Teresa's chin jerked up at such frankness, Maggie explained, "As far as I'm concerned, that's one of the most natural feelings involved in being a mother. Any woman with children who says there has never been a time when she wanted to simply chuck it all and run away is either lying or so out of touch with herself as to be pitiful."

Teresa toyed with her quiche, not really hungry. "How did you keep from giving in to that impulse?"

"I didn't. In the beginning, when we had very little money, there were times when I went without a pair of stockings, a bottle of nail polish, things like that just so I could hire a baby-sitter for a few hours a month. It wasn't that I wanted to go anywhere special. I just needed to be away for a little while, to be reminded that I was something besides a mother." She smiled faintly. "There was a small park across from the local hospital. I used to sit there on a bench and watch the people go by. How's that for strange?"

"It wasn't really. You missed your work."

"But I felt I shouldn't. It seemed so . . . ungrateful not to be satisfied with all I had. That's one thing at least that really has improved. Young women nowadays don't feel being a wife and mother should somehow complete them."

"On the contrary," Teresa said wryly. "From what I can see, marriage is more often than not viewed as a way station en route to future relationships, while having children is considered a luxury, if not outright indulgence.''

''Is that how Matthew feels?''

''Not about marriage...not really...I don't know. As for children, we haven't talked about them.''

''Why not? They're clearly very much on your mind.''

''It's difficult to explain. We're being...careful with each other.''

Maggie put her fork down. She blotted her lips with the linen napkin, then replaced it in her lap. ''When I was your age, and younger, I was very impatient with older people who claimed there was nothing new under the sun. That seemed to be a way for them to dismiss our concerns. But the longer I've lived, the more I've realized that while change does occur, a great deal also remains the same. What you're describing—this reluctance to confront each other because of the possible consequences—isn't that unusual a stage within a marriage. Your father and I went through it when I decided to go back to work despite his opposition, and I know Alexis and James experienced something similar, though the circumstances were personal and I won't go into them.''

Teresa had an idea they might have something to do with Winston's feelings for Alexis, but she didn't ask. Instead, she said, ''I'm not offended that you think what we're going through isn't all that unusual. On the contrary, I'm relieved. After all, you and Dad, and Alexis and James, came through it fine.'' She paused a moment. ''Didn't you?''

''No one can ever really know what happens in someone else's marriage, but yes, your father and I did survive that period and emerged more strongly committed to each other than ever before. If I had to guess, I'd say James and Alexis did the same. But for all of us, there was a price to pay. We had to come to terms with our true selves. We couldn't just go on accepting without question the roles society thrust on us.''

''My generation has some experience at questioning,'' Teresa pointed out quietly.

''But whenever any of you have challenged the accepted norm, it's been as part of a much larger group, not as individuals. There comes a time when you have to step away from the protection of the crowd and find your own answers.''

Sunlight fell on the wine in Teresa's glass, as though filtered through old yellowing lace. ''I'm trying to do that, but it's very hard.''

''At least you're better prepared for it than most people. Your writing inclines you to see experience as something to be used rather than simply endured.''

''Matthew said once that I had too much time to think about myself.''

''He couldn't have meant it,'' Maggie insisted.

''I think he may have.'' Teresa rose, picked up their empty plates and carried them to the kitchen. She returned with a chocolate mousse she had made that morning, knowing it was one of her mother's favorites.

They tasted it in silence before Maggie said, "This is marvelous. When did you start doing so much cooking?"

"When I finished my new book. I can't seem to get another one started."

"Are you worried?"

"Some. I'd hate to think that part of my life was over." In fact she was terrified to even admit the possibility.

"Can that happen? I've never heard of a really good writer who simply stopped."

Teresa laughed faintly. "You'd be surprised. There are all sorts of ways for writers to self-destruct."

"HOW IS TESSA?" Anthony asked later that night as he was getting ready for bed. Maggie was already there, sitting propped up against the pillows. Her face was cleaned of makeup and her hair was brushed away from her face. The reading lamp beside the bed illuminated the lines on her throat and around her mouth and eyes. He considered them badges of honor and thought she looked lovely.

"I'm not sure," she admitted, lowering the paperback mystery she had been absently trying to read. "She and Matthew don't seem to be as close as they might be, but she's thinking about having a baby."

"Did she say that right out?" Anthony asked, trying to conceal his excitement. There were few things he wanted more than a grandchild, though he had never actually said so.

"No...but she asked a lot of questions about what it's like to be a mother. Why else would she do that?"

"Maybe she's researching for a new book," he suggested as he stripped off his shirt.

"I don't think that's it. She finished the one that took so long and she hasn't started another."

"Well, then, maybe she's thinking a baby would help."

"I hope not. More marriages have gone on the rocks because of that mistake."

Hanging his trousers on the mahogany valet, Anthony frowned. "Do you really think she and Matthew are in that kind of trouble?"

"I don't know. Frankly, I don't think they do either."

He walked into the bathroom to put his underwear in the hamper and brush his teeth. When he returned, his frown was deeper. "Is there something we should do?"

She smiled and pulled the covers back for him. "What could we?"

"I don't know." He slid in beside her and lay with his arms folded behind his head. "She used to have simpler problems."

"Isn't that the truth."

"There must be something...."

Maggie put the mystery on her bedside table and turned off her light. She pulled her pillows flat and lay down close to him. "We have to be patient."

"That's what you always said when the kids were going through some stage or other."

"I don't want to make light of the situation, but maybe this isn't all that different. She and Matthew are both grown now; they have to work out their own problems."

He put his arm around her, drawing her nearer. Her skin smelled of the jasmine soap she had used in the bath. She rested against him lightly, her head in the crook of his shoulder. Anthony sighed deeply. "Were we ever that young?"

"A century ago." She laughed softly and raised herself far enough to be able to look at him. "Do you remember what it felt like?"

"It was . . . disconcerting. There was so much I wanted, but I was almost afraid to breathe for fear it would all slip away from me."

"And now?"

His chuckle was deep and rich. "Now is a lot better."

Her hand traced a teasing line down his chest. "You don't want to be twenty again?"

"Twenty? I wouldn't be thirty again." He turned suddenly, shifting her under him. "Any arguments?"

Maggie smiled and shook her head as she reached for him.

TERESA WAS ASLEEP when Matthew got home. He ate the rest of the quiche while standing by the kitchen sink. The terrier joined him and mooched a few bites. He woofed softly and thumped his thanks with the tail he had never quite grown into.

When Matthew came out of the bathroom the dog was on its blanket near the bed. He crouched down to pat it, doing his best to make no sound. Still by the time he got under the covers, Teresa was awake.

"Hard day?" she asked.

"Not really, just a bunch of meetings with Dad."

"How is he?"

"Fine. Why do you ask?"

"No reason . . . he seemed tired the last time I saw him. Anything new from the FCC?"

"They've agreed to the sale of the affiliates."

She sat up and ran a hand through her hair. "As many as you wanted to sell, not any additional?"

He nodded. "Yeah, it looks like we'll be able to take the first steps toward combining the networks."

"Thank God for Gerald Ford."

"You should write and tell him that. He probably doesn't hear it a lot."

His disparaging tone surprised her. "This is good news, isn't it?" she asked.

"I guess. Listen, don't mind me, I'm just tired."

"Of course . . . it's late."

He turned over on his side, facing her. "I don't think I got more than four, maybe five hours' sleep last night."

The sheet had ridden down, exposing his bare chest. She watched its steady rise and fall as she asked, "Why was that?"

"No particular reason."

But there has to be, she wanted to say. Tell me about it. Maybe I can help. Once she would have tried to coax it out of him; now she did not. There was only so much strength left in her. It had to be conserved.

"That's a pretty nightgown," he said suddenly.

She was surprised to discover that his eyes were open. A moment before they had been closed. "It's new."

"I like the color." He touched a blunt-tipped finger to the curve of her shoulder, drew it across the hollows of her collarbones and let it drift slowly downward to the shadowed cleft between her breasts. "Among other things."

"I thought you were tired."

He moved slightly, insinuating a leg between hers. "I'm getting my second wind."

A memory intruded: of the small blue pill container with the dial marking off the days to ensure that none were skipped. It was in the drawer to the left of the double sink in the bathroom, where it had remained untouched for two weeks. Each day she had remembered the pills, had thought about taking one but somehow had not gotten around to it.

"Matthew . . . this might not be a good idea."

He looked up, his eyes already dark with gathering passion. "Why not?"

"I've sort of been . . . forgetting my pills."

"Forgetting? You mean you haven't been taking them?"

"That's what I said, wasn't it?"

"No, not exactly. Never mind." He sat up and looked at her doubtfully. "Why have you been doing that?"

"I don't know. It just happened."

"Nothing just hap—"

"Would you let it go, please? I don't want to get into a big discussion.

He hesitated, wishing he could see her better but unwilling to turn on the light. "Look, if you want to . . . think about having a baby, I'm not against it. I just don't want to be taken by surprise."

"I'm sorry," she murmured into the darkness. "I should have said something."

Looking at the ripe curve of her breasts opalescent against the dark covers, he was filled with an unexpected sense of tenderness. She was usually so self-possessed and assured, he could almost relish the note of genuine uncertainty in her voice. Except that underneath it all he really did love her, whatever that meant, and he didn't want her having regrets, especially not about anything to do with him.

"Teresa . . . it's okay. I'm not upset. Maybe it's a good idea for you to stop taking the pills. I've never been convinced they were a hundred percent safe. If you want to do that, but not . . . you know, get pregnant, I think we might still have some condoms around.''

She turned over, staring up at him. ''From when?''

''Before you started on the pills.'' What had she thought—that he'd been buying them for some other reason?

That had occurred to her but she'd dismissed it instantly. Whatever problems they might have, she didn't believe infidelity was one of them. ''Aren't those kind of old?''

He laughed softly. ''They don't have expiration dates.''

''Oh . . . well then, maybe we should. . . .''

''I wonder where they are,'' he said.

''Are you sure you brought them with you when we moved in here?''

''Pretty sure, but I'm not positive they got unpacked.''

''Then they're in one of those boxes in the basement storeroom.''

Basement, at this time of night? They looked at each other tentatively. ''Uh . . . do you think we might . . . ?'' Matthew began.

''It seems sort of silly to go all the way down there. . . .'' Teresa broke in.

He took a deep breath, trying hard not to look at her nipples, which had tightened and were thrusting against the thin material of the nightgown. "I wouldn't want to jeopardize you. . . ."

Her gaze followed his and she flushed slightly. "Actually, I think this is a safe time of the month."

"Are you sure?"

"Not completely. . . but almost."

Still he hesitated, seeking some sign from her, some assurance that she wouldn't feel later that she had been cajoled or manipulated into anything. It took her a moment to realize what he needed.

Her hands on his shoulders were gentle but insistent. He slid onto his back as she smiled down at him. Slowly she bent forward. With the tip of her tongue she traced the shape of his mouth, circled the square thrust of his chin, found and savored the pulse in his throat. His skin was warm, almost hot, and faintly salty. She lingered over it, dampening the fine hairs on his chest with catlike strokes.

Matthew could not remain still. His hands gripped her arms above the elbows, moving upward to her shoulders, flexing as they slid down her back to the curve of her buttocks. Her nightgown had become tangled around her thighs. He pulled it up and slid his hands underneath the cool silk, touching her skin with soft, almost tentative gestures as though he still was not absolutely sure of what was happening.

A low moan broke from him when her teeth found each of his nipples in turn. He kicked the covers back impatiently and grasped her hips. "Take this thing off."

''Not yet . . . soon . . .''She slid down further, tracing the line of hair over his flat abdomen until it began to thicken at his groin. There she paused, nestling her head against him. He smelled of sweat and musk, the intrinsically sensual smell of the aroused male. His urgency pressing against her cheek increased her own, made a mockery of the self-control she was trying so hard to hold on to.

She sat up and pulled the gown over her head, emerging from it in a tumble of disarrayed hair and flushed skin. For a moment she remained upright, the gown still in her hands, watching him rise beneath her.

''Teresa . . .'' The entreaty woven through each syllable of her name drew her abruptly back to full awareness. She tossed the gown aside, hearing the softly sibilant whisper as it fell to the floor.

''I love you like this,'' she murmured against him, ''needing me so much.''

''It should be mutual,'' he gasped as she nibbled gently on the tip of him.

''It is, I promise.'' That was the truth, more even than she really wanted to admit. She had said once that being close only when they made love wasn't enough, yet right then it seemed everything and more. She didn't have to wonder why this time should be different from all the others. For the first time she was consciously opening herself to the possibility of pregnancy. What had been simply a mutual giving of pleasure had suddenly assumed far greater significance.

Slowly, cherishing every instant, she lowered herself onto him. Her hands were braced against his shoulders, her elbows locked. He stared up at her, his eyes hooded and the skin drawn taut over the sculpted bones of his face. "Lovely, you're so lovely." Gently, he cupped her breasts, imagining them filled with milk. His passion took an abrupt leap forward, making him rear up into her. "Sorry," he gasped, "don't want to hurt you."

"You aren't . . ." She could barely speak. The fire inside was burning higher and higher, reaching past her heart to the center of her mind, burning away the cool layers of thought, leaving only raging hunger. She felt herself falling into the whirling vortex of sensation and instinctively tried to fight against it, though only for a moment. Quickly enough she yielded and let the undulating waves take her; they were a shimmering path she had traveled many times before yet whose ending was always new.

This time glittering gold awaited her, molten and stirring with forces that were part of her but also vastly beyond her. She saw a shadow at the heart of the gold, watched as it transformed into Matthew's face, straining with his own fulfillment, and plummeted into hers.

Only much later did she lift briefly out of the enveloping blanket of sleep, lifted on a single thought:

it was two weeks since she had stopped taking the pills; she might already have been pregnant.

A PALE PINK DAWN edged hesitantly against the heaviness of night. Wisps of gray clouds hugged the horizon. The air was hazy, lacking the brittle coldness of recent nights when the temperatures had flirted with freezing. Spring seemed finally to be settling in.

Alexis turned away from the window to look at James, still deeply asleep. He had been wakeful most of the night; she was relieved he was finally getting some rest. Her hand strayed to her throat as she studied him, running over the familiar signposts that should have reassured her that he was well. Should have, but did not.

Something was wrong; she had known that for some time though she had not consciously acknowledged it. There had been only a vague, niggling concern at the back of her mind growing slowly more compelling, finally demanding all her attention and honesty.

Once before in their marriage, she had feared that James was hiding something from her. Then she had thought—incorrectly as it turned out—that he might be having an affair. Now she would gladly have accepted another woman in his life rather than the alternative that seemed increasingly a certainty.

He was ill. She saw it in a multitude of small things that each by itself would have gone unnoticed but taken together added up to an ominous whole. There was the fatigue that had at first seemed simply a normal by-product of his years and the long hours he worked, but that had slowly emerged as much more serious. He simply did not have the normal energy even of a man his age, and considering that there had been a time in the not too distant past when he could best men considerably younger than himself, that worried her deeply.

He had stopped smoking, something she had been trying to get him to do for longer than she could remember. Suddenly, without explanation, he had simply quit. Through sheer willpower, he had overcome a habit many people found impossible to break. His motivation must have been enormous, but he would not reveal it.

There was more: he had recently shown a willingness to share at least some responsibility with Matthew, also something she had tried to bring about for years but that, in light of all the other changes, did not give her any pleasure. He no longer seemed to enjoy the same foods, forgoing steaks, butter-laden baked potatoes and other such dishes with the explanation that he was watching his weight. Never much of a drinker, he had cut alcohol out entirely.

She should have been relieved that he was being so sensible, but in James—a man fueled by his passions—that pallid quality, however appropriate it might be, could not be regarded as cause for celebration.

Was age simply catching up with him? That was the most reasonable explanation and also the least acceptable. It seemed an affront to nature that anything so magnificently strong, confident, noble in the furthest sense of the word, should be brought down by nothing more than the accumulation of years. Life, she thought, should not be its own defeat.

She walked closer to the bed, going carefully so as to run no risk of waking him. His hair, still thick and mostly black though shot through with strands of silver, was disheveled by his earlier restlessness. She smoothed a strand of it from his forehead with a touch so light as to be imperceptible. In sleep, some of the years fell away from him. The lines etched into his weather-beaten features faded slightly, reminding her of how he had been what seemed like scant days ago.

Strange how he existed for her in so many forms, all but the present one long vanished, yet all held simultaneously within her memory. She wondered if it was the same for him. Did she still exist for him as the young woman she had been when they met, defiant and wary yet drawn to him almost against her better judgment? Was she still the young bride, reluctant mother, stubborn opponent, grudging partner she had once been? When he looked at her whom did he see? They had been so much to each other for so long. Without him, there would be . . . what?

She couldn't think of that. It brought a deep, twisting pain as though a carrion bird was clawing at her vitals. She wanted to rip it out and cast it away but could only shut it tightly in a locked closet and listen to the beating of its wings.

He stirred slightly in his sleep, as though aware of her scrutiny. She stepped back from the bed, taking shelter in the soft dawn shadows filling the room. Her eyes behind the lids felt dry and gritty. She longed to lie down beside him and share his rest, but she was afraid to, fearful that he was somehow slipping away from her and if she once let down her guard, he might be gone forever.

She shivered, despite the warmth of the room. This above all she had feared: to become so dependent on another person as to know death twice, once through him and once alone, that second death being no more than an affirmation of the first. For a long time, she had fought against such a love, until finally she had realized that to be without it was to exist in the shadowy reflection of life rather than in its bright substance.

She had chosen the brightness, thinking to gather it to her like faerie's gold with which to pay the bill that would ultimately come due. Now she thought she glimpsed the total and wondered how she had ever imagined she would have enough.

Chapter Twelve

GRAHAM SAT behind his large metal desk strewn as always with galleys, correspondence, invitations and the like, all demanding immediate attention, all postponed for at least the moment. He leaned well back in the comfortable swivel chair occupied by generations of *The Literary Quarterly* publishers. It had been his for twenty-five years; sometimes it seemed to have shaped itself to the contours of his body, if not his mind. Other times, he wasn't so sure.

"*Newsweek* liked it," he reminded Teresa as he spoke into the phone. A thin, nervous assistant editor tiptoed in with the first draft of a review. Graham gestured at him to leave it on the desk. "So did the *Washington Post*. What do you care what those idiots at the *Times* think?"

"I have to care," she protested quietly. "They gave both my other books good reviews, but they really hated this one. So it's obviously an objective opinion."

"Would you mind explaining to me how you arrived at that?"

"Obviously if they were prejudiced against me for any reason, they would have simply ignored all my books or given them all bad reviews. But they didn't, so they must be right.''

Graham sighed deeply and made a minute adjustment in the alignment of his left cuff. ''To begin with, there is no *they*. The *Times Book Review* is no more some great monolith than my own poor rag. There is simply a collection of reviewers and editors, every one of them with an ax to grind. In addition to which, you've always known women writers have a particularly tough time being taken seriously.''

''But they still liked the first two, so . . .''

''Teresa, dearest, tell me something. Has being pregnant rotted your brain as well as destroyed your waistline?''

''That's not nice, Graham. I admit I might have put on a few pounds, but—''

''You look lovely, which you should know perfectly well. My point is that those first two books were nothing compared to this one. You were just getting warmed up for the main event. It was easy for them to give you nice little pats on the head when you weren't any threat to them. But now you've moved into the major leagues. They have to sit up and take notice, and what they see scares them.''

''Why? I didn't say anything outrageous. There's hardly even anything original in that book.''

''Oh, lord,'' Graham groaned. ''Why are authors so overwhelmed with self-confidence? Why do they have such vaunting egos? Nothing original? I found it pungent, disturbing, insightful, riveting, to quote from the review I wrote. And I was being restrained, seeing as how we're friends. At least half a dozen other major—I give myself that—reviewers really let loose and praised it to the skies. So why this infantile, not to say maniacal obsession with the friggin' *Times*?''

''It's the one my publisher reads.''

''The *one*? He's not allowed more than that?''

''I don't know . . . they had a meeting . . . all they talked about was the *Times* review. Clare called me afterward. She says she may not be able to buy my next book.''

''Are you working on one now?''

''I'm . . . trying. It's hard.'' Mainly because she kept falling asleep at odd times, like every hour or so.

''Then don't worry about it. Let the bastards stew. If they're stupid enough not to recognize what they've got, plenty of others will.''

She laughed shakily, a faint sound that seemed very far away to him. It wasn't, of course. She was no farther than her parents' house out on the island. But he worried about her nonetheless and wished he could see her, if only to reassure himself.

''Look,'' he said hesitantly, ''you are feeling all right, aren't you?''

''For someone who can't keep a piece of dry toast down, I'm doing great.''

''I don't suppose you could have considered adopting. It's always struck me as much tidier.''

"I wanted it this way," she reminded him gently. "Besides, Matthew's ecstatic."

"How nice for him. I suppose his dry toast is staying down fine?"

This time her laugh was firmer, more like what it had been until two months before when her pregnancy had, in swift succession, been confirmed and become debilitating. After the disappointments of the past year, when she had been so certain she would become pregnant quickly but had not, she couldn't really resent the changes her body was at last experiencing.

Teresa said, "It's true he can't share the entire experience, but he's doing his best." In fact, Matthew was involving himself to what she regarded as a remarkable degree, hurrying home early from the office, reading baby books, often simply staring at her with rapt attention as though he expected her to bud. She kidded him about it, but she was also very touched.

"It's just as well you're out of the city," Graham said. "The weather's awful."

"It's lovely here, though I'm barely allowed to lift a finger without somebody rushing to scold me. Actually, I'm in real danger of being spoiled."

"It wouldn't do you any harm," he told her gruffly. They hung up a short while after Graham had tried to convince her yet again that one bad review, even if it was in the friggin' *Times*, was not the end of the world.

Teresa wanted to believe him, but couldn't quite manage it. She drifted through the rest of the day, lying by the pool, sleeping off and on, occasionally trying to read. After lunch, she wandered back into the house and flipped through the notebook she had brought with her in hopes that she would be inspired to work.

The blank pages taunted her. She felt as though she had returned to the same point she had been at years ago when she was first starting to write. There was no sense of order or discipline, no idea of how to begin or where to go. Even as she told herself that she was a fool to let the biases of a single reviewer affect her so strongly, she couldn't shake off her lethargy. Late in the afternoon, she tried to reach Clare but couldn't get through.

She gave up finally and tried to think of more pleasant things. Maggie had told her that the baby might be affected by her moods, and though she didn't quite believe it, she didn't want to take chances either. While she stayed at the house, Matthew was commuting each evening to be with her. Since he had taken over for Winston, he was working harder than ever. If he had suggested staying in the city, she would have understood, but she much preferred being with him.

Because he didn't usually get home until after 10:00 P.M., they sat up talking for several hours, then slept late. Teresa dreaded the moment of waking when the nausea struck her, but at least it was more tolerable if Matthew was there to help. She had quickly gotten over her embarrassment at his seeing her in such a state and learned to accept his care.

"I had no idea it would be like this," he admitted the following morning as he pressed a cold compress to her forehead. She had just retched into the bowl he was holding even though there had been nothing in her stomach. When she lay down again weakly, he took her hand. It was cold and slightly clammy. Her eyes were closed, the lids all but translucent. He could see thin blue veins in them. "Teresa…maybe you'd better check with the doctor again."

"He'll only tell me what he already has," she murmured.

"There are pills you could take. He told you that."

"But he also said they're strictly a last resort. It's better for the baby that I don't take anything. Don't worry," she added, squeezing his hand, "everyone agrees the first three months are the roughest and I'll be past them in another few days."

Matthew wished he could be as confident that she would soon be better. Before leaving for the office, he found Maggie and asked her to check on Teresa even more often than she usually did. "I'm really worried about her," he explained. "She insists this is normal, but I've got a bad feeling."

"I'll keep a close eye on her," Maggie promised. She didn't discount Matthew's concern, especially not since it accorded with her own. In each of her own pregnancies, she'd gone through bouts of morning sickness, and as a nurse, she had ample evidence of how common the problem was. But Teresa's difficulties seemed to be exceeding tolerable limits.

"When you're feeling a little better," Maggie said as she came into the guest room immediately after Matthew left, "I'd like you to get on the scale. We should check to see if you've lost any more weight."

Teresa protested it wasn't necessary, but only halfheartedly. With her mother she was more willing to acknowledge what she would not admit to Matthew, namely that she was becoming very frightened. Leaning on Maggie's arm, she made it into the bathroom. The mirror showed a slender young woman with deep shadows under her eyes and a pinched look around her mouth. Teresa glanced away hastily.

"Two more pounds gone," Maggie murmured, staring down at the scale. She tried not to show how much that alarmed her. Minor weight reduction wasn't that unusual during the first trimester if morning sickness was severe, but Teresa had already lost seven pounds in the past month; she was passing over the line from slender to thin.

"Honey, I'm sorry to say this, but I think you'd better see the doctor."

"I have an appointment next Wednesday," Teresa murmured as she got back into bed. There were spots in front of her eyes and she couldn't seem to keep her head erect. It was a relief to lay it down again on the pillow.

"You shouldn't wait," Maggie insisted. "The risk from those pills is small compared to what you're going through now."

"The baby. . . I don't want anything to happen to him." She clasped her hands over her still flat abdomen as though they could somehow protect the small being growing inside her. As Maggie watched, a single tear slipped down her cheek, then another.

"I'm calling the doctor," Maggie said. She hurried from the room before she, too, began to cry.

Teresa had selected her obstetrician carefully, after considering half-a-dozen alternatives. In the end she had chosen a three-man practice to make sure a doctor familiar with her case would be on hand no matter when she went into labor. On her two previous visits, she had found the care to be both courteous and thorough.

Maggie had the same reaction when she talked with the young woman who scheduled appointments. "Of course, Mrs. Gargano, if there's any possibility that your daughter or the baby is in danger, she should come in immediately. The only problem is getting her here." The doctors' offices were on the West Side facing Central Park, a scant two blocks from Teresa and Matthew's apartment, but at least an hour's drive from the island.

"I really don't know what to do in this situation," Maggie admitted. "It might be best to get her to the local hospital, but that seems rather extreme."

"Wait just a minute, I'm putting the doctor on."

When she had done so, Maggie quickly established that she was not only his patient's mother but also a nurse. "That's a break," he said. "Could you get more information for me? Her blood pressure, to start with."

"I'll call you back in five minutes."

When Maggie returned to the bedroom, she thought Teresa might have fallen asleep. She hoped that was the case so that she could do what she had to without worrying her. But as she gently wrapped the pressure cuff around her daughter's arm, Teresa asked weakly, "What are you doing?"

"Just getting a reading for the doctor, that's all."

"Oh . . . does he think this is anything serious?"

"He doesn't know, honey. Without seeing you and with so little data, it's hard for him to tell. Now just hold still a minute." She placed the stethoscope in her ears and gently squeezed the small balloon, keeping her eyes on the gauge. In her years as a nurse, Maggie must have done exactly the same thing tens of thousands of times. But this was different. She could hardly bear to look at the numbers.

"I'm okay. . . aren't I?"

"Sure, honey, don't worry about it." Maggie removed the cuff and returned it and the stethoscope to the small medical bag she had brought back with her from her war service and had never replaced, although the equipment inside had from time to time been updated. The bag had seen her through all the assorted accidents and illnesses of three lively children. Only very rarely had anything happened to them that was beyond her ability to cope with. This was one of those times. "I'll be right back," she said softly as she left the room.

"It'll have to be the hospital," the doctor said when he heard how far below normal Teresa's pressure was. He hesitated a moment before adding, "I suppose I don't have to tell you what's happening?"

He didn't. Maggie had seen enough similar cases in the emergency room where she had worked when she first returned to nursing to realize that Teresa was bleeding internally. If the baby wasn't already dead, it would be soon.

The ambulance Maggie called arrived within five minutes. Two white-jacketed attendants lifted Teresa onto a stretcher. On the sheet where she had been lying there was a dark pool of blood. Maggie quickly pulled the covers back over it.

The day was long and sad. Matthew arrived within forty-five minutes of Maggie's call, having broken every speed limit between the IBS garage and the hospital. He listened to what the doctor said but seemed to take very little of it in. All that really registered was that he had been too late to help her.

Long after she had been sedated and had fallen asleep, he stayed beside her. Her face was ashen, the only color in it came from the small wounds where she had bitten down hard on her lower lip. Traces of blood showed there. He wiped them away with a damp cloth and tried very hard not to weep.

TERESA RECOVERED SLOWLY from the loss of the baby, though physically she was well enough to leave the hospital within days. She and Matthew returned to their apartment. Anthony and Maggie had tried—with Matthew's support—to convince Teresa to stay with them a while longer. She courteously but firmly refused, saying that she needed the more familiar surroundings of her own home. What she did not say, though they guessed, was that she could not yet be in the place where her child had begun to slip away from her.

There was a great emptiness at the center of her being. A place that, until recently, she had not even known existed ached dully. Encounters with children were acutely painful. In the park or on the street, whenever she saw or heard them, she hurried by quickly, her eyes averted and her attention desperately focused elsewhere.

Instinctively she turned to the solace of work. A book was beginning to take shape within her mind. She said nothing of it to anyone, but little by little, in small increments, it began to emerge. The leaves beyond her window turned orange and gold. They drifted around her feet when she walked the dog in the park and blew in swirling gusts between the trees.

Vendors selling roasted chestnuts appeared on the street corners. On the television, Jimmy Carter hammered away at Gerald Ford. She tried to take an interest, found she could not and gave it up.

Talks began between the upper management of IBS and UBC regarding a possible merger. Matthew was deeply involved in them, as well as anchoring the nightly news. After Winston's retirement was announced, ratings had briefly slumped, but they had since recovered and even increased slightly. Whenever Teresa and Matthew went out together, she was struck yet again by how many people recognized him. She remembered his embarrassment years before when he had first begun to be noticed and thought about how far from that he had come. Cloaked in a solid, steady confidence, he gave every sign of being very comfortable with himself, his career and his future.

The loss of the baby saddened him, but he was not in any way affected as she had been. Even though she had never felt the child move, it had still been vividly real to her. She had imagined it swimming in the dark silence of her body, its tiny arms and legs fluttering, budlike fingers groping toward the light it was never to reach. Sometimes she woke from dreams in which it spoke to her. The words never lingered yet she felt reproached.

"It wasn't your fault," her doctor told her very firmly when she went in for a checkup. "As sad as it is, these things happen all the time. The best thing you can do for yourself is get pregnant again as soon as possible.''

It wasn't that he was unsympathetic; on the contrary, he had told her that his own wife had suffered two miscarriages before the birth of their first child. When he spoke of those losses, his eyes went to the small plastic cube on his desk that held photos of his family. There was a question in his gaze as though he was searching for the other faces that should have been there.

She thought about what he had said and decided he might be right. Her desire for a child remained as strong as ever. Even when she remembered how sick she had been and realized the same could happen again, the longing did not change. In that way, at least, pregnancy seemed to have something in common with writing. Both wrenched life out of its comfortable path, twisted it into a new, odd shape, and finally—with suitable flourishes—disgorged results that could run the gamut from exhilarating to anguishing.

''I don't see how you can compare the two,'' Matthew insisted when she brought up the subject with him. ''Writing doesn't endanger you.''

She could have made some profound comment about the risks of creative endeavor, but she knew it wouldn't be appropriate. Stamped on his face was the memory of how she had been in the hospital, pale, weak, pulled into herself like an animal that had been tortured. While he had not been able to fully share her grief, the depth of it had not escaped him. Not for anything would he want her to go through that again.

"It won't necessarily happen a second time," she insisted, even though she knew the possibility certainly existed. Three miscarriages, the doctor had told her, before they would consider that she had any real problem.

"I just don't know," Matthew said. "Couldn't we wait a while?"

"I suppose, but—"

"Good. I'd really prefer that. Besides, you're writing again. You don't want to interrupt a book."

That much at least was true, but the way her new novel was going, she had no idea when it might be finished. She had sent an outline to Clare but had yet to hear anything. Although she wondered occasionally what she would do if it was turned down, she didn't let herself dwell on that.

Election night came and went. Teresa cared most about where IBS placed in the ratings. She was thrilled when Matthew and his news team placed first even though CBS beat them by minutes with the prediction that Jimmy Carter had won.

"Who ever heard of a president called Jimmy?" Graham groused a few days later when she dropped by his office. At his suggestion, she had begun doing some reviewing for *The Literary Quarterly*. She approached it with trepidation, concerned that she would never be able to criticize a fellow writer's work. To her surprise, she found that she could bring an objective eye to the efforts of others, perceiving what they had tried to achieve and to what extent they had succeeded. As an unlooked for by-product, reviewing gave her more confidence in her own work, which she suspected had been Graham's intention all along.

"Mandy says he's going to have problems making good in his promises to buck big government. She doesn't think he won by a big enough margin to be able to pull that off."

"It sounds as though she's become very interested in politics since she got out of law school. Do you think she has any thought of going into it for herself?"

"I don't know.... With a little more seasoning, she might be suited to it. Heaven knows, she's telegenic enough."

"Like her mother," Graham agreed. "That's one of the things that used to annoy me most about Alexis—that she refused to rely on her looks."

"You don't really think she should have?"

"No, of course not. But back then I wanted nothing so much as for her to have some weakness, if only to provide less of a contrast to me. Vanity would have been a good one; insecurity would have been even better. Unfortunately, she was immune to both."

"Everyone has weaknesses," Teresa said gently. "Even Alexis."

"It might be more correct to say that she has points of vulnerability. Her son, for instance, and James."

"She loves them."

"That's the catch, isn't it? Did she ever tell you what happened to our mother?"

"No . . . but I've heard rumors."

"She killed herself. Alexis found the body. She was very calm about it, went and called our father at the office. When he got home, she was sitting on a couch with her hands folded in her lap, waiting for him."

"Did you think that meant she didn't care?" Teresa asked, trying to conceal her shock.

"On the contrary. It made me afraid for her. You see, the night after our mother's funeral, I couldn't sleep so I was wandering around in the hallways of that huge stone monstrosity where we lived. I heard her crying in her bed. It was the most tragic sound I've ever encountered. I wanted to go to her and offer some comfort."

"Why didn't you?"

He turned in his chair so that he was facing the window and she was looking at him in profile. There was a slight pouch under his chin and the skin of his throat had the dry, crepe-paper look of age. "Because I knew how much stronger she was than me. At least that was the excuse I used. I suppose deep down inside I was ashamed of feeling more anger than sorrow."

"I'm writing about a character now who loses his wife to cancer and never forgives her for abandoning him, even though he knows perfectly well that she had no choice."

Graham sighed. He turned back to his desk and flicked absently at the corner of a stack of papers. ''Mother had known that only Alexis and the servants were home, and none of the staff went into her quarters unless she rang. She wanted Alexis to find her.''

''What a horrible thing to do to a child.''

''Oh, I don't think she meant it that way. It was as though she trusted Alexis more than anyone, and perhaps also because she wanted her to know the truth, before the discreet cover-up could start, as it inevitably did. The undertaker did a marvelous job; mother really did look as though she was merely sleeping. When I saw her, I felt so . . . cheated. As though there had to be more to death than that. Instead, she seemed about to jump up at any moment, laughing and saying the whole thing had only been a joke.'' His pale-gray eyes met Teresa's. ''Alexis knew better. She had looked straight into the face of death. It could never be a mystery after that.''

Teresa straightened in her chair. The images in her mind were painful ones, of a daughter burdened by knowledge she should not have had and a son left to wonder why it had been withheld from him. Had that been the beginning of the bitterness between them that had led eventually to such a long estrangement?

''You must know,'' she said softly, ''that I think it's time you and Alexis reconciled.''

He placed a pencil in careful alignment with the one next to it, positioning them so that they were exactly parallel. ''When I first contacted you,'' he said without looking up, ''I was convinced that was what I wanted. But since then, I've begun to wonder. It's so much . . . safer this way. Through you, I've come to know all the family, including Alexis. I understand what it's like to love them and be loved in return. Yet it's a secret love—vicarious, I suppose you could say—with none of the risks of the real thing.''

''Are you satisfied with that?''

''I don't know. In retrospect, my life seems to have been a long flight from reality. I have never found it particularly pleasant, yet only very rarely is it truly escapable. For me, in this instance, it is. I keep thinking I should take advantage of that.''

Teresa did not try to dissuade him; the decision was his. Much as she believed he would be making a mistake to go on as he was, she would not try to insist that he do otherwise. She would only hope that over time he would come to reconsider.

After she left Graham, she dropped by Alexis and James's town house to return several books she had borrowed. At that hour, no one was home except the staff. She paused to chat briefly and to admire the several new additions to James's art collection. He had developed a taste for American primitives and was becoming known as something of an authority.

She was leaving just as Jim rounded the corner, walking swiftly despite the stiff-legged gait caused by the prosthesis. He saw her and grinned. ''Hey, I didn't know you were coming over today. Got time for a cup of coffee?''

''Sure, provided I won't be taking you away from your studies.'' She smiled as she gestured at the overloaded book bag slung over his shoulder. ''It looks as though you've brought home half of Columbia's library.''

''I found some great stuff for a paper I'm working on, really gives it a whole new dimension.'' He laughed and held the front door open for her. ''Can you believe me saying a thing like that? If anyone had told me a few years ago that I'd be fascinated by six-teenth-century English literature, I would have suggested the poor jerk get some help.''

''It could be worse,'' she teased. ''You could have decided to specialize in pre-Columbian pot shards or something equally relevant.''

''Hey, listen, that stuff could be very relevant. Everything's part of everything else, after all. It's just one big jigsaw puzzle. Fit in enough of the pieces and we may start to see the picture.''

''When you get a clue, let me know.''

''Oh, I think you've already found a few your-self,'' he said as they reached the den at the back of the house. Jim went off to see about the coffee and came back with a plate of freshly baked shortbread. ''Just something to tide us over.''

''Hmmm, delicious. I think the cook's partial to you. Who else gets stuff like this?''

He settled back on the couch, his leg stretched out in front of him. ''Hey, I'm a sweet guy, haven't I ever told you that?''

She smiled and shook her head. Whenever she was with Jim she had to resist the urge to simply stare at him as though if she watched long enough, the secret of how he had done what he had might be revealed. Somehow in the past few years he had emerged from the numbing darkness he had been locked in when he returned from Vietnam. The man she saw now before her—as tall as Matthew, well built, handsome—might have been a completely different person.

Few vestiges of who he had been before Vietnam remained. There was still the same gentleness but none of the insecurity and bewilderment that had led him down such a dangerous path. All that had been burned away, not in an instant but as though acid had fallen drop by drop on the surface of his soul, slowly eroding it. The results might have been ugly and tragic, but in this case they were anything but. She was reminded of etchings she had seen, their lines carved out by the steady hand of the artist turning what would otherwise have been destructive into an instrument of beauty.

She stayed a while longer talking with him. They hadn't seen each other in several weeks so there was catching up to do. As they chatted, she felt his gentle scrutiny and knew he hadn't asked her to come in simply because he wanted company. He cared about her and needed to be reassured that she was truly healing.

When she compared what she had been through to his own experience, she was embarrassed by her grief. While no one could ever truly gauge the extent of another's suffering, she did not imagine they were equivalent. Yet Jim had never suggested that was so. By his very sympathy, he acknowledged what had happened to her and seemed to imply that for her, too, out of destruction could come creation.

Chapter Thirteen

SHORTLY AFTER JIMMY CARTER'S inauguration, Teresa and Matthew went away on vacation. It was the first trip of any real length they had taken together since their honeymoon; in between there had been only long weekends snatched here and there. For once, Matthew left anything resembling work at home and Teresa did the same. She had reached a natural pause in her new book where she thought it best to let it alone for a while. Over the years she had learned to know the difference between when such pauses were genuinely necessary and when they were simply a means of procrastination. As they headed south toward the Caribbean, she left the book behind with a clear conscience.

They had rented a house in a private enclave on Barbados. It sat on a bluff above the beach, surrounded by high stone walls softened by flowering hibiscus and bougainvillea. Discreet servants saw to their needs. Food and drinks appeared at regular intervals, sand was swept off the tiled floors, the bed was changed and fresh towels laid out. Aside from that, they were left to themselves.

Teresa had been a little nervous about that; later Matthew confessed that he had been, too. For so long they had lived surrounded by distractions. In their absence was a tentativeness that could not be disguised.

At first, they were very polite with each other. "Would you mind if I turned on the radio?" Matthew asked the second day in the house. He had glanced at the only clock, in the kitchen, a moment before and seen that it was almost noon. Someone, somewhere, must be broadcasting news.

"No, of course not," Teresa had assured him. They sat down and listened together to the local station. The big story was about a squabble between the two major political parties. There was no news from the States except a mention of bad weather.

Matthew clicked off the radio with a laugh. "I guess nothing's going on back home."

"It's very wise of everyone to hold off doing anything until you get back," she told him with teasing solemnity. "After all, if you aren't there to report it, it isn't official."

"Brat," he said mildly. "Want to go for a swim?"

The water was crystal clear. Floating in it on their stomachs, they could look down through the scuba masks and see schools of iridescent fish darting back and forth. Occasionally something larger swam by, a dark shadow in the water that they viewed from a respectful distance. The sun was warm on their bodies afterward as they lay on the beach, handfuls of golden sand trickling through their fingers. Behind them, amid the palm trees and fluttering sea grass, doves called softly to one another.

"This isn't too hard to take," Matthew admitted as he stared out over the water. Nothing interrupted his line of vision between the edge of the sea and the horizon. They might have been completely alone in the world. "I could even get used to it."

"I like that," Teresa murmured drowsily, "bring the man to paradise and he admits it isn't too bad."

He laughed and trailed a finger down her bare back. Having confirmed that their privacy was total, neither had felt compelled to bother with a bathing suit. At first, standing naked in the sun and air, Teresa had felt almost unbearably self-conscious. But she had quickly come to savor the sense of special freedom and intimacy it gave, as well as the response it provoked in Matthew.

"Be careful," she told him, "that you don't get sunburned anywhere vital."

"Maybe I need more lotion rubbed on," he told her with a friendly leer.

"Remember what happened last time I did that?"

"Vividly."

So passed that afternoon and a good portion of the night that followed. At dawn, they woke as though by mutual accord and watched the sunrise together, then went back to bed and recreated for themselves the vibrant spectrum of colors that had streaked the sky.

"We have to find some way to do this more often," Matthew said afterward as they sat on the stone patio overlooking the water. "It seems incredible all the time that has gone by without our really getting away together."

"We've been busy," she reminded him gently. The utter peace of her body resonated through her, making her more conscious than ever of how long it had been missing.

He reached out a hand across the small distance separating them and stroked hers lightly. "I'm glad you said 'we,' although to be honest, I know it's mainly my fault."

"There's no fault involved. We're both very ambitious; we want to accomplish so much that there hasn't been time for anything else."

"I've been wondering about that," he said almost to himself. "Maybe it's not a good idea to try to look into the future and imagine what things will be like, but that's what I seem to be doing these days. Sometimes I wonder if it will all have been worthwhile."

"All what? Your work?" Surely he didn't mean their marriage?

"That . . . and other things. I can't help but think that I tend to put off too much, telling myself that I'll get to it eventually. What if eventually never happens?"

"Matthew, I . . ." She sat up on the lounge chair, moving away from his touch. Wrapping her arms around her knees, she said, "I know what you mean; I've felt the same way myself. We both act as though we have all the time in the world when of course we have nothing of the sort.''

He nodded, thinking with something akin to disbelief that he would be thirty-seven in a few months. It seemed only a year or two ago that he had been in his mid-twenties, and little longer than that when he had been a child. Where had all the time gone?

''Maybe we're growing up,'' he suggested with a half smile that didn't quite mask his unease. ''Realizing we aren't immortal must be part of that.''

''And wanting to be, at least in some little way, seems to be, too.''

''What do you mean?'' he asked, though he had a fair idea he knew.

''I'm reluctant to bring it up again, but—''

''A baby?''

She sighed and looked away, out over the water. ''I don't want to wait much longer.''

''Lots of women are having their first children at thirty-five, even older.''

''I may want more than one.''

That hadn't occurred to him. He could barely grapple with the idea of a single child, let alone multiples. ''We've never talked about more. . . .''

''We've barely talked about it at all. You know how we are.''

This time he knew the 'we' was no more than a courtesy. She really meant that he was the one who shied away from personal issues. Worse yet, he couldn't deny it. He had come to realize over the years that her attempts early on in their marriage to get him to open up more had been justified and that he should have tried harder to make them work.

"All right," he said at length. "You don't want to wait any longer, and I guess I don't either. I just pray everything works out this time."

So did she; though it was years since she had last gone to church, she found a reassurance in prayer she had never encountered before. Sometimes she wasn't sure whom she was praying to—herself or some higher being. And sometimes she genuinely didn't know who—or what—was answering. It didn't seem to matter, not so long as the result was a measure of acceptance of whatever might come to pass.

By early summer she was pregnant. Much as she had hoped to conceive again, she nonetheless had an almost superstitious fear of acknowledging that it had happened and put off going to the doctor until a second period was skipped. Even then, after he had confirmed it, she didn't want to think about what was happening inside her.

Telling Matthew was hard. She waited until a weekend when he was home. They had gone for a walk in the park with the dog and, on the way back, started to talk about redecorating the apartment. That seemed as good an opening as any she was likely to get.

"We could use some new furniture, and maybe paint the small room next to your den," she said.

"We've never used that for anything."

"I know." She bent down and scratched the dog behind its ear. Her hair fell over her face. "But we're going to need it next spring."

Silence, then the touch of his hand on her shoulder, so tentatively that she thought she might be imagining it. "Teresa . . . are you sure?"

She nodded, straightening up. "I went to the doctor yesterday."

"I see . . . you're all right?"

"Everything's fine," she assured him with a smile. "I'm a little tired, but I haven't felt anywhere near as sick as I did last time."

"Maybe that's a good sign."

"Maybe." She took his hand and they started out of the park. "Let's not talk about it right now, okay?"

He agreed reluctantly. There were dozens of questions he wanted to ask her, but they were all echoes of the one big question: Would she be all right? Reasonably he knew she would be, even if this child, too, was lost. But reason had nothing to do with what he was feeling. Deep inside him in a hidden part of his soul where he had rarely ventured, he feared for her. Trying to imagine his life without her was impossible. It simply wouldn't be his life.

They agreed not to tell the family yet and events conspired to help them keep that promise. Mandy announced she was getting married to a fellow lawyer in her firm. Having made up her mind, she didn't want a long engagement. Her husband to be, a hardheaded young man from Boston's South Side, agreed. The ceremony took place on a Saturday early in September at the Church of the Transfiguration, where Alexis and James had been married twenty-nine years before.

As he walked down the aisle with his daughter on his arm, James felt a tightness in his chest that for once had nothing to do with his heart condition. He had woken that morning knowing there was something very important about the day but, for an instant, unable to remember what. When it had all come flooding back to him, he had known a mild sense of shock at the idea that he had a daughter old enough to be getting married. It was as though he was being confused with someone else.

Looking at himself in the mirror while he shaved, he thought he could almost glimpse the man staring back at him from behind his own eyes. If he could have spoken, what would the man have said? "Congratulations, sir, that's a lovely daughter you've got?" No, he had never been that polite. Maybe, "Hey, fellow, got any more like her at home?"

He had laughed at that just as Alexis came into the bathroom to remind him that they had to leave for the church soon. For a moment, their glances met in the mirror. Softly, she said, "Yes, it is startling, isn't it?" He nodded and went back to his shaving, concentrating on the simple task rather than looking into his own eyes again.

A reception was held after the ceremony at the Plaza Hotel. At Mandy and Tom's insistence, the guest list had been kept down as far as possible. Nonetheless some five hundred people crowded the ballroom to celebrate the new couple. Among the many notables attending were the governor, three senators, stars from all the major networks, along with men—and a few women—whose faces might mean little to the public but whose names rang loudly in boardrooms across the country.

Winston had come back from his newly built home on Maui to attend the wedding. Several hours after the festivities began, he and James found a quiet corner toward the back of the ballroom.

"You're looking good," James said as they sat down on a couple of gilt and velvet chairs. Actually, he thought the former anchorman looked better than good. Since his retirement, Winston seemed to have shed about ten years. His lean face had filled out a bit, the pouches under his eyes were almost gone and he was tanned and fit.

"I do a few laps in the pool every morning, play a little tennis, get in some writing. It's not a bad way to live."

"That's good to hear," James said. He had a glass of club soda in his hand, but he wasn't drinking it. Hal had mentioned recently that it was high in salt, which he should be avoiding. "When you retired, some of us were a little worried that you might get bored."

"So was I," Winston said with a laugh. "Hell, to be honest, I was scared to death of it. But I figured I wasn't really retiring, not as long as I kept my hand in writing, giving the occasional lecture, that sort of thing. The funny part is I find myself doing more work than I'd ever anticipated."

"I read that book on recent foreign policy you brought out last year. It was about the best I've seen on the subject."

"Thanks. It did well enough to make me want to try my hand at another. But enough about me. How's everything at IBS?"

James shrugged, "About the way you'd expect."

"Still working on the merger?"

He nodded. "It's slow going. The FCC is looking over our shoulders every step of the way. They're insisting we can't do anything that will result in a single network controlling more than one quarter of the total viewing audience in any single market."

"Do you think that's unreasonable?"

"Depends on whether or not a few exceptions can be made. You know as well as I do that there are places out there lucky to be served even by one network. We sold off the affiliates that would have given us half or more of a market; now we're working on getting the number down further."

"What does Alexis think of all this?" Winston asked as he reached inside the breast pocket of his tuxedo for a cigarette, only to remember for perhaps the hundredth time that he had quit the year before.

"That it's the only way for us to go, and I have to admit, she's right. The only alternative is to have at least one of the networks pass out of our hands, at least so far as day-to-day management goes."

"You don't believe Matthew can juggle both of them?"

James shook his head. "He's got a way to go before he can handle even one. Which isn't to say I don't think he's good; he is, but two networks are beyond any person's control. Besides which, even I wouldn't expect the FCC to sit down under that."

"No . . . it would be hard to argue they were really separate companies that just happened to be headed by one man."

"Damn government," James muttered, glowering at his club soda. "Interferes in everything."

Winston raised a hand and beckoned to a passing waiter. "You used to be more of a liberal."

"You mean with Kennedy? At least he had class."

The waiter took Winston's order for a Scotch and water, made sure James wasn't ready for a refill and departed.

"Carter fascinates me," Winston said. "I keep trying to figure out if he really believes what he's saying."

"Isn't that the trick with any politician?"

"Certainly, but I've never been so perplexed before. On the one hand, I see a man who appears genuinely intelligent, even brilliant. On the other, there's a degree of naïveté that simply stuns me. I have a bad feeling we're headed for trouble.''

James shrugged and eased his tie away from his collar. "When have we not been?"

"True, but there's a good side to that. After all, if all hell didn't break loose regularly, what would we put on the air at 7:00 P.M. every night?"

"I can just see it now," James said with a chuckle. "Devoted viewers are gathered in living rooms across America, roll intro, cut to Matthew looking appropriately serious, and Matthew says, 'Sorry, folks, there's no news tonight, so here's a lineup of your favorite commercials instead.' It'd be great. Chances are at least half the country would never notice."

"Remember when Agnew was trying to get us to put on 'good' news? A couple of radio stations actually tried that until they found out nobody was listening." Winston spoke lightly, but his thoughts were more serious. Beneath their banter, he sensed a weariness in James he had not felt before. Weariness and something more, pessimism that seemed so unlike him as to make Winston think he must be imagining it.

"It's funny," James said, "all that stuff with Ford, Nixon, and the rest of them, seems to have happened a long time ago, but things that really did take place decades ago seem much more recent."

"I know what you mean. Sometimes when I think that it's been more than thirty years since the war ended, I can hardly believe it."

"Plenty of kids growing up today don't know what you mean when you say 'the war.' And who can blame them; they've had a couple more since."

Out on the dance floor, Mandy and Tom were waltzing. She had learned how years ago as part of the upbringing considered proper for a young woman of her class. He had hastily mastered the rudiments the week before but seemed to be making a pretty good job of it.

"What do you think of your son-in-law?" Winston asked.

"I don't really know him yet, but he seems all right. At least Mandy's settling down. Say, did I tell you Jim brought a lady friend over the other night?"

"Somebody from college?"

"You could say that. She teaches medieval literature. Her name's Charlotte something-or-other. I think she's a couple of years older than him. Has a good sense of humor, easy to look at, too. I liked her."

Winston smiled inwardly. That was high praise from James who, so far as he knew, had never before approved of any of Jim's friends. Of course, there had been good reasons for that, which thankfully no longer existed. "Is there any chance Jim might get involved in the business at some point?"

"I don't know...we've never talked about it. Frankly, I'm reluctant to do anything that might put pressure on him. He's had more than enough as it is."

"Still, it could happen. Or Mandy might come in. How do you think Matthew would take to that?"

"Good question," James said thoughtfully. "He takes after me in some ways; likes to run his own show."

They sat in silence for a few moments, watching the dancers. Winston affected not to notice when James slid a small pill from his watch pocket and swallowed it. Out on the floor, Alexis was dancing with Tom, while Anthony was doing the honors with Mandy.

"I suppose I should get back to it," James said.

Winston cast him a quick look. "It'll be winding down soon. I'd just relax if I were you."

James was ready enough to accept the suggestion. Beneath his evening clothes, his skin felt clammy. His hand, when he lifted it to brush aside a stray lock of hair, shook slightly.

Winston hesitated. He didn't want to overstep himself, yet he could not forget that he and James shared a rather special relationship. They both loved the same woman; the fact that she had long ago chosen James over him did not change that. "Look...it's undoubtedly none of my business, but have you seen a doctor?"

James's mouth tightened. For a moment Winston didn't think he intended to answer. Finally, reluctantly, he said, "I see one regularly. A heart man. He's doing everything he can." In answer to Winston's unspoken question, he added, "Alexis doesn't know."

"Are you sure?"

"No...perhaps...Let's put it this way, she hasn't said anything."

"Don't you think you should talk with her about it?"

James sighed deeply. He rubbed the bridge of his nose tiredly. "If you were me, would you tell her?"

"We're very different in some ways. I wouldn't be able to keep it from her."

"Because you'd want her help?" When Winston nodded, he went on, "But she can't help, not really, though she'd certainly try. All that would happen is that she'd end up feeling helpless. I'm determined to avoid that."

"There are things that can be done. The proper diet—"

"I've already taken care of all that. What can be done, has been. For the rest, I just have to wait and see what happens." As he spoke, he wondered why he was trusting Winston to keep his secret. In part it was because he knew the other man would never do anything to hurt Alexis. But beneath that was another reason. He was alerting him to the fact that she might suddenly need someone to lean on.

"You put me in a quandary," Winston said, a wry smile twisting his mouth.

"How so?"

"I'm a nice enough guy to want to see you recover fully and live to a ripe old age. But I'm human enough to at least wonder what it would be like if you didn't."

Far from being offended, James laughed. "You're frank, at least, I'll give you that. I never could stand people who said one thing and meant another."

"Too complicated," Winston agreed. "Life's tough enough without messing it up with a lot of fakery."

"If you had to come out here suddenly...how long would it take?"

"Start to finish, not more than twenty hours or so." He smiled suddenly. "Of course, I won't count on it. Stubborn as you are, you'll probably outlive us all."

Though he knew Winston was deliberately trying to lighten his mood, and appreciated that, he could not quite manage it. Softly, he said, "Never that. I haven't the courage for it."

IN THE AFTERMATH of Mandy's wedding and his discussion with Winston, James made the decision to offer Matthew a position as vice president of IBS. The new job would mean leaving his job as anchorman, and one of the reasons James had put off discussing it with him was his fear that Matthew might turn him down.

Few men could command the attention of the American public as he now did; his evening news broadcast regularly vied for first place with Walter Cronkite's. Between the two of them, viewers had a clear choice—the older, wise father figure, or the young, sincere son they might all wish they had. Preference split about evenly.

Now James would be asking him to give that up and instead accept the relative anonymity of the executive suite. Though he believed Matthew would want the position eventually, he wasn't at all sure that he was ready to accept it. And if he was not, what then? The special need that had driven him to confide his condition to Winston did not extend to Matthew. Pride, above all, forbade him from being completely honest with his son.

Shortly before Labor Day, they got together at James's invitation in a private dining room on the top floor of IBS headquarters. The room, furnished as a similar accommodation in a very affluent household, had floor-to-ceiling windows commanding a view of the East River and beyond it Brooklyn and Queens. On any given day, a dozen or so executives and guests would have been enjoying that view as they sipped their preluncheon drinks and chatted amiably. But on this particular day, there was only Matthew and James.

"Tomato juice," James said to the waitress who came to take his drink order. Matthew felt the sudden need for something stronger. His father looked particularly grim, and he wondered again at the purpose of the meeting. In an effort to get him to divulge it, he asked, "Everything proceeding all right with the merger?"

"Fine," James said, which revealed precisely nothing. "How are things at home?"

"Fine. Teresa sends her love."

"Is she feeling all right?" In the aftermath of Mandy and Tom's wedding, the family had finally been told about Teresa's pregnancy. As expected, they were apprehensive, but they were also all being careful not to add to the pressure with their worries.

Matthew nodded. "You know she's had a lot less trouble this time, but even that seems to have passed. She's really glowing."

"Good, that's how it should be. I hope she's taking care of herself."

"She doesn't have much choice. I keep a close eye on her."

The waitress arrived with their drinks. James ignored his; Matthew took a swallow of a fairly decent white wine. "I haven't been up here in a while. Still have the same chef?"

James nodded. "François what's-his-name. Seems to do a pretty good job."

If Matthew remembered correctly, the gentleman in question had run the kitchen of a five-star restaurant before being lured away to IBS. There had been a time when James cared about such things, but apparently no longer.

They chatted about nothing in particular as they sat down to lunch. The indirection of their talk made

Matthew apprehensive. It wasn't like his father to engage in pointless conversation. Still, he knew it would do no good to try to rush him into explaining what was on his mind. Matthew knew only one person more stubborn than himself and he was sitting across the table from him.

"I saw last week's ratings right before I came up here," James said at length. "You're number one again."

Matthew laughed a little self-consciously. "I never feel really good about beating Uncle Walter. But I'm always consoled by the likelihood that by next week he'll be back on top again."

"You like the contest though, don't you? The striving to be the best. In a way I envy you. You're in one of the few lines of work where you really know, almost moment to moment, how well you're doing."

"That brings its own kind of pressure."

"I suppose. What I'm trying to say is that in my position, for example, things are different."

Matthew frowned. What was his father getting at? He waited, pretending interest in the fileted fish.

"I've gotten the impression," James said finally, "that you would like more responsibility here at the network."

"I've hardly made a secret of it." His throat was tight. Was this the moment he had sometimes feared would never come? Now that it might suddenly be upon him, he felt a rare sense of uncertainty as he wondered how he would respond.

"You realize responsibility has a price?" James asked.

"Doesn't everything?"

"Maybe. To lay it out, I'm offering to make you vice president of programming, reporting directly to me and overseeing day-to-day management of the news, sports and entertainment divisions. Since you've had experience in two of the three, I think you'll fit in fairly easily. I've talked with Dom and he'll give you all the help he can."

"About Dom, do you get any feeling that he thinks he should have been considered for the job himself?" Matthew genuinely wanted the answer to that, but he also asked it simply to buy himself time as he struggled to assimilate his father's announcement.

"Are you kidding? He's got too much sense. You may wish you did, too, before very long. That is…if you take the job."

"And give up the anchor?"

"That's it."

Now that the choice was his to make, Matthew was surprised to discover how difficult it was. He had wanted this for so long; why should he hesitate now? Yet he did, because he sensed there was something more than what his father was telling him. "Why now?" he asked. "Why are you suddenly offering me this?"

"It isn't sudden," James countered. "We've been heading toward this for years; you know that."

"I never felt any assurance that you would acknowledge it."

"So now I am. What's the problem?"

"No problem. I just want to know where I stand.
You're telling me that you'll give me day-to-day control of everything except finance and operations?"

"Those are Anthony's areas."

"I know that, and I'm just as happy to stay out of
them. But where does that leave you?"

"You'll report to me."

"That can mean a lot of things."

"In this case, it means exactly what it says. I
expect to be kept fully informed of everything you
do."

"That sounds as though you'll be second-guessing
me."

"Only," his father told him succinctly, "if you
screw up."

Matthew didn't comment on that. Instead, he said,
"You realize none of this can happen until we find a
new anchorman."

"I'll leave that to you."

Finding a replacement for himself proved harder
than Matthew had anticipated. It wasn't that he
thought so highly of his own abilities as to believe no
one could match them, rather that during his tenure
in the job he had—despite the high ratings—come to
know his own deficiencies and wanted to avoid du-
plicating them. What he hoped to find was someone
who had his strengths without his weaknesses.

As though that weren't difficult enough, he had to contend with his mixed feelings about leaving the news division. He had been a reporter for some fifteen years and had grown used to living at the center of events. He would miss that, even though he knew he would only be giving up one kind of power for another that, in the long run, might well prove to be far greater.

Teresa's reaction to his father's decision surprised him; she seemed to have expected it. When he tried to get her to explain why, she said only that since James was no longer a young man, it was natural for him to begin preparing for retirement. Matthew supposed she was right, yet he still found it hard to believe that his father would willingly put himself out to pasture.

Throughout that fall and into early winter, Matthew watched innumerable hours of videotapes featuring anchormen from stations around the country. He began by concentrating on the IBS and UBC affiliates, figuring that it might be best to try to find someone already within one or the other organization. Several possibilities were identified this way, but none really excited him.

"I think I've got a clear enough idea of what I'm looking for," he told Anthony when the two of them discussed the search. "That's not the problem. The difficulty arises in finding someone who's similar enough to me to hold the audience we've already got but different enough to firmly establish his own identity. The last thing I want is a replacement who comes across as a copy instead of an original.''

''That makes sense,'' Anthony agreed, ''but don't lose sight of the fact that as far as the affiliates go, there's no arguing with success. They like what you've accomplished and they're going to be upset enough that you're moving on. If they get the idea that we're tampering with a winning formula, we'll never hear the end of it.''

''We may have to put up with that because the more tape I look at, the more I like an idea I've been kicking around for a while now.''

Anthony sat back in his chair, prepared to listen. ''What's that?''

''An anchor team consisting of a man and a woman. It would set us apart from everyone else and give us a degree of balance that's long overdue.''

''I don't know,'' Anthony said slowly. ''While it's true women are more accepted now as correspondents and on the morning shows, I'm not sure the public will go for one in the evening slot.''

''It would be a risk; I don't deny that. But I think we should take it.''

''Have you talked with James about this?''

Matthew shook his head. ''Not yet. We're meeting this afternoon.''

''Let me know what happens. If the two of you decide to pursue it, I'll do whatever I can to keep the affiliates in line.''

Matthew appreciated that, just as he appreciated James's willingness to at least give the idea a chance.

"I'd like to see who you have in mind for the team," he said after hearing him out. "We could try a few run-throughs in the studio, get something on tape and see how the chemistry works."

The "chemistry"—how the members of the team interacted with each other—would be all important. If one or both were overburdened with ego and disinclined to share the spotlight, the results could be disastrous. Even before drawing up his final list of possibilities, Matthew had decided that whoever ended up being picked, both would have to be paid exactly the same and in all other ways treated as complete equals. That further narrowed the list at least in so far as the men were concerned; only those candidates who seemed likely to be able to accept a woman on such terms survived the next to last cut.

Early in January, 1978, a little-used IBS studio on the West Side became the scene of trial run-throughs conducted under tight wraps. Candidates were smuggled in and out of New York by private jet, lodged at hotels under false names. No unauthorized personnel were allowed anywhere near them. Every possible precaution was taken to prevent leaks to the media, the other networks and the affiliates.

The strategy worked; by March, as Teresa's thoughts turned to decorating the nursery, Matthew was ready to accept the position that would make him second-in-command to his father and prepare the way for his eventual succession.

Chapter Fourteen

TERESA AND MATTHEW'S SON was born early in the morning of April 3. He arrived in the world with an outraged scream but settled down quickly when he was laid at his bemused mother's breast. Teresa had been fully conscious throughout the birth, with Matthew at her side. Her labor had lasted about ten hours and had been a little easier than she had anticipated. Or so it seemed once she saw the results.

The small body and already evident personality of her son astounded her. Nothing she had read or seen had prepared her for the reality of him. He was so complete, so perfect, and he had come from her. The sense of achievement she felt was as exhilarating as any she had experienced with her writing, yet it was leavened by awe at the nature of the mystery in which she had been almost an unwitting participant. It was as though through him she glimpsed a tiny corner of a vastness so immense as to defy all comprehension.

On a more mundane level, William Joseph Callahan lost no time establishing his priorities. He required a perpetually full stomach and a constantly dry diaper. Given those, he was the picture of benign contentment; without them he was, as even his doting grandparents admitted, horrendous. When his eyes screwed up shut, his tiny fists flailed and his rosebud mouth opened to emit an outraged bellow, he somehow managed to project not an image of infantile dependence but of tyranny personified.

"I've never heard anything like this," Matthew said the fourth night after they brought William—no one had yet dared to refer to him by a diminutive—home.

"The doctor did say he had a remarkable pair of lungs," Teresa mumbled. It was 4:00 A.M. William was nursing greedily, as he had at 2:00 A.M., midnight, 10:00 P.M. and so on. Every two hours, so regularly that clocks could be set by him, he demanded to be fed. The process took about forty-five minutes, after which he deigned to sleep, briefly, before the cycle resumed.

Teresa had lost track of what it felt like to be rested; she existed in a numbing cloud of weariness where the only reality was her son's demands. Matthew did his best to help, but so long as she was breast-feeding, there was relatively little he could do except offer moral support.

"This can't go on much longer," he said when she had returned the baby to his crib and they were trudging back to bed.

"Don't be so sure. I've heard of babies who were several months old before they slept through the night."

"Months? That's not possible. No one could survive it."

"I think you may be right." She stifled a yawn and
slid under the sheets. Her body was still sore but the
sheer pleasure of an almost flat stomach made up for
a lot, or at least it would have if she had been alert
enough to enjoy it.

"I don't know what we've got that baby nurse
for," Matthew muttered. "She's the only one in this
apartment who's sleeping through the night. Although how she manages it with the racket he puts
up . . ."

"Ear plugs. I checked."

"Smart. I don't suppose we could . . . ?"

They looked at each other and shook their heads
regretfully. Teresa curled down at Matthew's side.
He put an arm around her shoulders. Moments later
they were both asleep, until the next summons from
the tiny despot.

Bathing her son the following day, under the careful eye of the nurse, Teresa was struck by how quickly
he had come to identify her touch apart from all others. She had only to pick him up for him to respond
instantly in a way he did for no one else. At the mere
sound of her voice, he opened his eyes. When she
smiled, he smiled back, never mind what anyone said
about it being only gas. If she put him down before
he thought she should, he cried as though heartbro-
ken.

The effect was at once highly gratifying and astonishing. She was vividly aware of being part of a
vast stream of women encompassing the entire world

and stretching far back in time, who had felt the same responses, done the same things, experienced the same awe.

Once she would have resented being lumped together with so many others, seemingly stripped of her individuality; but now she found a certain comfort in the experience, if only because it kept her from feeling completely overwhelmed. What those other women had accomplished, she could, too—given a minor miracle.

About a month before William's birth, Teresa had finished her latest novel and mailed it off to her agent. As the full burden of her pregnancy made itself felt, she had put all thoughts of the book out of her mind. When, shortly after William's one-month birthday, Clare Danvers called to say she was about to make an offer, Teresa was too tired to muster more than mild pleasure.

She vaguely remembered Clare saying something about changes at the publishing house that she believed would be to Teresa's benefit, but that was a bit too complicated to focus on. The advance offered for the book did register with her, if only because it was significantly larger than any she had been paid before, but even that did not jar her out of her utter absorption with motherhood.

On a bright, sun-filled day in May, William was christened at the church Anthony and Maggie attended. Mandy and Tom were his godparents. Jim was there with Charlotte; they were sharing an apartment near Columbia and had announced their intention to marry eventually.

Teresa's brothers—Tony, Jr. and Joe—were both on hand. Tony's wife of three months, Irene, was with him. Joe had recently broken up with the girl he'd been seeing, to his family's secret relief, and was talking about starting his own business, something in computers.

Maria Gargano was on hand, as were Elizabeth and Will Lawrence who had come up from Virginia. Both elderly now, they traveled little but had been unwilling to miss seeing their first great-grandchild.

To Teresa's mingled frustration and pride, William behaved perfectly throughout the entire ceremony and the party afterward, effectively quashing any bid she might have made for sympathy. She couldn't really mind though because lately he had been showing some compassion. He had taken to sleeping four or five hours at a time, allowing his frazzled mother to get some desperately needed rest. Slowly she was beginning to rediscover what it felt like not to be continually exhausted.

"He really is a good baby," she went so far as to say one evening shortly after the christening as she and Matthew strolled along Central Park West. He was pushing the carriage, in which William gurgled contentedly. She had charge of the dog, who adored the latest human to enter its world and had to be forcibly prevented from jumping into the carriage with him.

Matthew, loving father though he was, was not fooled for a moment by William's placid demeanor. "Good compared to whom," he asked, smiling down at his son, "Attila the Hun?"

"Do you hear what your father's saying about you, sweetheart?"

William smiled tolerantly. In the weeks since his birth, he had filled out quite a bit. His rosy cheeks were now plump, his elbows and knees dimpled. The dark down he had been born with was gone and the hair that replaced it looked as though it would be the same brownish gold as Matthew's. Like all babies', his eyes were blue but Teresa thought she could see hints of hazel. Long discussions about whom he took after had led to the conclusion that he resembled no one so much as himself.

That impression strengthened as spring gave way to summer. The baby nurse left and Teresa, with some trepidation, hired a comfortable Nicaraguan woman to whom William took without demur, perhaps because she swiftly gave him to understand that though he was undoubtedly an extremely impressive baby, he had nothing she hadn't seen plenty of times before.

Though Teresa was still nursing, she could now be away from him for several hours at a time without hearing his lusty protests resounding throughout the apartment. Seated at her desk looking out over the park, she slowly began to write again, not with any clear plan in mind but with a sense that one would eventually emerge.

She was following the trail of a promising idea on a warm afternoon in mid-September when the ringing phone abruptly shattered her concentration.

HAL LANDIS had recently put James on a new drug in the hopes that it would stem the arterial blockage that was responsible for his eroding health. At first there had been some indications that the medication was working, but that did not last long and in its aftermath James experienced increased difficulties.

"We've reached the point where surgery has to be considered," Hal had said during James's last visit. "You've been incredibly lucky not to have had a heart attack by now. I attribute that mainly to the changes you made in your diet and just generally taking better care of yourself, but I'm not sure how much longer that will be enough. The blockage is definitely becoming more severe. Sooner or later, it's going to kill you."

Nothing he said surprised James. He had been aware for quite a while of the signals his body was sending him, telling him that time was running out. As Hal said, he had been lucky, but no one could count on luck to last forever. "What are you recommending?" he asked calmly.

"Bypass surgery to remove the damaged artery and replace it with a graft. The procedure has been done countless times by now and the success rate is very high.''

''I'll think about it.''

Hal hesitated a moment, then nodded. ''All right, just don't take too long.''

James didn't really need to be told that. He understood the urgency of the situation only too well, but that didn't mean he was willing to be rushed into anything. Even before Hal had brought up the possibility of bypass surgery, he had checked the procedure out for himself and agreed the chances looked good. But even under the best circumstances there was always some possibility that the odds would work against him. Before he took so irrevocable a step, he wanted to make sure no loose ends were tangling.

Plans were almost complete for the merger of UBC and IBS into a new network to be known as the United Broadcasting System (UBS). James would be chief executive officer of the new firm and Alexis would serve as president. Anthony would continue to direct finance and operations, while Matthew ran news, sports and entertainment.

Shortly after Labor Day the heads of all the affiliate stations that would make up the new network were flown into New York for a week of what James referred to as ''pep rallies and cat parties.'' They went away reassured that their profits were not threatened by the merger; on the contrary, they stood to make more money than ever. Whether that would actually turn out to be the case remained to be seen, but at least any tendency to jump ship at so critical a point had been minimized.

Throughout the long days spent with the affiliate heads, James knew that his condition was steadily worsening, but he was confident that no one watching him could tell except for the one person who knew him better than he knew himself. Soon he would have to talk honestly with Alexis, but that had to wait until the crucial affiliates' meeting ended.

It did so on a Friday afternoon; James had an appointment with Hal Landis immediately afterward. The results of the examination were not good. ''You're walking a tightrope,'' Hal told him, ''and I've got news for you, buddy, the net's shot full of holes.''

''I'm not arguing,'' James said. ''How soon can you schedule the surgery?''

''I'll give you the weekend to straighten out any family matters. Check into the hospital Monday and we'll do it the following day.''

That was sooner than James had expected, but he was just as glad there would be little time to dwell on what might happen. He went home intending to tell Alexis, but he did not get the chance.

TERESA PICKED UP the phone absently, her mind still on the sentence she had just written.

''Hello . . . ?''

''It's me,'' Matthew said. ''I just got a call from Alexis. Dad's in the hospital.''

Her hand tightened on the receiver. "What happened?"

"I'm not sure yet. He was on the way home in a cab and had some kind of attack. The driver had the presence of mind to rush him to the emergency room at Lenox Hill. Alexis is there now with him."

Though Matthew spoke quietly, Teresa did not mistake his feelings. Beyond the simple fact that he loved his father, he must be stunned by the abrupt realization that James was not, after all, the indomitable figure he had always appeared. Gently, she said, "Juana will stay with William. I'll meet you at the hospital."

He agreed and hung up a moment later. She spoke briefly to the nursemaid, explained what had happened, accepted her sympathy and called downstairs to ask the doorman to get her a cab. It was there by the time she reached the lobby.

James was in the intensive care unit; Alexis sat in a small room outside, speaking with Hal Landis. He had just come from examining James and was very worried by his condition.

"What happened to him was as close as it's possible to come to a heart attack and not actually go through it. Even as careful as we're being, there's no guarantee it won't happen at any moment and, if it does, we may not be able to save him. I'm sorry to have to lay it out so bluntly for you, but if he doesn't have immediate surgery, I can't be responsible for his life."

Alexis sat with her hands folded in her lap, her ankles placed neatly together. At a quick glance, she seemed perfectly composed. Only a closer look revealed that her entire body was trembling, set into motion by the resonance of fear so profound as to be barely endurable. "Will the surgery save him?" she asked, her voice so low that Hal had to lean forward to hear her.

"I don't know," he said honestly. "There's a good chance, but no guarantees. All I can tell you for certain is that without the bypass, he may not make it through the night."

"Then there's no choice, is there? It has to be done."

By the time Matthew arrived, Alexis had signed the consent forms and James was being prepped for surgery. Hal spoke briefly with them both before going in to scrub. He would be assisted by two of the top cardiac specialists in the city but, as he had said, there still were no guarantees.

Teresa reached the hospital shortly after Matthew. She met Mandy by the elevators and they went up together. "I can hardly believe this is happening," the younger woman murmured. "Dad's always seemed so . . . invulnerable."

"He'll be all right," Teresa said, though she was far from feeling so confident. She could not think of her father-in-law dying, yet she feared that possibility might be all too real. The sight of Alexis's ashen face confirmed that.

"How is he?" she asked quietly as she took the seat
next to Matthew. Mandy sat on the other side, holding her mother's hand.

Briefly, Matthew explained what had happened
and what was going on at the moment. "Dr. Landis
said the surgery could take as much as ten hours.
He'll be down to talk with us as soon as it's done."

Throughout the afternoon and into the evening,
more people arrived. Anthony and Maggie came
from the island; Jim and Charlotte came down from
Morningside Heights. No one spoke very much, but
there was comfort in simply being together.

At dinnertime, Alexis insisted they have something to eat, though she refused to do so herself. A
member of the hospital's public relations staff arranged for sandwiches, soup and coffee to be brought
in. A waiting room had been set aside strictly for their
own use and every other possible courtesy was being
extended.

Still nothing could speed up the slow passage of the
hours or ease the fear that weighed down on them all.
Different ways were found to deal with it. Jim and
Mandy sat in a corner talking quietly together while
Tom and Charlotte got acquainted. Maggie and Anthony stayed close to Alexis, doing their best to keep
her mind on other things even though they knew that
wasn't really possible.

Matthew moved restlessly from one group to the
other, unable to settle anywhere for very long. Teresa had to leave briefly to go home and feed Wil-

liam. When she returned, Matthew drew her to his side.

"How is he?" he asked.

"Fine. He was sleeping when I left."

"He's not giving Juana any trouble?"

Teresa shook her head. "She swears he's a little angel."

"That woman's a born diplomat." His eyes went again to the clock. "It's taking so damn long."

"The doctor said it would."

"That can't be a good sign." He spoke very softly so that no one else could hear, but the drum-tight tension in his voice was unmistakable.

"You don't know that," Teresa insisted, squeezing his hand. "James is a very strong man."

"But still a man . . . If only he'd told me he was sick. I've been thinking about this, and I can't believe he didn't have some warning."

"Perhaps asking you to take on more responsibility was his way of telling you."

"He could have been more open," Matthew insisted. "It wouldn't have cost him anything."

Teresa didn't comment on the irony of his expecting his father to behave any differently from the way he himself would have had their positions been reversed. She knew Matthew was too intelligent not to be aware of his inconsistency. For the first time, he was personally experiencing the repercussions of such stubborn self-containment.

"Do you think Alexis knew?" he asked after a moment.

Teresa cast a quick look at her mother-in-law. She was reminded of how Graham had described Alexis's apparent calm in the aftermath of discovering her mother's body; it had made him afraid for her. Now Teresa felt the same way. "She knew, though I don't imagine James told her, at least not directly."

"It makes no sense to have kept something like that to himself." A note of anger crept into his voice. "He wasn't being fair."

"No, he wasn't. But he was certainly doing what he thought was best." She had to stop herself from saying anything more. Now was not the time to comment on the dangerous pride of men that made them so afraid of ever being perceived as anything less than strong and whole.

Her gaze met Jim's across the room. Of all of them there, he knew best what his father had faced and would continue to face if he survived. She wished he and Matthew were closer, that he might help his brother to understand and accept.

Hal Landis came down from surgery about an hour later. All conversation ceased the moment he entered the room as everyone's attention focused on him. He looked tired and worn, but he managed a smile as he directed his comments to Alexis but somehow managed to include them all. "I've got to hand it to James. He's either too tough to die or too stubborn, and at this point I don't much care which it is.''

There was an instant of silence as this news was assimilated, then Jim spoke what each of them was feeling as he said softly, ''Thank God.''

Alexis had sagged in her chair. All the courage and strength that had kept her going was used up. She could only nod silently when Hal told her she would be able to see James in the recovery room, but for no more than a few minutes and she would have to be alone.

''I'll go in with you, of course, but the rest will have to wait here. There would be no point to your seeing him anyway. He won't know anything that's going on before tomorrow afternoon at the soonest.''

Alexis supposed that might be the case, but that could not prevent her from feeling that James was somehow aware of her presence as she stood beside his bed, holding his hand tightly in hers.

He was very pale and the skin beneath his eyes looked bruised. There were red marks on the sides of his face that she supposed must have come from an oxygen mask. His lips were chapped and dry. A tube ran into his nose, another into his arm. Above the sheet, she could see the beginnings of the bandage that appeared to swathe his entire chest.

A nurse stood at the other side of the bed. She smiled reassuringly. ''He's doing fine, Mrs. Callahan. All his vital signs are strong.''

"He tolerated the surgery very well," Hal assured her. He saw no reason to mention that there had been a few moments as James was being taken off the pump that had kept his blood circulating during the most critical phase of the surgery when it had looked as though his heart might not start again. When it had, Hal had experienced a rush of relief as profound as any he had ever known.

Alexis nodded, though she had barely heard either of them. All her attention was concentrated on James. He looked so helpless lying there, all his great strength and energy unnaturally quiescent. It was almost as though he wasn't there at all, as if only the shell of him was left. She had to forcibly remind herself that was not the case. James was there, and for that she had the surgery to thank. If it had also exacted a high price, they would both simply have to accept that.

But in fact, as James slowly recovered, it became clear that the price had actually been very small. Though he refused to acknowledge it, his convalescence was briefer than usual as he experienced relatively few of the debilitating side effects possible after such major surgery. "When I said he was either too tough or too stubborn to die," Hal muttered one afternoon early in October, "I forgot to add that he might just be too damned mean. I've had some bad patients in my time, but he takes the cake."

"I couldn't agree more," Alexis said serenely. They were sitting in the living room of the town house where she had asked Hal to join her after examining James. After ten days in the hospital he had threatened to check himself out if Hal didn't agree to his release. The compromise the two men had reached, after a raging argument conducted at the top of their lungs, had meant James got his way but only if he followed the doctor's orders to rest at home, take his medication and have no contact with the office. That last part in particular was causing no end of trouble.

"He thinks as long as he doesn't actually go into the office, he's following my instructions," Hal groused as he sat down on the couch. "Half a dozen phone calls a day are supposed to be fine."

"That's nothing," Alexis said, pouring them each a cup of tea. "I go in for several hours each morning and promptly get interrogated the moment I get back."

"You shouldn't tell him anything. Maybe after a while, he'll give up."

"James, give up? Are we talking about the same person? He'll never admit that he wasn't completely recovered the moment he got off the operating table. In fact, I think he's busy forgetting he was ever sick to start with."

"Damn idiot," Hal muttered, not unkindly. "Of course, I can't deny he's making an excellent recovery."

"That being the case, perhaps we should let him go on as he is, provided, of course, that he doesn't try to do anything really outlandish."

"Like what?" Hal asked warily. He had come to know Alexis a good deal better in the past few weeks and greatly admired her. Not only did he consider her a remarkably attractive woman, he was by no means oblivious to the intelligence and strength that made her the only person capable of exerting any control whatsoever over James.

"I hesitate to even guess what he might be capable of at this point," she said matter-of-factly. "But I do know he's thinking about making a tour of the Orient sometime soon."

Hal put his teacup down. "How soon?"

"I believe he said something about next month."

"That's absolutely impossible."

"You and I know that, and I suspect James does, too, somewhere deep inside. The trick is getting him to admit it without making him think he's going to have to lead a very limited life from now on. That would be completely intolerable to him."

"It also wouldn't be true. The surgery was a great success. I don't mind admitting he had the benefit of some of the best work I've ever done. He'll have to accept very few restrictions in the future, nothing more onerous than staying on some of the medication he's taking now and sticking to the diet he's been on for years anyway. As far as other things go . . ." He broke off, slightly embarrassed even though he had discussed such matters hundreds of times before.

Alexis graciously helped him out. "James is concerned about our sex life. It's always been very important to us. If he thought the surgery had disabled him in that regard, I'm not sure he would really want to recover."

"The surgery. . . ?" Hal repeated. He hesitated a moment, then asked, "Are you telling me that there was no interruption in your. . . uh . . . marital relations until he had that attack in the cab?"

Alexis nodded. "Rather remarkable, I suppose, in light of his condition. That more than anything made me wonder sometimes if my suspicions about his health might be unfounded. He has incredible willpower and lets very little get in the way of what he wants to do."

Hal shook his head admiringly. "All I can say is that for all his orneriness, he's the kind of patient who makes a doctor look good. Tell him if he'll just take it easy for a few more weeks, he won't be disappointed with the results. As for the trip, there's no reason why you can't make it, but not for a few more months. At least let me feel needed that long."

"We both deeply appreciate all you've done," Alexis said as she walked with him to the door. "If James is a little lax about showing his gratitude, it's only because he hasn't quite accepted what happened. But he will," she added. "I'll make sure of that."

The doctor left smiling. He might almost have felt a twinge of sympathy for the indomitable man lying upstairs, if he hadn't thought him so extremely fortunate in his choice of wife.

Alexis returned to the living room after he had gone. She wanted James to sleep and knew that if she went to him, he would stay awake, insisting that she tell him everything Hal had said and then arguing with all of it. The immense relief she had felt at his survival was giving way slowly to a determination to make the most of the new chance they had been given.

Always before their lives had been dominated by work, both his and hers. That was how they had each wanted it, and she had no regrets, but now she wanted something different. She had reached the point where the power she had striven so hard to achieve as the only woman president of a television network no longer seemed so important. She was ready to move on to a new stage of life where more personal objectives held sway.

She needed to gather up the wisdom gained over the years and make some sense of all she had learned. She felt the urge to begin putting things in order, placing them in neat bundles, returning borrowed items and reclaiming her own, almost as though she was starting to close a house up for the winter. Before the cold wind blew, she wanted James and herself to be settled well within each other, so that they could never truly be parted.

Standing at the tall window, gazing out at the soft evening shadows falling over the city, she breathed a silent prayer of thanks for the second chance they had been given and a promise that it would not be allowed to go to waste.

Chapter Fifteen

FOR MATTHEW, the months when his father and Alexis were touring the Far East were a time of personal testing and discovery. In their absence, he learned how much he had been unconsciously counting on them to help him should he encounter problems he did not know how to solve.

While his experience in the news and sports divisions and the stature he had earned during his time as anchorman proved to be great assets, they could not completely disguise the fact that he had moved up to an entirely new level of responsibility and authority.

Whereas before his only concern had been to report the news accurately and objectively, he now faced far more complex situations. Numerous conflicting forces had to be kept in balance. The demands of sponsors had to be weighed against the expectations of viewers. Special interest groups from the government to self-appointed gadflies had to be kept, if not placated, at least soothed. Union leaders, affiliate heads, stars, writers, directors, producers, all found their way to his office.

There were days when he felt as though if he had to listen to one more person's dissatisfactions, demands or advice, he would walk out and never return. How, he wondered, had his father and Alexis ever stood it? Only gradually did he begin to get his bearings and to realize that there was a brighter side to the situation.

Whatever problems his position as vice president might entail—and they were legion—the fact remained that he had an immense amount of power. So much that it was difficult for him to grasp. With his father and Alexis away, more and more decisions were made on his say-so. Certainly he consulted with Anthony, without whom he doubted he would have been able to navigate the rocky shoals of finance and operations, but in the end it was still his word that determined how millions of dollars would be spent and millions of viewers hopefully wooed.

''You've got a knack for this,'' Anthony reassured him one evening late in March when Teresa and Matthew were having dinner at her parents' house. William was ensconced on Maggie's lap, his attention caught by the story she was quietly reading to him. On the eve of his first birthday, he had mastered walking, insisted on feeding himself and had firmly rejected the concept of the afternoon nap. He also liked to talk and would carry on at great length, occasionally even saying a word others could understand.

Their lack of comprehension did not faze William. He had developed a broad streak of tolerance for adults, often laughing happily at their foibles. To Teresa's amusement, and his father's and grandparents' chagrin, television left him utterly unmoved.

About the only guaranteed way to get him to go to sleep was to turn it on. Books, on the other hand, fascinated him.

"'Gain," he demanded as soon as Maggie finished the story.

She smiled down at his brown-gold head. "Later, sweetheart. We're all going to have dinner now."

William began to frown, then remembered that he liked food almost as much as he liked books. "Awright."

"Thank you," Maggie said solemnly. She handed him to Anthony and smoothed her skirt. "He's growing so fast; he hardly even seems like a baby anymore."

"I'm not convinced he ever really was," Matthew said, regarding his son benignly. "Or at least he never realized it. As far as William is concerned, he was born king of the mountain and he seems determined to stay that way."

"I suppose..." Anthony ventured, "that it would be a terrible shock to him if you had another child."

"To him?" Teresa repeated. "How about to us? We're just beginning to feel more or less sane again."

"Actually," Matthew said, "that might not be a bad idea. I kind of like larger families."

Teresa looked at him incredulously. "You've never said a word before about having another baby."

"It was just a thought. We don't have to make any decisions right now."

"I should hope not," Maggie interjected. "The roast is almost ready." She shot Anthony a chiding glance. He shrugged unabashedly, settling William into his high chair with practiced ease.

"When is the new book coming out?" Maggie asked Teresa as the cook brought in the first course.

"In two weeks." She didn't want to talk about it very much; the publisher had high hopes for *The Flowering Thorn,* but after her last experience, Teresa was not so sure. She had tried to prepare herself for the worse, but since she couldn't even imagine what that might be, she hadn't had much success so far.

"They want me to go on a publicity tour," she told her parents as she kept one eye on William. He was enthusiastically waving a piece of roast beef in the air but looked as though he eventually intended putting it in his mouth. She didn't know why she had brought up the tour; it was a real bone of contention between her and Matthew. Although he had said little since she first mentioned it, he had made it clear he didn't want her to go.

"Doesn't that mean you'd be away from home?" Anthony asked.

Teresa nodded, casting a quick look at Matthew who kept his eyes averted. "For about two weeks."

"That's a long time to be away from the baby." Her father glanced worriedly at William who, in prompt duplication of his expression, stopped smiling and frowned.

"He's old enough to do without her for a while," Maggie insisted. "Besides, she has her career to think of."

Writing as a career was a relatively new idea to Teresa. She had always thought of it as something she did simply because she had no choice. In the final analysis, it wasn't all that different from eating or sleeping in terms of being an absolute requirement of her life. But with the advance for *The Flowering Thorn* she had begun to see that there was another side to what she did; the business side that both puzzled and attracted her. She wished Matthew could understand that but he didn't seem able to.

''The thing is,'' she said, ''I said everything I had to about the book in the book. There's nothing to add. If I have to go on talk shows, I have a horrible feeling I'll be mute.''

''You'll do fine,'' Matthew said unexpectedly. As much as he didn't want her to go, he also didn't want her to stay home simply because she was afraid. ''You've been around television all your life, you're beautiful and you have the kind of personality that comes across great on camera. What could be better?''

''A stand-in,'' Teresa murmured even as she warmed to his praise. Maybe later that night he would like to show her exactly how beautiful he thought she was.

''I am not ready to have another baby,'' she told him as they were driving home. William was asleep in his car chair in the back seat, no doubt dreaming of roast beef and books. Traffic was light and they were making good time.

"I didn't think you were," Matthew said. "But perhaps we should give it some thought."

"There's no room in the apartment for a second child."

"I've been thinking about that already. Now that William is walking, the place seems a little cramped. What do you say we buy a house?"

"You mean in the suburbs?"

He nodded. "I was thinking of Connecticut. We could get something on several acres, plenty of room for William and the dog, not to mention us and whoever else might eventually come along."

"But if we did that, you'd have to commute."

"That's a drawback, I'll admit, but I think the pluses would outweigh the minuses. Besides," he added with a grin, "Connecticut is supposed to be heaven for writers."

"Only because there's no state income tax," she muttered, struggling to think of herself amid verdant lawns and bubbling brooks, with perhaps a few old stone walls thrown in for good measure. Though she had grown up in the suburbs, she had been happy in the city and was somewhat taken aback to think of leaving it.

Nonetheless, Matthew insisted and Teresa finally agreed that after she returned from the publicity tour, she would think—only think—about looking at houses.

In the days immediately before she left, Teresa came as close to panic as she had ever been. Nervous about how well she would hold up on a schedule that covered twelve cities in fourteen days, she could barely sleep or eat. Worse yet, as the time neared for her departure, Matthew became more and more distant. He took to working even later than usual and when he was home, he said barely a word to her.

Finally, the night before she left, she could stand it no longer. She was in their bedroom packing when he came in, saw what she was doing and turned to leave.

"Wait a minute," she said, holding the sweater she had been about to fold. "I'd like to talk with you."

He leaned against the door molding, his hands jammed in his pockets. "What about?"

Teresa bit back a sigh. She really didn't need this; couldn't he see that? "Don't you think you're being a little unreasonable? After all, it isn't as though you haven't been away plenty on business."

"I don't know what you're talking about."

"Of course you do," she said, determined to be patient. "You're treating me like some kind of leper when I'm not doing anything different from what you've done innumerable times."

"It's not the same," he insisted. "When I travel on business, it's because I have no choice."

"Neither do I. Doing well on this tour could have a tremendous impact on sales."

"Why should you care about that? We certainly don't need the money."

She shook her head, dazed by the sheer scope of his incomprehension. "I care about reaching as many people as possible. You know I've never been one of those writers who work in splendid isolation, never giving a thought to her audience.''

As he continued to stare at her unresponsively, she corrected herself. ''No, I guess you don't realize that. How could you when you know almost nothing about what I write or why.''

''Are you going to start that again? I thought we'd settled it years ago.''

''All we did was shove it aside,'' she said, jamming the sweater into the suitcase without thought to how it wrinkled. ''Like so much else. But now I think maybe we'd better clear the air.''

There was a note of determination in her voice Matthew had never heard before. It made him very wary. ''You're nervous about the tour and you're looking for some way to blow off steam. That's fine, but don't take it out on me.''

Teresa inhaled sharply. No matter what he said, she absolutely was not going to lose her temper. ''Has it occurred to you that every time we have a difference of opinion, you do your best to make it seem that the problem is strictly mine and you have nothing to do with it? That's unfair to me, but worse yet you're deluding yourself.''

''Look,'' he said, straightening away from the door. ''I'm tired, I've got a lot on my mind and I am trying my damnedest not to tell you what I really think of your going off and leaving our son when he's at the stage where he cries the moment he loses sight of you. But since you seem so determined to, as you say, clear the air, here goes. I think you're being selfish in the extreme. You're not thinking about anything except yourself. Frankly, I'm very disappointed.''

Teresa's cheeks burned. The shock of his blunt words made her legs feel weak. She sat down quickly on the side of the bed. ''Do you think it's easy for me to leave him?'' she whispered, staring at Matthew.

He shrugged. ''What else am I supposed to think? You're going, aren't you?''

''Because I have to. This is a chance I may never get again.''

''That's ridiculous. There will be plenty more books.''

''Maybe, maybe not.'' Her back stiffened as shock turned to indignation. ''I can't believe you're really this obtuse; you're deliberately refusing to understand. I could go on for decades doing good work and still never have a publisher willing to promote me again this way. This is my time; I have to take it.''

''No matter what the cost to William or myself?''

''Wait a minute. I thought you were only objecting to my leaving William. How did you get into it?''

''Of course I'll miss you.''

''That's very nice to hear,'' she said, letting the edge on her tongue show. ''But you've been away numerous times when I needed you, and I didn't try to make you feel guilty about it. Don't you think you should reciprocate?''

''I didn't say I particularly needed you,'' he insisted defensively. ''I'm just used to your being here when I come home.''

She didn't answer, only stared at him as the lameness of his assertion resounded between them. At length, she said, "If you honestly believe that, you're an even bigger fool than you're making yourself look right now."

Matthew flushed angrily. The last thing he wanted to do was argue with her, but he couldn't seem to help himself. What she was doing caused him to feel threatened on some level so fundamental that he could barely comprehend it. "Thanks a lot. It's nice to know what my dear wife really thinks of me."

"Oh, for God's sake!" Averting her eyes, she said, "I don't mind William being childish, he's entitled. But you're not. Can't you stop hiding behind your righteous indignation and admit what's really going on here?"

"I'm sure you're willing to enlighten me."

She lifted her eyes to the ceiling for a moment, then brought them back to his flushed face. Quietly, she said, "You're jealous." When he didn't comment but only stared at her as though what she had said was so utterly incomprehensible as to be meaningless, she went on determinedly. "You believed for years that you wanted to be a writer, but you drifted further and further away from it until now you're doing something entirely different. That was your choice and I think it was the right one. You're doing important work well, so why do you feel compelled to deny me my chance to do the same?"

"I've never denied you anything," he protested. "You do exactly as you like."

"No, I do not! I do what I have to; it isn't the same thing. My work is hard; it takes an enormous amount out of me. So does yours, but at least you have someone to come home to who understands and tries to make things easier. I'm tired of doing that and never getting the same back. I need your support, and I damn well will not settle for less!"

"You're getting hysterical. Calm down or you'll wake William."

Teresa's teeth ground together. A dozen responses sprang to her mind, but she uttered none of them. Instead, with deadly calm, she said, "That kind of attitude is beneath contempt. I think you'd better plan to spend the night in the guest room."

"I'm surprised at you," Matthew sneered. "That's such a cliché. What makes you think I'm willing to be tossed out of my own bed?"

"It doesn't matter," she said wearily. "You sleep there or I will. Either way, I don't want to be near you right now. I need time alone."

"You're about to have two weeks of it, honey," he said as he realized she was serious and in angry rejection turned toward the door. "Enjoy yourself. I sure as hell will!"

Matthew was gone before she woke the next morning. Ducking her head into the guest room, she saw that the bed was rumpled as though he had slept poorly; the sheets and blankets half tossed on the floor. Somehow the sight of that made her feel even worse than she already did. Her head was aching and her throat felt raw as she went into the kitchen.

William was in his high chair. He grinned and chortled when he saw her and held out his arms insistingly. She picked him up, rubbing his back gently, and caught sight of Juana's sympathetic expression. Embarrassed, she looked away.

An hour later, as she was en route to the airport, she felt no better. William had cried when he realized she was leaving, and though she knew from experience that he would calm down within minutes and be playing serenely before she even reached the curb, she still felt as though she had suddenly turned into a child abuser.

Matthew's scathing criticism had made her acutely aware of the essential conflict in her life between her responsibilities to her family and to herself. She loved her husband and her son but she also loved her work, and she didn't believe that she should have to apologize for either side of her nature. Literally millions of other women faced the same difficulties, but whereas that anonymous sharing had comforted her during pregnancy, it did not now.

She saw no evidence that anyone had come up with a solution to the problem. Choosing not to marry or not to have children struck her as no better an answer than choosing not to work. Either way the woman ended up missing a great deal. No matter how she looked at it, it simply wasn't fair. Men had never faced such a choice, so perhaps they shouldn't be expected to understand. But she had imagined that loving someone conferred a certain measure of empathy. Apparently she had been wrong.

Ironically in light of her mood, the tour was a great success. Her problems with Matthew made it impossible for her to concentrate enough on what she was doing to be made nervous by it. As a result, she sailed through interviews, smiling, chatting comfortably, winning the approval of audiences across the country. All the while her mind was firmly elsewhere.

She called home daily to talk with William. His vocabulary was expanding rapidly and they carried on some real conversations, which invariably made her miss him all the more. Still she was reassured that he was doing well. About Matthew she wasn't so sure. Juana said he was coming home early every evening to be with his son, which eased the worry engendered by that parting crack of his about enjoying himself. If the Nicaraguan woman thought it strange that Teresa didn't phone when her husband was there, she said nothing of it.

By the second week of the tour, *The Flowering Thorn* was selling out at bookstores across the country and was believed to have a shot at the pinnacle of commercial approbation, *The New York Times* best-seller list. Moreover, reviews were uniformly excellent. It looked as though Teresa might have pulled off the nearly impossible—a book popular with both the public and the critics. At the insistence of the publisher, the tour was extended to a third week.

By the time she came home, she was exhausted, could barely talk and had only the dimmest recollection of where she had been. There was nothing but a

jumbled mass of impressions—television studies
peopled by smiling interviewers with very bright
teeth, airplanes with very bad food and hotel rooms
that all looked identical. She wanted nothing so much
as to take refuge in her own home and never come out
again.

Juana met her at the door, clucked in dismay and
quickly took her suitcase. William was playing in the
kitchen, where he had his own set of pots to bang together. He looked up when she came in, smiled contentedly, said "'Lo, Mama" and went back to
playing.

Teresa started to cry. She couldn't help herself. The
tension of the past few weeks combined with the
worry over her personal situation had drained her.
She had no more strength left. It was all she could do
to follow Juana docilely as the nursemaid led her to
her bedroom, insisted on helping her out of her
clothes and made sure she slipped underneath the
covers before tiptoeing out of the room.

For a few moments she lay awake, staring up at the
ceiling and wondering how on earth she had come to
such a pass. Then the demands of her body overwhelmed all else and she slipped gratefully into sleep.

Matthew got home later than usual that evening.
He had known Teresa was due back and had been
hesitant about how she would behave toward him or
indeed how he should act toward her. The past three
weeks had given him ample opportunity to reconsider his behavior. He had alternately derided himself
for being a pompous idiot and assured himself that he

had been completely justified. Between those extremes was the niggling suspicion that nothing was as clear-cut as he would have liked to believe, but that he had not yet allowed himself to consider very closely.

Juana had retired for the evening when he arrived. William was fast asleep in the nursery. He murmured softly when his father looked in on him but did not wake. Matthew lingered there a few minutes, then wandered out to the kitchen and got himself a beer. He drank it standing by the sink, stretching out the time until he would have no further excuse for not going into the bedroom.

When he did, he found it dark and silent. Puzzled, since it was only slightly after ten o'clock, he walked cautiously toward the bed. As his eyes adjusted, he could make out Teresa, as deeply asleep as William had been, but with nothing like the same look of contentment. She slept curled up into a tight little ball, something he had seen her do only when she was in pain or very worried. Her hair, shoulder length and elegantly styled, hid part of her face, but he could still see that her brow was slightly puckered, as though even in unconsciousness sad thoughts pursued her.

He bent down slightly, studying her more closely. There were shadows beneath her eyes and the hollows in her cheeks were deeper than usual. She must have lost weight on the tour, as well as not getting much rest. Anger flared through him. Why hadn't she been looked after better? He touched the back of his hand lightly to her face, careful not to wake her. Her skin was cool and the bones beneath it felt almost unbearably fragile.

A long sigh ran through him. He thought of all the emotion expended over the past few weeks—the anger, worry, resentment—and wondered what the point of it had been. All that really mattered to him was that she was there, back in their home and their bed. Until then he hadn't let himself realize that she might not return, which was crazy since she would have died before leaving William.

Maybe that was the problem, he thought tiredly as he pulled off his clothes. He didn't like the idea that she had come back because of their son rather than because of him. She had said he was jealous. Sadly he wondered if she knew how close she was to the mark. Some part of him didn't want to share her with anything, not even herself.

It was a shock to realize that he wasn't better than that. Slipping into the bed beside her, he resolved to give it some careful thought at the first possible opportunity. For the moment, all he could do was gently gather her close to him and be grateful simply that she was there.

IN THE AFTERMATH of the publicity tour, Matthew and Teresa returned to the carefully polite behavior they had resorted to in the past when circumstances became too much for them. No mention was made of the argument they had had the night before her departure, though it remained very much on their minds. Although neither thought avoidance of the problem was in any way a solution, both realized that a cooling-off period of sorts might be helpful. They each made a special effort to be cordial and considerate, often going to elaborate lengths to avoid even the possibility of giving offense.

"I'll be home late tomorrow night because of a meeting with the legal staff," Matthew explained one morning at breakfast. "There's a problem with some of the contracts for next season."

Teresa nodded and retrieved the spoon William had just tossed on the floor. "I hope it's nothing serious."

"I don't think so, just time-consuming." He smiled faintly. "Like everything else. Sometimes I'm tempted to suggest Dad and Alexis come back full-time."

"They both look great," Teresa said, glad of the relatively safe topic. James and Alexis had returned from their three-month tour looking not unlike young lovers back from a joyful honeymoon. They had both become interested in Far Eastern art and were helping to sponsor an exhibit scheduled to tour American museums later in the year. While they came into the office a few hours a day and continued to sit on the board of directors, they left no doubt that they were enjoying their lessened responsibilities.

"Dad told me he wished he'd started taking off more time years ago," Matthew said with a sigh. "He seems to have gotten a whole new lease on life."

"I'm happy for them," Teresa said sincerely. Whatever the problems with her marriage, she cared deeply for her in-laws and was delighted to see them so content. It was only too bad that it had taken such a close brush with tragedy to make them realize the true importance of what they had together.

She wasn't about to let the same thing happen with her and Matthew; sooner or later they were going to have to come to some sort of understanding. But not just then when so much was happening.

The Flowering Thorn stayed on the best-seller list for close to four months. Movie rights were sold and, to her considerable surprise, Teresa was approached about writing the script. She turned the offer down on the grounds that she had no experience but was very gratified to have been asked. Meanwhile, she was hard at work on a new book. The advance for this one reached into six figures and prompted another spate of trouble with Matthew.

Since their marriage they had essentially lived on his income, which had become more considerable with each passing year. Like her, he had a trust fund but rarely drew on it. The bills were paid by his extremely high salary, first as an anchorman and more recently as network vice president. That had always vaguely bothered Teresa, since she had money of her own and saw no reason for them not to be using it.

The few times she had discussed it with Matthew he had placated her by saying that the funds were being invested for William and any other children they might have, so it was hardly as though they were going to waste. He had strongly suggested that she shouldn't worry about it. Unable to think of the trust fund money as really her own since she hadn't earned it, and well aware that her writing brought in very little, she had not pursued the matter. But now she felt constrained to do so.

"If you're serious about getting a house," she said, "there's absolutely no reason for me not to help pay for it."

Matthew frowned. He had brought up the subject of the house again because he thought it would be something pleasant they could safely do together. Also, it would help foster the implication that their marriage was on, if not solid ground, at least not on thin ice either. Now it appeared that there were problems with that plan that he had not envisioned.

"Why don't we look at houses first and decide how much we want to spend?" he hedged. "Then we can discuss how to pay for it."

Teresa went along reluctantly. She didn't want to be put in the position of buying a ridiculously extravagant house simply to make her income necessary. It was bad enough that the real estate agent, upon realizing that she was dealing with the heir apparent to one of the largest networks and his wife, the best-selling author, fell all over herself showing them the most choice real estate available.

After tramping through the dozenth sprawling, drafty mansion in the space of two days, Teresa called a halt. "I think we can agree," she said firmly, "that it would be ridiculous for us to live in any place like this. It's too big and too formal, plus we wouldn't have any use for at least half the rooms. I want someplace smaller, more personal and,'' she added firmly, ''more realistically priced.''

To her great relief, Matthew agreed. That left only the real estate agent to be disappointed, and she managed to hide it well. They began to look at somewhat more modest housing, if only in relative terms.

Teresa remained dubious. The question of money aside, she wasn't at all sure that she wanted to leave the city with its museums, bookstores, shops, park, all the places she went when she couldn't write. Up there what would she do? Garden? That had limited appeal. Entertain? Matthew had alluded to the need to socialize more in his new position. She didn't mind that but could hardly think of it as a really absorbing activity.

Not until they came across the fieldstone house nestled among oak and maple trees with a brook running nearby and a tiny waterfall did she begin to think suburban life might not be too bad. ''Two hundred years ago,'' the real estate agent enthused, ''this was the site of a grist mill. If you're interested, you can find references to it in the town records.''

''What happened to it?'' Teresa asked as she moved William from one arm to the other. If allowed to walk, he promptly wandered off and had already had to be retrieved twice.

''It was torn down around 1880, but the original home of the family that operated it was combined into the present house. As nearly as anyone can tell, it makes up the kitchen and family room. There's a marvelous beehive oven." So saying, she led the way inside.

Teresa fell in love with the house before she had been in it five minutes. Everything about it fascinated her, from the nooks and crannies beneath the stairs to the slightly crooked floors and the big bow windows overlooking the garden. It was a place of high ceilings, sun-filled rooms and a rare sense of the past and present mingling harmoniously.

"I'm sure you'll be happy here," the agent said as Matthew wrote out the check for the binder. In the face of Teresa's insistence, he had finally broken down and agreed that they would split the cost of the house, though he claimed it was only for tax purposes.

"It's loaded with atmosphere," the agent added.

Also spiders, mice, bats, owls and squirrels, all of whom were nicely settled in and showed no inclination to leave. The spiders Teresa didn't mind since she rationalized that they ate other bugs. The mice would probably get the hint if she brought in a cat. As for the rest . . . she took one look around the shambles of the attic and threw up her hands. The wisest strategy seemed to be to seal it off.

"We don't really need an attic," she told Matthew. "Not when there's so much storage space in the basement." Actually, she had her suspicions about what was living down there but saw no reason to mention them.

"I'll take care of it," he assured her, leading her to wonder if he had any idea what he would be getting into. He went off confidently to the hardware store to purchase traps, wire mesh, nails and one of every kind of hammer ever made. "First we catch everything that's up there," he explained when he returned, "let it go somewhere far from the house and cover over the entrances they were using. That's all there is to it."

Except that the traps did not work. Even baby bats were apparently too smart for them, while the squirrels and owls regarded them with disdain. Succulent bits of bait laid out each night were gone the next morning, but with nothing to show for them.

"This isn't working," Teresa said after they had been in the house for a couple of weeks. Fall was passing quickly; the trees had already begun to lose their crown of orange and gold. She knew that if they didn't find new homes for the menagerie soon, she would be stuck with them until at least the next year since she couldn't bear to evict anything in the winter. "We have to try something more dramatic."

"Like what?" he asked, regarding her dubiously across the breakfast table.

"I don't know. Something that will make them want to leave."

Ingenuously, he said, "I have to work late tonight. Why don't you see what you can do?"

"I could let William loose up there," she suggested direly.

"Not unless you want the ASPCA after us."

Their son chortled happily and waved bye-bye to his father. Teresa sighed. Looking at William, she said, ''Your mother is a big deal, best-selling writer now. She should not have to cope with things like this.''

William grinned agreeably. He broke off playing with the dog and lifted his arms imperially. ''Go up.'' Reluctantly, she did as he bid. William liked the attic. He seemed to think the wildlife there existed for his express amusement, and he took great care to point out every evidence of it to his reluctant mother. Spotting a bat hanging upside down under a rafter near the ceiling, he chortled his glee.

Teresa took a deep breath, reminded herself that she had never been squeamish in her life and that this was not the time to start, and swung the broom she had brought in more or less the right direction. The bat woke with a high-pitched squeak and darted away. After several minutes of chasing it around the attic, William laughing gleefully all the while, it apparently decided to seek quieter accommodations and flitted out the window. Half a dozen or so of its cousins followed in due course.

That done, she nailed the wire mesh over the window, set up the new traps she had bought—the ones the man at the hardware store absolutely swore would work—then collected a very grubby William and carried him downstairs for a bath.

It wasn't until much later that evening, as she waited for Matthew to come home, that she realized the whole silly business had filled her with an unexpected sense of satisfaction. It made her realize just how important the house had already become to her, not for its own sake but because of what it seemed to represent—a silent promise on her part and Matthew's not to give up on each other as so many couples seemed inclined to do, but instead to make every possible effort to work out their problems.

Sitting in the cozy den with the curtains drawn and a fire gently glowing, she listened for the sound of his car and prayed they would succeed.

Chapter Sixteen

JIM AND CHARLOTTE were married quietly at Christmas. They had been planning it for some time and insisted that no fuss be made, but the occasion was still a very special one for all the family. Because Charlotte's father had died several years before, she asked James to give her away, saying that he had, after all, had experience. He left no doubt that he was honored to comply.

In retrospect, the happiness of that day was particularly poignant, coming as it did only a few months before the death of Grandfather Will Lawrence. He passed away quietly in his sleep without suffering, for which everyone tried to be grateful. Still he was sorely missed and Elizabeth did not want to stay on in the Virginia house without him. She moved to the cottage recently built on Maggie and Anthony's property and found comfort in being close to her daughter.

The swift, remorseless passage of time was made even clearer when, on a warm summer night not long afterward, Maria joined her Joseph. Teresa had spent the previous day with her grandmother, having brought William to visit. Maria had delighted in playing with him and had said, as they were leaving, how happy she was to have lived long enough to see the future. Teresa wept when told of her passing, but she found solace in the knowledge that a part of Maria would always be with her.

While time raced by for some, it lagged for others. The news was filled with stories about the hostages taken at the American embassy in Tehran early in November of the previous year. As the election campaign heated up, it became clear that there were only two issues—the shambles of the economy with inflation running rampant and the hostages who seemed to stand for American strength and pride ground into the dust.

Teresa felt no surprise when Ronald Reagan won, nor any particular relief. She had ceased to look to any one man to lead the country out of its troubles and had come to the conclusion that the solution had to lie within each individual. For herself, she resolved to make a beginning by tidying up some personal loose ends.

For several years now she had been trying to convince Graham to get in touch with Alexis. He had been extremely reluctant, fearing her rejection. But as he approached his sixtieth birthday, he seemed disposed to reconsider. "I suppose all she can really say is no," he ventured when Teresa brought the subject up again. He tried to smile. "God knows I've heard that often enough."

"I don't think she'll say it. On the contrary, I won't be surprised if she jumps at the chance."

Graham made it clear he considered that highly unlikely, but he did finally agree to Teresa at least telling Alexis about their friendship. "Just so long as she doesn't think badly of you because of it," he said. "I couldn't stand that."

"She won't," Teresa promised, swiftly making plans to see her mother-in-law. She found her at home on an early December morning, having just come from the doctor.

"I hate checkups," Alexis said as she poured them both cups of tea. Outside the wind was raw and snow was forecast. "But ever since his heart problem, James has insisted we both have them regularly."

"Is everything all right?" Teresa asked. She didn't want to intrude on anyone's privacy, but she hated the thought that there might be any problem.

"I'd say we're both perfect," Alexis said with a smile, "except that it would sound immodest. Now tell me about that extraordinary grandson of mine."

Teresa obliged, trotting out the latest pictures of William and promising to bring him over soon. When that was taken care of, she was silent for a moment before getting around to the reason for her visit. "I have something to ask you that I think you may find surprising but that I hope you'll consider carefully."

Alexis nodded but said nothing, preferring to reserve judgment until she heard what Teresa had to say. Despite that, it was impossible to hide her surprise as her daughter-in-law said, "For some time now, your brother, Graham, and I have been friends."

Alexis's hand went to her throat. She shook her head bemusedly. "I had no idea you knew each other."

"He wrote to me about one of my books and we started meeting for lunch. Right at the beginning he said that he hoped once I had gotten to know him, I would consider bringing the two of you together."

When Alexis stiffened and would have spoken, Teresa went on hurriedly. "But that was years ago and even though I've offered to do it several times, he always puts me off. He's afraid, you see, that you'll reject him."

"Did he give you any hint why that might be?" Though she spoke dryly, Alexis could not hide her dismay. She had gone white and a pulse fluttered in her throat.

"I know about the rivalry between you when you were growing up, how you believed you should have been your father's heir but instead he left the network to Graham. And I know what you did about it, carefully mustering your resources until you were able to take over UBC. Graham also told me what motivated the takeover, namely your conviction that he was involved in James's captivity in North Korea. He says he wasn't, by the way, but I don't think he expects you to believe him."

"Do you?" Alexis asked very softly, her eyes locked on Teresa's.

"Yes, I do. I think he made some bad mistakes when he was younger, which he deeply regrets, but I don't think he was ever capable of doing anything of such magnitude.''

"So you think I deluded myself?''

"No . . . not exactly. I think you needed something to spur you on what must have been an extremely difficult course. You hit on that and it worked, but that doesn't mean your suspicions were correct.''

"That's what James has always said,'' Alexis admitted softly. "Oddly enough, over the years I've come to believe him.''

Teresa was surprised; she hadn't expected her mother-in-law to so readily admit that she had been wrong.

"Don't misunderstand me,'' Alexis said. "I have no regrets about doing what I did. Graham should never have been entrusted with UBC. He was in the process of destroying it when I took it over. However, I don't take that to mean that simply because he was an incompetent executive he lacked all human decency.''

She sighed deeply and looked off into the middle distance, as though seeking the answer to a puzzle she had never quite been able to solve. "I can't really explain why I believed what I did, except that it was an extremely difficult time for me. For several months after James disappeared over there, it was impossible to get any firm word of his condition. The State Department and Pentagon both tried but failed. I think they were coming around to the idea that he must have been killed when Anthony and I were

suddenly approached by representatives of the Red
Chinese. They told us that not only was James alive,
but he would be kept that way if we cooperated.''

''By slanting the war news?''

Alexis nodded. ''It was particularly ironic in light
of the fact that the falling out between myself and my
brother and father had occurred because I objected
to their cooperating with the McCarthyites who were
claiming that Communists had infiltrated every as-
pect of American life. I still believe those charges
were false and were used simply as a means of un-
dermining basic freedoms, but that doesn't mean the
Communists wouldn't have liked to do what the
McCarthyites charged. They may very well have
made other attempts besides the one with us. However, I don't believe they ever had much success.''

''We don't have to talk about this if you find it too
painful,'' Teresa said gently, ''but I have always been
puzzled as to how you thought Graham was able to
have any impact on what happened to James. He
wasn't even in Korea, was he?''

Alexis shook her head. ''No, but he had been with
the Pentagon during World War II.'' She hesitated a
moment, glancing at the younger woman. ''You say
you know Graham well?''

''Enough to understand that his life hasn't always
been easy. It never is when someone lives against the
accepted norm.''

Alexis nodded, satisfied that she grasped the situation. ''Back then homosexuals were subject to
blackmail, coercion, all sorts of dire consequences

simply because of society's hypocrisy. They had no choice but to stick together and help each other. I conceived the notion that some of Graham's friends at the State Department and Pentagon were working with him to discredit James and through him the network in order to cost us our licenses. If we had lost them, Graham would have been able to buy us out very cheaply and instead of me ending up with UBC, he would have been running IBS."

She smiled faintly. "It sounds crazy now, I know. But believe me, there was a time when it seemed to make sense."

"Since it doesn't any longer," Teresa ventured, "does that mean you'll meet with Graham?"

"I don't know. . . . It's been so long. I'm not sure we have anything to say to each other." The anxious look she cast Teresa made it clear she hoped that wasn't the case.

"I think you'd be pleasantly surprised. He's a very different man from the one you knew. I can't claim to know for sure, but I think he simply needed to find his own niche. He's done that, and in the process helped a lot of people like myself. But he's still basically alone and at his age that's hard."

"Yes . . . it would be." Alexis absently twisted her wedding band, the only jewelry she habitually wore besides the slim gold watch fastened around her wrist. She glanced at that as she said, "I suppose I could call him now."

Teresa bit back an exclamation of relief. She knew none of this was easy for her mother-in-law and she didn't want to put more pressure on her by raising expectations too high. Instead she calmly said, "He's usually in his office at this hour."

Alexis nodded. She got up and walked toward the door. Turning slightly, she said, "I think I'll use the phone in the den."

"I can give you the number if you like."

She shook her head. "No, thanks, I already know it."

Teresa was left to puzzle over that, coming finally to the only possible conclusion. Alexis had no reason to know how to reach *The Literary Quarterly* unless she had considered calling there in the past, perhaps several times.

So much for having pulled off a great coup, she thought wryly. It was looking more and more as if she had only convinced Alexis to do what she had been thinking about for some time anyway. That being the case, she considered leaving. Since she had no real part in what was happening, it didn't seem right to hang around to learn the results. But just as she was gathering her things together, Alexis returned.

She still looked pale but was smiling, if a bit shakily. "We're getting together for lunch tomorrow. It's funny, he doesn't sound different at all except for what he says, of course."

"Of course," Teresa repeated, finding that made sense after a moment. Graham had changed a great deal over the years, but he was still Alexis's brother. There was a bond between them that not even years of estrangement could completely erode. Perhaps it would be enough for them to make a fresh start.

"Thank you for this," Alexis said softly as she walked with Teresa to the door. "It's been on my mind for quite some time, but I needed to be pushed to do something about it."

"I just hope it works out."

"It will, not all at once of course, but over time." Alexis's confident smile faded slightly as she added, "I'm only sorry we let it go this long."

That, of course, was something that could never be changed. The years, once gone, were lost beyond recovery. Teresa thought about that as she drove back to Connecticut. She, too, was letting time pass without making the best use of it. That was going to have to stop, though she didn't quite know how.

THE FLOWERING THORN had been published in paperback a year after it came out in hardcover. Once again it made the best-seller lists, where it hung on solidly week after week. The movie was due for release shortly, and was expected to prompt yet another spurt of sales.

Teresa was working on a new book and finding this one a little easier as she seemed to have gained some in confidence. William was in play school several mornings each week where he mingled with other toddlers, to whom he took with unexpected ease.

"He's a natural leader," the teacher told Teresa. "They all flock around him." That was apparently fine with William, who seemed to enjoy helping the children who were not quite as adept as himself. He also showed a tendency to be protective of those who were frightened or simply at loose ends.

"Matthew was the same," Alexis said when Teresa shyly confided her pride in her son during a phone conversation. "He was always looking out for someone else. Sometimes it was hard to tell what he was feeling himself. He always kept his thoughts rather hidden."

Tempted to say that he still did, Teresa was silent instead. To speak of such a personal matter seemed disloyal, yet she could have done with some advice. Not that it would be fair to burden Alexis with her problems when she had enough of her own. Since her first luncheon with Graham, they had met several times and were slowly becoming friends. That being the case, Alexis naturally wanted her brother and her husband to meet. James, who had been the one to always insist on Graham's innocence, was nonetheless reluctant.

"I suppose I should have expected this," Alexis said. "I was estranged from my family when James and I married, so he never had anything to do with them. It's a bit much to ask him to start now."

"Perhaps he'll come around," Teresa suggested, "when he's had time to think about it more."

Alexis said she hoped so. They talked a while longer. After she hung up, Teresa settled in front of the television with William on her lap. She had decided to watch the Reagan inaugural, if only to see if the hoped-for release of the hostages would actually happen. William, who normally disdained anything on the small screen, for once showed signs of interest.

Teresa's cheeks were damp when the news came that the men and women held captive for some fourteen months were at last free and on their way home. Wryly she acknowledged that the juxtaposing of the inaugural pageantry with the hostage release made for incredible programming. The anchor team Matthew had selected were making the most of it, undoubtedly drawing more viewers to augment their already high ratings.

She wondered if he missed being able to cover the spectacle himself, but when he came home and she asked him that, he said he didn't. "Of course, sometimes I get nostalgic about all the excitement, being at the center of a breaking news story, that sort of thing. But you were right when you said I had made the correct choice. What I do now suits me better."

She thought it was remarkably generous of him to admit that and tried hard to show him that she appreciated it. For several months relations between them seemed to ease at least a little. They were less rigorously polite, more relaxed and natural than they had been in some time. Until Matthew dropped a bombshell that sent Teresa reeling.

He chose to do it the night of William's third birthday. A dozen children from the play school had been invited to a party. Later in the day, after the small guests had left, the adults had enjoyed a pleasant dinner. James and Alexis were there along with Anthony and Maggie. On the spur of the moment, Teresa had decided to make it a real family get-together and had also invited Mandy and Tom and Jim and Charlotte. Mandy was expecting her first child and looked radiantly beautiful. She and Charlotte spent a great deal of the evening in a corner talking quietly, which caused Jim to give them several nervous looks.

Dinner was a relaxed, noisy affair with everyone talking at the same time amid a great deal of laughter. William fell asleep halfway through, worn out from all the excitement, and managed to look suitably angelic as his father carried him upstairs.

When he returned from tucking his son in, Matthew sat down beside James and grinned wryly. "You know what I was just thinking? I can remember you putting me to bed when I wasn't much older than William. Somehow I never really thought of myself doing the same thing, but it sneaks up on you, doesn't it?"

"If you're lucky, it does," James said. He was tanned from a recent vacation in the Caribbean and looked exceptionally fit. From across the table, Alexis smiled at him tenderly.

"William's a terrific little kid," James went on, "but I have to tell you, I wouldn't mind a few more grandchildren."

"That's what I tried to tell them a few years ago," Anthony put in. "All I got for my pains was a talking-to from Maggie."

"Which you richly deserved," she quickly added. "Teresa and Matthew are doing a wonderful job with one child. They shouldn't be rushed into having more. Not," she added after a moment, "that it wouldn't be nice."

"See," Anthony gloated, "even she wants you to have another." Turning to Teresa, who was blushing slightly, he said, "You've finished that new book, haven't you, sweetheart? And didn't you say you wanted to take a break before starting another?"

"I . . . uh . . . thought I might try my hand at gardening," she said weakly.

"Gardening?" Her father raised his eyebrows. "You employ a gardener. What do you want to do—put the poor man out of work?"

"No, of course not. I just thought I'd put in a few more flowers, grow some vegetables, that sort of thing."

"Grow children instead," he advised her firmly. "They come out better in the end and last a lot longer."

"I'd say that you sound exactly like an Italian grandpa," Maggie insisted, "except that your own father would never have presumed to butt in like that. At least he had too much sense."

"Shows what you know. He regularly took me aside and told me I'd have an easier time keeping you in line if you stayed pregnant."

"He what?" Maggie exclaimed. As the others laughed, she shook her head ruefully. "I should have known better. Men never learn."

That set off a friendly argument about the foibles of males and females that lasted the rest of the evening. Teresa joined in, but her attention was only partly captured. She kept looking at Matthew, wondering what he thought of their fathers' comments. Once he had seemed interested in having another baby, but lately the subject hadn't come up. The possibility that he might have given up on the idea made her feel oddly bleak.

She needn't have worried. Shortly after the last guests left, as Matthew was helping her to clear up, he suddenly asked, "I don't suppose there's any chance you're pregnant?"

She almost dropped the tray she was carrying. Not until she put it down carefully on the kitchen counter did she answer him. "You know I'm on the pill."

"You stopped taking it once before."

"That was different." How exactly, she wasn't sure but she did know that she had outgrown such behavior. "I wouldn't do something like that again unless we'd discussed it first and agreed."

"You mean you might . . . if we talked about it and decided we both wanted another baby?"

She wiped her hands on her apron, noticing as she did so that they were shaking. "I don't know. We haven't talked about it."

"But we could." He ran a hand through his hair, not quite looking at her. "I don't know about you, but I'd like to have another child. Being with William has made me see the world in an entirely different way. He makes me feel at once very adult and responsible, but also new and untarnished. I'd like to experience more of that.'' He broke off, suddenly self-conscious. ''Maybe I'm not making any sense.''

''Yes, you are,'' Teresa said quickly. ''I have the same feelings when I'm with him. He gives us far more than we can ever give him. Although,'' she added with a smile, ''I'd never tell him that. He's arrogant enough as it is.''

He grinned in return. ''That's certainly true. Where do you suppose he gets it from?''

Her eyebrows rose fractionally. ''I couldn't begin to guess.'' More seriously, she went on. ''Anyway, I don't think we should even consider having another baby until things improve between us.''

She had thought he might insist that they really weren't doing badly at all, everything considered. When he did not but instead merely nodded, she felt a tightening in her stomach. It was one thing to know the problem existed; it was quite another to try to drag it out in the open again. Each time she had tried before, she had gotten nowhere. The temptation to put it aside yet once more was very strong, but she could not quite bring herself to give up all hope that a solution might be found.

''Matthew...'' she said quietly as she gathered her courage, ''I want you to know that I love you dearly. I always have ever since I was a little girl. That love has changed over the years, but it's never lessened. In fact, it's grown stronger. But,'' she added before he could speak, ''that doesn't mean it can make everything all right. It can't; we have to work at it.''

"I know that." He took a step toward her, then stopped. "Why is it," he asked gently, "that people always seem to have very serious discussions in either the kitchen or the bedroom?"

"Maybe there's something about those places that brings out the basics."

"Such as being honest with each other?"

She nodded, hoping he wouldn't notice how tense she was becoming. Something warned her this discussion was going to be different from the others. She didn't quite know how she would handle that.

Matthew reached out suddenly and put his hands on her shoulders, turning her around. He unfastened the apron and removed it, then took her hand. "When it comes to basics, I prefer the bedroom."

She went along without protest. Whatever mess was left to be cleaned up could wait. There were more important matters to attend to.

Matthew clicked on the light, let go of her hand and went into his dressing room. She stood in the middle of the room, waiting for him. He returned within minutes, holding a book she was startled to recognize.

"I've read it twice now," he said, holding up *The Flowering Thorn*, "and I want to go back and read your earlier work. You're good, Teresa. I have to admit it hurt me a little to realize you'd done it all on your own."

"My own . . . ?"

"I certainly didn't help. If anything, I made problems for you by refusing to realize what you were trying to accomplish. That was very insensitive of me; I apologize.''

''Matthew, I...'' She broke off, looking at him. He seemed very uncertain, as though waiting to hear how she would respond. ''I don't know what to say. We've always had a good marriage except for the problem over my work. I never felt that you understood it, but I also realize that I didn't try to explain.''

''You did,'' he reminded her softly, ''several times.''

''Not really. I was too busy feeling put upon. Somehow that spurred me to keep going.'' She laughed faintly, embarrassed. ''Awful, isn't it?''

''Not really. Maybe it would have been different if we hadn't always known each other, but as it was, we each had such a firm image of what the other was like that they've been very hard to break.''

''That's true. I know I still have a tendency sometimes to rely on you too much.''

He smiled crookedly. ''This from the woman who single-handedly fought off an army of bats?''

''William has never forgiven me for that. He thought they were pets.''

''Speaking of William, I know the old prejudice against only children has been pretty well debunked, but I still think it wouldn't do him any harm to have a brother or sister.''

''Maybe not,'' Teresa agreed. ''But what about his poor sibling? Have you thought what he—or she—would be in for?''

Matthew laughed and shook his head. "Trust you to think of that. What about the poor parents, namely ourselves? We could have another William, you know."

She sat down on the side of the bed and regarded him solemnly. "Perhaps, if we were very lucky."

He joined her there. "Do you think we might be?"

"I don't know." She turned slightly, so that she could look at him. "I'm very glad that you read my book, and I appreciate what you said, but I still think we have a way to go. It would be very easy to distract ourselves with another child when we should really be concentrating on each other."

"Sometimes," he said after a moment, "you're so smart that it scares me."

"We've never really had a chance to put each other first," she said, ignoring his comment. She knew her own intelligence, its reach and its limitations, but not for a moment did she believe he was really afraid. The time for that was past. "At first it was because we both worked so much, but we can't keep doing that forever. Something has to give eventually."

"My job..." he began, only to break off. She was tempted to jump in, to say that she understood, but she had done that too often in the past. This time he needed to say what was on his mind.

"My job is very demanding," he said finally. "I really had no idea how tough it would be when I took it on, and frankly I don't think that's going to change. Dad's made it clear he intends to retire completely in a few years. When that happens I plan to take over for him as head of UBS.''

''Why? I'm not suggesting you shouldn't,'' she added hastily when he looked at her. ''I'm just curious about what's propelling you along this course.''

''You mean you think I may simply be trying to live up to my father's expectations? I admit there was a time when I would have done that, just as there was a time when I wanted nothing so much as to rebel against him. They were both stages I went through on the way to becoming myself.''

He was silent for a moment, then said quietly, ''Sometimes I look inside and I see things I don't quite like. When I was younger, I had a nobler vision of myself that hasn't turned out to be accurate. For one thing, I want power, partly for what I can achieve with it but also for its own sake. I don't want other people determining what happens in my life; that's for me to decide.''

''There's nothing wrong with that. You're a leader, not a follower.''

''But that means I tend to think I know what's best for others, when I don't always. For instance, I was wrong when I thought you should concentrate on William and me to the exclusion of all else.'' He shook his head ruefully. ''Lord, was I wrong. You have to keep reaching people with what you write; it would be a crime to do otherwise.''

''I couldn't,'' she said softly. ''It's too much a part of me. But so are you, Matthew. That's what's been so hard for me: trying to combine different parts of my life that seemed determined to be in conflict.''

''They don't have to be,'' he said softly. ''We can work it out. Not all at once, that would be unrealistic to expect. But little by little, one day at a time. Don't you think so?''

''Yes,'' she murmured, watching the play of light over his face, realizing for perhaps the thousandth time all that this man meant to her. ''Yes, we can, little by little.''

''It might take the rest of our lives,'' he said almost as though he was warning her.

She smiled, all the way to her eyes. ''I could stand that.''

''So could I.'' His hands on her were very gentle, hers on him were a bit less so. Need grew swiftly between them. The same as it had always been, yet different.

A bit unsteadily they undressed each other. That was something they hadn't done in quite a while, and their fingers were a little clumsy on zippers and buttons, but eventually they managed. Naked, they stood for a moment beside the bed, not touching except with their eyes.

''You're so beautiful,'' Matthew said. ''It sounds trite, but it's really the truth. You will always be the most beautiful woman to me.''

''I feel the same way about you,'' Teresa murmured as she touched his chest lightly with one hand. ''Did you notice tonight how our parents looked at each other? After all these years, they're still lovers in every sense of the word. I've seen that before but I've only begun to realize what it means. They know something we're just starting to learn.''

He nodded, his hand capturing hers, closing gently around her wrist. ''About love. They could tell us things, about the problems they've overcome and how they did it, but they won't. Some things belong only to the two people involved.''

She shivered slightly, not because the air was chill. ''They show us though, by what they have together.''

He drew her closer to him, savoring the warmth of her body against his. ''Where do you suppose we'll be when we're their age?''

She looked up, meeting his eyes. ''Here? Like this?''

He laughed, very softly. ''I hope so. Oh, Tessa, how I hope so.''

''You haven't called me that in years.''

''It was a child's name; you didn't like it.''

''And what is it now?''

''A woman's. My wife's. My love's.''

''You know,'' she whispered into his shoulder, ''being Tessa isn't so bad.''

''Are you sure?''

''Remember how smart you said I am? There's no way I'll make it that easy for you.''

He laughed deep in his throat. ''I could persuade you.''

''You're welcome to try.''

He did, through the dark, sweet hours of the night, making her forget how long they had been married, how many years they had been lovers, making everything new and fresh. And she, in turn, did the same.

Together they rediscovered each other as a man and a woman, brought together by fate, bound by love, troubled by the problems of their age, yet determined to rise above them.

In the privacy of their hearts and minds, they put aside the barriers raised by doubt and pledged again their trust in each other, this time truly understanding what it meant.

What they forged that night was at once a new beginning and an affirmation of everything that had gone before. There would be problems ahead, for that was the very nature of life, but they would face them together, finding in each other the strength to take whatever might come and shape it into something good.

They would build on the past to create the future, as their parents had done, as their children would do, in the legacy of love that was its own beginning and that had no end.

Daughter of a wealthy senator, wife of a ruthless tycoon, she had everything a woman could want... except love.

Barbara Delinsky

WITHIN REACH

Danica Lindsey was locked into a loveless marriage until she met Michael Buchannan. But even as their souls became one, a scandal threatened to destroy forever their chance of happiness!